Macy

a novel

Macy

a novel

APRIL McGOWAN

WhiteFire Publishing

This is a work of fiction. All characters and events portrayed in this novel are either fictitious or used fictitiously.

MACY

WhiteFire Publishing
13607 Bedford Rd NE
Cumberland, MD 21502

ISBN: 978-1-939023-40-7 (digital)
          978-1-939023-39-1 (print)

For
Ken, Madeline, and Seth

"But those who hope in the Lord
will renew their strength.
They will soar on wings like eagles;
they will run and not grow weary,
they will walk and not be faint."

~ Isaiah 40:30 (NIV)

One

They say there is a time and a place for everything. I could tell by the way Arthur held his fork, this was neither. It swiveled in his hand, looking more like a stabbing device than an eating implement. The pieces of salad fell from the tines onto the booth's laminate tabletop, splattering it with red Catalina French salad dressing. As if listening in, the restaurant seemed to go peculiarly quiet.

He leaned toward me. Steel gray eyes stared me down. "You're what?"

"We're going to have a baby." I whispered, certain everyone had turned their attention on us. Then the busboy dropped a tray of dirty dishes, and a half-eaten portion of chicken-fried steak hit the big trucker at the bar, and gravy coated the wall. They no longer cared about two strangers in the back, their lives at a sudden impasse.

I curled a strand of red hair around my finger, gripping it tight. My husband's gaze bore down on me, and everything around us went still. It reminded me of the time we stayed over in California during one of their earthquakes. The breeze stopped and the birds quieted like someone'd tossed a blanket over the whole place. Then it came on us, shaking me to my core, tossing me from my comfortable seat.

I gripped the table. Arthur shook his head at me, and disgust curled his lips into a false smile. "I'm a long-haul trucker. We live in our sleeper cab. We don't have a house." He listed things in a cold, detached way that told me his stress level had reached an all-time high. I also noticed he left the biggest issue off his list. He never wanted children. Until the moment I took the pregnancy test, neither had I.

"Would you like some herb tea?" My hand shook as I lifted the silver teapot toward him.

His eyes refocused on me. "Tea?"

I motioned to the basket of mixed teabags the waitress had left for us. "To calm you down."

I waited for him to yell. Maybe take a swing at me. But he didn't. Instead, Arthur did something that surprised me. He got up, tossed money on the table, and walked out. Stunned, I didn't move. He must have needed time to think. After all, I'd had a week to process the idea. He'd come back in a while, and we'd figure out what to do. Arthur could be a hard man, no one knew that better than me. The baby would change all that.

A picture of a house nestled in the trees, a garden out back, and maybe a dog to keep us company while Arthur was out on the road, formed in my mind. I touched my stomach, daydreaming, until a familiar rumble startled me back to the present. I peered out the window, tipping to the side to see the parking lot, and saw diesel smoke bellow out of the chrome stacks.

He was warming up the truck. I took fast bites of my lunch, not wanting to make him wait for me any longer, but my stomach rebelled. I'd get a to-go box and take it with me. And the tea—that'd be just the thing to settle my stomach on the road. I almost got the waitress's when I heard the engine shift from idling to engaged. My hand froze mid-air and I watched as if in slow motion. Our big rig pulled out of the parking lot and past the window where I sat. The brown cab, splotched with dirt and oil from thousands of miles on the road, moved across the front parking lot of the restaurant, pulled out, drove to the light, then turned the corner out of sight. My heart raced, but my legs went numb.

He'd left. He'd be back, he had to come back. I read the maps for him. He probably went to get supplies to let me finish lunch. We were overdue on an oil change—hadn't he noticed the shop up the road? I nibbled my food, glancing out the window between bites, sure he'd come pulling in any minute. Any minute.

A full hour later, I still sat in the booth. The waitress refilled my hot water pot. "You okay, honey?"

I started to say what we all say when a stranger asks such a question. I started to tell her I was fine. Instead, when I opened my mouth, a sob came out.

"He's gone," I managed to get out and then swallowed hard, realizing a new point of panic. "I don't even know where I am." The smell of fried potatoes and eggs wafted off the waitress and traipsed over to my nose. My stomach churned.

"I'm sure he'll be back."

I glanced at her hopeful blue eyes. Her name tag said DONNA. The lines around her smile and age spots on her hands showed her to be in her mid-fifties. "They all come back."

"I didn't think he'd leave." I shivered even as others around me shed their jackets. Maybe I was going into shock.

"Come with me, sweetie." She pulled me up from the booth and led me down the hall, past the kitchen entry—where I held my breath—to a door painted white with a seventies confetti sparkle. After pulling out a key, she unlocked it, revealing a long shadowy staircase.

"We've got a small apartment up there. Just a studio." She paused, her voice softening. "It's unoccupied. Go lay down a bit. Life always looks better after a nap."

At the very suggestion of a nap, my body went on autopilot. I trudged up the stairwell and she closed and locked the door behind me. For a moment, I considered if I'd been voluntarily kidnapped. As I topped the stairs, I found a cozy room with a kitchenette. In the corner sat a daybed, all made up, as if waiting for me. I headed toward it, past the love seat and small coffee table, my eyes focused on the pillow. Everything was clean, dust free, hair free. I lay down and turned my face into the bedding. As the aroma of baby powder dryer sheets met my nose, I gave in and cried myself to sleep.

The smell of coffee woke me. I cracked my eyes and took in my surroundings. It hit me again that I'd been abandoned, and I buried deeper under the comforter. A bright light came in through the window sheers as the sun rose. I heard rustling in the kitchenette and saw Donna's back.

"What time is it?" My croaky voice surprised me. I must have cried harder than I thought.

Donna turned and gave me a soft smile. Her eyes held regret. "Sorry, didn't mean to wake you. It's just a bit after five."

"Five? In the morning?" I sat up too fast and the room spun.

Donna rushed over and kept me from toppling off the bed. "I

peeked in on you after closing last night, and you were sleeping hard. You looked like you needed the rest."

I'd been there all night. We'd been married for seven years and not once had I spent the night away from Arthur. He'd never even let me go home for a visit.

"I've got coffee in the kitchen."

Autopilot kicked on, because otherwise I'd be sobbing. "Thanks." I looked around and saw a door. "Is that the bathroom?"

"Sure is. You go clean up—fresh towels inside. Feel free to take your time. You come on down for breakfast when you feel up to it." She patted my back and headed out of the room. Her heels clicked on the stairs as she tromped down. "I'm locking you in, but you can flip it from the inside. It's just to keep wanderers out."

"Thanks," I called. Bracing myself against the bed, I got up and waited for the room to still again. Low blood sugar ran in my family. I remembered hearing my mama complaining about it when she was pregnant with my sisters and brother. That must be what was wrong with me. Heading into the bathroom, I found not only fresh towels, but a bottle of shampoo, soap, packaged toothbrush, and toothpaste. A shiny clean hairbrush sat on the mirror shelf. And a fresh package of underwear, amazingly just about my size, lay on the back of the toilet. Tears pooled in my eyes.

Glancing into the mirror over the tiny sink, I caught sight of matted red hair and mascara stains running down my cheeks. I hoped I hadn't ruined Donna's pillowcase. In the shower, I ran my soapy fingers over the tiny hump I imagined on my stomach. Realistically, the baby couldn't be showing yet—but something felt different. Firmer. As I stepped from the shower, emotionally lighter, nausea washed through me. Before I knew it, I was over the toilet, vomiting bile.

My mother survived this four times, and toward the end of each one, resentment began to show. As it was only my third time throwing up, I didn't feel bitter yet. Maybe that would come later?

Fully clothed and cleaned, I felt more human. My toast had gone cold. A real breakfast sounded good. I headed downstairs, thinking about how I could pay back Donna for her kindness—and for the breakfast I would eat. My hand protectively covered my stomach. I needed to figure out what to do next, but I couldn't get my brain to engage. I didn't have any cash on me. I needed to find my bank. Regret passed over me. I'd worked hard to save my secret money for emergencies.

Being abandoned qualified.

The restaurant murmured with early morning customers, sipping coffee from their mugs in zombie-like trances. I could almost see the light of life begin to sparkle in their eyes. The aroma of ham and eggs and all things breakfast-like cozied around me.

"There you are." Donna gave me a bright smile and motioned me to a booth. "What sounds good this morning, sweetie?"

"An omelet, some hash browns, side of fruit?"

"Coming right up." Donna turned to go.

I caught her arm and motioned her to come closer so I could whisper my shame. "Donna, I don't have any money right now."

"It's on me." She winked.

Again, I was taken aback. It'd been a long time since I'd met anyone who didn't want something for, well, everything. Worries rushed through my head. All of my things, though few, were with Arthur. I had no clothes. I had no job. I had no means of getting a job. Reading road maps for the past seven years, and raising my siblings before that, didn't qualify me for much of anything. While my schoolmates were finishing high school and working at the Fresh Freeze, I directed my husband across the country. My meager savings wouldn't last long at all.

Donna put the plate before me. "What's your name, honey?"

This woman fed and housed me, and I'd never even introduced myself to her. I blushed. "Macy Stone."

"So, Macy, what are your plans?" Donna tucked her order pad into her apron pocket and sat down across from me.

Panic threatened to pop the lid covering my emotions. I had never been on my own. I thought marrying Arthur would take care of my future and give me the freedom I'd dreamed of. Bit of a mistake there. "I need a job."

"Just so happens, I'm down a waitress. You ever waitressed before?"

I shook my head.

"I can train you, but you need to assure me you're in for the duration. I don't want you skipping off to the next place as soon as I get you broke in."

I almost laughed. I'd never skipped anywhere. And I had no place to go. "What if Arthur comes back?" My question was a hollow one.

"If he comes back, then you can go with him. If you want to."

My eyes locked on hers. If I wanted to?

Have you ever looked at a lion in a zoo habitat too small for it? You'd expect it to pace back and forth, yell and carry on to be let out. But it just sits there with all the hope squeezed out of it. The idea that there could be something else doesn't enter its mind anymore. It was just waiting. Waiting for the next rain, for the next meal, for the next time little kids made growling noises at it.

That had been me. But for the first time in my life, I wondered if there was something more.

Two

Donna handed me a job application and a pen. As I ate my omelet, I considered what to put for my address. I didn't have one. Arthur and I had a P.O. box service who would forward our mail around the country when we needed it, but I could hardly use that.

As if I'd spoken my worries aloud, Donna came over with a slip of paper in her hand. "This is the address of the apartment upstairs."

"I can't stay there," I protested. But inside, there was nothing more I wanted to do. The idea of looking for an apartment, leaving this place, made me edgy. Besides, I trusted Donna. I hadn't met her husband— the cook—yet, but if she'd married him, he couldn't be that bad. It'd be comforting to live there. Safe. Besides, if Arthur came back…I wasn't sure of my thoughts yet. Either I'd be glad to be easily found, or I'd be glad to have Donna and her large, spatula-wielding husband at my side telling him to leave me be.

"Yes you can. I've talked it over with Nick. You'll pay rent from your salary."

Rent. The word scared me. I had never lived on my own. The only practical experience I had with bill paying was Arthur fuming over the truck loan and the gas credit card receipts he sent into the contract company for reimbursement. I'd never paid for utilities.

I'd never paid for anything.

"How much is the rent?" I asked that rather than what I'd be paid.

"Say two-hundred-fifty a month, utilities included? Sound fair?"

I had no idea if it was fair. But I did remember what our truck payment was, and it had to be ten times that. "Sounds good." I gathered my courage. "How much will I make?"

Donna smiled. "We pay minimum wage, plus tips. And you'll get three meals the days you work."

Having been on the road with Arthur for the past seven years, I knew restaurants, and this one was off the beaten path in small-town Oregon. I also knew waitresses and how their wages were made up in tips. Most places didn't pay minimum wage out of the gate. I started to suspect I was a charity case. I began to say as much, but I noticed the hopeful look in Donna's eyes. She genuinely wanted me to stay.

"Sounds more than fair."

Donna squeezed my shoulder, her eyes twinkling. If I didn't accomplish anything else in the next few weeks, at least I was making her happy by staying there. That was something. I filled out the form and put down the address, the first permanent one I'd had since I left home with Arthur. It gave me reason to pause. I stared at the words *home address*, and a warmth seeped inside me I hadn't felt for a long time. Not since being at my grandmother's house.

Those times were rare moments of peace when I could get away from taking care of my brother and sisters and have Grandma's full attention. She and I would plan the day, as if I were the only grandchild she had. We'd cook, can fruits and vegetables, and talk about boys—or what I wanted to be when I grew up. I never knew. Grandma always expected great things from me.

I stared out the diner window at the dancing leaves and empty chips bag playing chase in the wind. A child and his mother passed by, and the boy dove down on the bag with both feet, crushing it under his tennis shoes.

Minutes later, I passed Nick my job application. He wiped his large hands on the food-stained rag hanging from his waist. Usually, men made me edgy. I was often surprised by what they said and did. I glanced at Nick. He gave what could only be called a loving look at his wife. She nodded to him.

"Says here you live upstairs." He winked at me. "Guess if you're late, we'll know how to find you."

I tried to laugh, but, every muscle in my body tensed.

"Donna's going to train you. I can't tell you how much we need dependable help around here. We've got Toby." He tipped his head to the busboy, who I now noticed was more of a bus-man. "But, he's no waitress. And besides, I need him as my assistant chef and head bottle washer." His brown eyes, so dark I couldn't see the pupils, glanced back at my application. "Let's give each other two weeks. If you don't like us, no hard feelings. And if we find things aren't working out with you, then I hope for the same."

As an abandoned pregnant woman with no job experience whatsoever, I couldn't have hoped for more. I had a job and a place to live in less than twenty-four hour's time. "Thanks. I'm grateful."

"Don't be grateful yet. This place gets hopping around breakfast and dinner. You and Donna will have to hoof it. We'll wear you out." He took my hand in his. I felt small and young and foolish in his grasp. He gave it a squeeze and turned back to making hash browns. Donna led me down a side hall from the kitchen. It opened into a smallish room with a stand of painted green lockers and a washroom. She took a piece of masking tape and put it on the door of one of the lockers, then wrote my name on it with a Sharpie. Donna gave me a warm smile and handed me a hanger with an apron and button-down white shirt, an order pad, and a ring with two keys.

"The keys are to the restaurant's back door and to your apartment."

The pressure of responsibility they bestowed on me, a stranger, grew heavier. I now had access to their life's work at all hours.

"Donna." I stared down at the keys. "Why are you doing this for me?"

"Now, now. Can't a body be helpful? You need help, so do we. It's a mutual arrangement as far as we see it." She patted my shoulder. "I'll have the locks changed by the end of the day. Use those until then."

I could see the honesty in her eyes, but there was something else there. Something I wasn't sure of, but not worried about. Just curious. Maybe she'd tell me one day. I was too glad for a place to stay to ponder it much more.

"You get changed in the washroom and come on out. I'll have you setting tables and taking orders in no time."

After I changed, Donna enlightened me on the organizing and running of the diner. She started with the subject of wiping down tables with bleach water and filling ketchup bottles, followed with table settings and coffee-mug etiquette. Having eaten in diners more times than I could count, I was nonetheless fascinated at the inner workings of the routine. After explaining the simple digital cash register to me and laughing at my nervousness (it still looked shockingly complicated), she had me sit down at the bar and study the shorthand she used to take orders. It was straightforward, but there was so much to learn.

SOS for sauce on the side. NS for no sauce. CB for cheese burger. T-b for T-bone steak. CHX for chicken. BLT for bacon, lettuce, and tomato sandwich. PAT for patty and LNK for link sausages.

My head spun. I listened intently as she took a couple's order, watched her scratch out the shorthand and give them a kind smile as she filled their glasses with water. Donna passed me and winked as she attached the order to the spinning silver disc over the hot counter.

"Order up."

"Got it," Nick called back. Without looking, he reached over, grabbed the slip and tucked it under a metal slat over the grill. He read it off and slapped frozen patties on the grill as she poured dressing into cups and served salad, reaching into the pass-through without looking up and grabbing a plate of fries he'd just placed. They mesmerized me with their fluid mind-reading actions. Glancing back down at the list, I started committing everything to memory. It reminded me of my times tables all over again. Only this time, I did it because I wanted to.

Donna passed me with an armful of dishes balanced precariously and a coffeepot in her other hand. I flexed my arm muscles, sure my tiny frame would be found lacking.

Donna caught me staring. "Don't you worry, now, you'll grow into the job." She gave me a wink and moved on, shifting the tray around customers' heads, dipping and bending as if doing a dance.

Toby came by and motioned to the notes. "Learning her chicken scrawl?" He had a deep, warm voice and light gray eyes. It'd been a long time since I chatted freely with a man closer to my own age. There was nothing intimidating about him. I flashed back to yesterday, and the tray he'd dropped. Clumsy but nice.

"Hey, I heard that." Donna came by and gave him a gentle shove.

Toby smiled at her and leaned close to me. "I'm Toby Stinton." He put out his hand and took mine in a friendly shake. You could tell a lot about people by their hands. His were strong but not overpowering.

He wasn't trying to overcompensate for anything by crushing the life out of my fingers. "I'm glad you're here. We can really use the help." There was that look in his eye, the same one Donna had. I almost asked what it might mean, but Donna called him away to clear tables.

I sighed, still overwhelmed but beginning to get the rhythm of the place—organized chaos. They were like a family. It was a good feeling. A safe feeling.

The diner door opened with a jingle. From the corner of my eye, I saw a man the size and shape of Arthur, and my breath caught. Heart pounding, I glanced in his direction. It wasn't Arthur. Thank God, it wasn't Arthur.

Then I was certain. If Arthur came back, I'd be thankful for big Nick and his spatula.

Three

The day passed in a haze, and I was once again plodding up the stairs to the little apartment. I couldn't quite think of it as mine yet. This new life still seemed temporary. I locked the door behind me. Donna told me I had the only copy of the key—her assurance increased the sense of security building in me all day.

I put down a to-go container on the tabletop, and the aroma of fried chicken and mashed potatoes called me. Glancing around my little haven, I noticed the touches of comfort added since last night. There were fresh flowers on the table in a ceramic vase. The refrigerator was running. I found it fully stocked. A sticky note affixed to the outside told me Donna had picked up a "few things" I might need.

As I opened the cabinets of the kitchenette, I found a set of butterfly-patterned dishes and glassware. They weren't new but were free of cracks and chips. And clean. I could tell from the soapy smell and wet sink that Donna had snuck up here before the locksmith came and gotten the place ready for me. Where she found time to do that between training me and serving lunch and dinner, I had no idea.

Besides the kitchen table, love seat, coffee table, and daybed the only other pieces of furniture were a whitewashed armoire and partially stocked two-shelf bookcase. I opened the doors of the armoire and found some simple shirts and pants. A couple summer dresses and a jacket rounded out the wardrobe. In the drawers were a set of towels and a spare set of sheets. It was strange to find most of the clothes would fit me perfectly. Donna couldn't have shopped for me today, could she?

I pulled out a larger T-shirt, pair of sweat pants, and a fresh pair of underwear from the package I'd left behind that morning and headed to the shower. When I got out, I opened the cabinet and found a box of garbage bags under the sink. I stashed my dirty clothes in one and made sure to hang up my work shirt and apron.

Staring at the bag, I realized another need: clean clothes. I couldn't afford to go to the laundromat yet. I'd do them by hand. I needed to buy soap, though.

Clean and comfortable, I sat down and ate my dinner under the pinkish light of the setting sun slipping past the only window. The quiet seeped into me like the warmth from the radiator register sputtering in the corner. I looked out on the side street, watching couples walking here and there, holding hands and laughing. Down farther sat a movie theatre showing an old classic, and a line of customers streamed around the corner. The bright lights around the marquee flashed a welcome.

Someone else might feel lonesome, but I didn't. There was a newness to it all that captivated my imagination. I was no longer in charge of three little ones at home while my mother nursed my dying father. I was no longer tied to the road with Arthur. I could do what I wanted, when I wanted. If I had my money, I'd walk to the drugstore and buy a magazine and come back and read it. Or maybe take in a movie. Or stretch out on the bed in any direction I wanted. After sharing a twin mattress in the small confines of our cab with Arthur for the entirety of our marriage, the idea of not sharing anything with anyone appealed to me.

I really needed to find my bank. Before I could locate the phonebook, the phone rang, and my heart flew into my throat. Glancing around, I spied it hanging on the wall next to the bed. It was an old rotary style, custard yellow. I hesitated to answer. Who could be calling? The phone stopped ringing. As I lowered my arm, it began again, jarring my senses and rattling my nerves. I realized I'd have to answer it.

"Hello?"

"Macy?" An unfamiliar man's voice responded. "Macy, it's me, Toby. I wanted to let you know Donna had me go and buy a few staples for you and get the dishes done. And you know I'm good at dishes." He chuckled at his own joke. "Things were a little dusty. I didn't want you to think some stranger had been poking around your place."

"How'd you get in here?"

"I did it before Donna had the locks re-mastered."

I didn't respond. Part of me was disturbed that Toby had been in my apartment without me, even though nothing inside belonged to me.

"I hope everything's okay?" His voice sounded uneasy, and I remembered he was Toby. Clumsy, nice Toby.

"Sure. Thanks."

"I could show you around town tomorrow. We're only open until three on Sunday. I mean, if you'd like me to. As a friend."

Toby was too nice for me to lead on. But for some reason I couldn't manage to say what I was thinking. Instead, I hoped for his friendship. It had been a long time since anyone wanted to be friends with me. A long time since I'd been in one place long enough to get to know someone besides truckers and their wives, or girlfriends, or tiny grumpy dogs.

"I'd like that."

"Great. See you tomorrow."

I hung up the receiver and pondered vaguely where he got the number. But then I saw it clearly printed on the phone. For a moment, my hand hovered, and I wondered if my mother knew Arthur had left me. Instead of giving it any more thought, I retreated to the table and finished my supper. I'd find a phonebook later.

If Arthur hadn't told my mother, then I wouldn't. Not yet. She'd done her best to ignore me these past few years, there was no point changing things now.

That night, as I fell asleep, I watched the pattern of the marquee lights play across my ceiling, like my own monochrome aurora borealis. Peace enveloped me. My last thought had nothing to do with worry, and only to do with the unexpected love I felt for my baby.

The next morning, or what I assumed was morning from the gray light filling my apartment, I woke to the sound of the phone ringing over my head. If I stayed past the two weeks, the first thing I'd do was move it across the room. And cover it with pillows. My pulse thumped so wildly in my ears, I couldn't hear what they said when I answered.

"Sorry, who is it?"

"It's Donna. I realized you don't have an alarm clock. We open in an hour. If you want breakfast before you start, be down fast."

I thanked her for the wakeup call.

Sitting up, I realized I might be a lot more like my mother than I wanted to be. As soon as gravity took effect, the nausea hit. I raced to the bathroom and threw up. Since arriving there, I'd found myself grateful for many things. Right then, I chose the clean toilet.

After donning a white shirt and my old jeans, I headed downstairs to see if my stomach could hold breakfast. As I ordered oatmeal and toast, I realized Donna might not know about the baby. The whole place must have heard my talk with Arthur, but could it be they didn't know? Would they decide they didn't want me around once they did?

Donna transferred my order to the bar where I sat. I liked it there, watching Nick cook, watching Toby chop vegetables and mix eggs and tear open packages of shredded cheese. They moved with the fluidity of Olympic relay racers, passing the baton without looking. Or in this case, bowls of chopped bell peppers and tomatoes.

Donna brought me a cup of mint tea. "This'll help settle your stomach."

I glanced up at her, waiting for judgment. "You know?"

"I overheard."

"Nick knows?"

"Yes, he knows."

"Toby?"

"It's not my place to tell. Nick needed to know because you're staying on our property and you're our employee."

Relief flooded through me. It wasn't that I wanted to lie to Toby. It was just that, for some reason, hiding who I was felt better than admitting the truth of my life. I was hungry for friendship, hungrier than I had realized. I knew the look he'd give me. I knew the things he'd say when I told him about my marriage—looks I'd seen a hundred times. I wanted to hold on to the idea that he was a possible friend for a bit longer.

"He'll figure it out here in a couple months, though." She gave me a smile. "There's nothing to be ashamed of. You're married." Donna patted my hand and walked toward the front.

I nod. *Married.* What did that mean to Donna? She flipped the closed sign to open and unlocked the front door. A short line of customers filed in, greeting her and hailing Nick. She smiled in pride as Nick called back and gave her a wink. Their eyes twinkled at each other. Not just smiled in admiration, but actually *twinkled.*

No one ever looked at me like that.

Toby came by and grinned in encouragement. As he cleared the first table, I saw Donna really did need my help. We'd gone from four people straggling in to a room full of hungry customers in a matter of minutes. I cleared my plate and grabbed my order pad. It was now or never.

Four

"You did great today." Toby gave me an encouraging thumbs-up as I sat exhausted at a back table, filling salt and pepper shakers. The clock showed two-thirty. The last of the lunch rush left and Donna turned the sign back to CLOSED. My feet and neck were racing to be first in the pain category.

"Thanks. I don't know about that, though. Nick had to call me to the counter three times because he couldn't read the order."

Donna came by and sat down. "Oh, sweetie, that's fine. The last gal who was here never could get it down. Nick had her in tears by the end of the day." I guess she could see the concern in my eyes, because she put a hand on my arm. "He's kind, but gets demanding when there's eleven orders in the queue and he can't read a single one."

I nodded. I'd be a bit gruff too. Nick sat down at a nearby table with a cup of coffee and a burger—protein style, wrapped in lettuce.

He caught me watching. "I can't eat wheat. Makes me sicker than a dog. If you get anyone who has food allergies, you let me know. I'm as careful as can be."

Every time Nick spoke, he ended up surprising me. As appearances went, Nick reminded me of Mel from the old TV show *Alice*. Well, younger, and with more hair. They both carried a spatula and wore white. And they were big. I kept expecting him to yell or carry on, but he didn't. If I was anyone from that show, I'd be Vera. The lost, muddle-headed, clumsy girl. Naive at first, and then jaded. I wanted to be Alice—starting over, taking life by the throat.

"Our daughter was the same way," Donna confided, but then she looked down at her order pad.

It was the first time I'd heard of a daughter. Nick's eyes darkened, and he went back to eating. Toby shifted from one foot to the other and then started wiping down the red, sparkly vinyl seats with a rag, moving away with each swipe.

"You have a daughter?"

Donna shifted her gaze out the window for a moment, then cleared her throat. "What are your plans for this afternoon?" She wore a forced smile, but I could see pain in her eyes. I took the hint and went along with the change of subject.

"Toby's going to show me around."

Donna reached into her pocket and pulled out an envelope. "Here's your day's tips. Payday's the end of the month, but I send your tips home with you. Keep track of them for taxes."

Sliding the flap of the envelope open, I saw several dollar bills, some fives, and a ten inside. Enough for a magazine or movie. Enough to buy groceries until I could find a branch of my bank.

Arthur gave me an allowance, but I always stashed it away in my account whenever we were near our bank. He met my physical needs, and there wasn't any place for us to store collectibles or the like, so I never spent it. Besides, we were never anywhere for very long. I didn't know if there was something, some kind of sign that Arthur would abandon me someday—but it seemed prudent at the time. When Toby showed me around later, I'd ask if they had a branch in town.

"I can't believe someone left me a ten." I didn't remember exactly pleasing any of the customers. Although I didn't think I'd angered anyone, many had cold coffee and empty water glasses. And I'd mixed up people's orders at least three times.

Donna smiled but avoided eye contact, and I guessed she'd padded my tips.

"You can finish by refilling the ketchup bottles and we'll call it a day. Don't forget to be here by six A.M."

Growing up, I'd never been an early riser. That, among many things, changed when I married a trucker. I could wake up at just about any time now, ready to move on a moment's notice.

"Will do. If there's a drugstore in town, I'll look for an alarm clock."

Toby tossed the cleaning rags in a bucket. "There's a thrift store near the library, but they aren't open today. I'll take you by Mat's Medical Mart."

The ketchup bottles took another half hour to fill. I stood and stretched my back, feeling it pop and crackle. "I'm going to head upstairs to change, and then you can start the tour."

I was back in ten minutes, wearing a gray hoodie over my T-shirt. Donna's eyes locked on the hoodie, and she bit her lip.

"I found it upstairs. Is it okay if I wear the clothes? They're just about my size." If she said no, I'd have to add clothes shopping to the top of my list.

"Sure. Yes. Of course." She waved me off, but her eyes pinched at the corners in a wince as if she was hurting. It was probably her legs—mine were aching.

As we headed out, Donna reminded me to use the back entrance when I came home because the diner would be closed. It reminded me once again of the trust they were giving me. My parents' shop and market were their lives. I didn't think my mother would ever give the key to the mini-mart to anyone, not even me. Instead of thinking about the past, I forced a smile and gave Toby my full attention.

"So, tell me about the town."

"We've got about ten thousand people living here in Bridgeville. We've got three grade schools, K through eight, and one high school. A sheriff's office, a library, and a handful of lawyers and doctors."

I thought of the baby. "Is there a hospital?"

"Over in Appleton. It's about forty minutes from here."

I filed the information away.

We walked downtown, which held multiple brick buildings circa early 1900s. A block back, I could see some Victorian houses mixed with 1970s ranch-style. The street we walked also served as the highway and central dividing line in town. I heard an ice cream truck in the distance, growing closer.

If there was one word I could chose for the town, it was nostalgic. There seemed to be a bit of everything I'd ever wanted in a place. I wasn't naive enough to think my life would be perfect, but the sense of belonging that rushed over me pushed those thoughts away. Funny how fast my roots were growing. Maybe I'd feel that way in any town I got to stay in for more than a few days. Bitterness and then disloyalty to Arthur and his way of life sliced through me. I pushed off the guilt and reminded myself of how he'd left me here. The ice cream truck grew closer, the melody deafening me as it passed.

"Want one?" Toby grinned at me. I was sure my face showed anticipation. As soon as I nodded, he gave chase, waving down the driver. It'd been a long time since I'd enjoyed an ice cream bar. My parents' mini-mart had a freezer case, but it wasn't like we kids were allowed to grab one whenever we wanted. They were a special treat on a hot day.

Daddy would close down the shop early and he'd holler, "Calling it quits." He'd wave me over from the yard between our house and the mini-mart and we'd choose one and walk through the woods to the nearby pond. My brother and the young ones were usually napping or playing inside, so more often than not, it'd be just the two of us, striding to the water's edge, our shoes stomping over the dry ground, chasing off the occasional crickets and other hiding creatures. We'd sit on a rock and talk about the day, skipping stones and chatting about whatever hard case he'd figured out. My father talked about trucks and cars like a doctor would talk about his patients. I'd often find him pondering the difficult ones in the kitchen, late at night. He took such pride in what he did, and he loved it so. He'd put my mother in charge of the mini-mart and gas station, but the shop was his domain.

Toby caught up with the truck and motioned me to hurry. The lyrical music competed with my voice. Through pointing and nodding, the driver got the idea I wanted a drumstick. After he pulled away, I ripped the paper off the top and savored the chocolate and nuts.

"This is great."

"Yeah. Probably the last time he'll be out this season. The rainy weather is supposed to start up tomorrow. Knowing Oregon, it could be months before we see the sun." Toby took bites of his Creamsicle. Just the idea of biting ice cream made my teeth ache. I shivered, trying not to watch.

We headed to a small central park and sat on a bench. It looked like the whole town was out, savoring the last warm day of September. Parents pushed strollers, kids played on the jungle gym, and dogs chased Frisbees. Big rigs hauling logs and cows passed by every once in a while. The fumes teased my nose. How long would it be before the aroma of exhaust and rumble of diesel engines quit nagging me?

Toby chatted along about his high school days and growing up in such a small town. I understood better than he knew, my town being even smaller. He looked at me as intensely as I must be looking at him, each of us hanging on to every word. The wind ruffled his straw colored hair, and he ran his fingers through it, pushing it back. I watched his blue eyes sparkle as he ramped up for another tale. It was a moment out of time, and I sat enraptured, watching his mouth move before I realized I'd lost the point of this one.

"Wait, what did you just say about knives and toes?"

"My buddy, Ross, and I would chuck pocket knives at each other's toes, to see who could get the closest. So this one time, his little sister Trina came screaming out of the house how she was going to tell—she was always following us and being nosey. Ross lost his concentration and slipped. His knife caught my toe. Blood went everywhere." He laughed, but I grimaced.

"That's funny?"

"No, but Trina passed out right on the grass." He kept snickering.

I still wasn't laughing. "What about your toe?"

"Oh, it was okay. I only had to get a couple stitches. Ross ran in the house and got me a towel, and spied a chunk of cheese. Before Trina got up, he tossed the cheese to the dog and started screaming that the dog ate my toe. I lay on the ground and moaned." He spoke with such animation and excitement I began to wonder if he was as lonely as I was.

I hit his shoulder hard. "You did not!"

"Sure we did."

"That's mean." I tried not to laugh, but as the eldest in a family with four children, I knew what nosey siblings could be like. Still, I'd never go that far. Probably.

"Ross got into a lot of trouble with his mom, but his dad understood. They made Trina promise not to follow us around anymore."

"I wouldn't have to promise anyone not to follow *you*." We laughed together. The sound startled me—I couldn't remember how long it'd been since I'd laughed. Sitting there felt right and comfortable. I didn't want to run out of ice cream and have to go back to my apartment alone. "What's Ross doing now? Is Trina still in therapy?" I bumped against him, waiting for him to expand on more antics, but instead, he stiffened.

"We don't see much of each other now." He shifted on the bench and concentrated on his ice cream. A cloud shifted in front of the setting sun, casting an orange haze over the park. Even though it was still warm out, I shivered. Moms and dads took the cue and started folding up blankets and plopping kids into strollers.

"I'm married." My outburst surprised us both. After my admission, I expected he'd go back to being Toby the busboy and I'd go back to being the new girl at the diner. Our friendship was as good as over.

Instead, he surprised me.

"I know. I saw you together the day he left you."

"Oh." Shame filled me anew at the thought of the witnesses to my abandonment.

"How'd you end up with him anyway?" His voice didn't hold condemnation.

It was a question I'd been asked more than a few times in my life. What was a young woman doing with an older man like Arthur? I'd often been mistaken for his daughter. In the beginning, I was full of the romance of the idea. Arthur waited to marry just the right person, and *I* was the right person. We were soul mates just like in the movies or on television. We'd beaten the odds and our love would carry us through. Like Laura and Almonzo in *Little House*, or Holling and Shelly on *Northern Exposure*—the latter being more familiar.

Seven years later, I wasn't sure about the truth of that. If our roles were reversed, even if we'd agreed to never have kids, would I have left my young husband in a strange town—with nothing?

"My father ran a gas station and shop on a northern truck route near Spokane. He'd do tune-ups and repair jobs for Arthur when he came through town. Over the years, we got to know each other. One day he asked me to marry him, and I said yes."

It wasn't that easy. There'd been an illness and a death and then a courting period. There'd been a time when I thought Arthur could do no wrong. He'd been there for us all while Daddy wasted away from cancer, calling and stopping in when his route allowed. He'd shifted business our way, kept us afloat. When my father died, he'd come and let me cry on his shoulder. When my family was wrapped up in illness and plans for death, Arthur listened to the despair of my broken dreams. My whole family was grateful to Arthur.

He'd been a hero in my eyes. My savior.

"You're so much younger. How long have you been married?"

"Seven years." My voice was just above a whisper.

"But you can't be more than twenty-five." Toby's eyebrows bunched together. I had the routine down pat. I'd tell him the truth, he'd give me a shocked look and change the subject. We'd never chat about anything of any importance again. That was how it always went.

"I was sixteen. My mother emancipated me to him." I turned my head away so I wouldn't see the look that made me feel dirty and cheap. Instead, I heard his voice consoling me.

"We all make hard choices in life. Some work out. Some don't." The tone in Toby's voice startled me. I turned back around to see if he meant what he'd said, but he stared down at the drips of orange and white ice cream melting on the sidewalk between his feet.

The silence dragged on for a while. Lots of things ran through my mind. All the explanations I'd given to people, given to myself. But I found I didn't need to give him any.

He glanced up at me. "Do you think he'll be back for you?"

Did I? "I don't know. I never thought he'd leave in the first place."

"Will you go with him if he does?"

That was the question I hadn't wanted to consider. I'd made myself busy trying to live in the moment, not looking ahead. My parents weren't religious people, but my grandmother was, and she took me to church every Sunday. She'd told me about right and wrong. She'd read the Bible to me every Sunday after brunch. When my mother gave me a day by myself, I'd head over to her house and bake cookies or pies, and she'd teach me something about God. The lessons I remembered most in the past few years was how much God hated divorce. Maybe she knew my dad wasn't going to last much longer, and she needed to give me just one piece of advice.

I'd made a commitment. Wasn't that what my mother told me every time I called early on to complain about things not being quite what I'd expected them to be?

"I haven't thought that far ahead, I guess."

Toby went quiet. I wasn't sure if I'd lost his friendship or not. He stood and put his hand out toward me. "We'd better get to Mat's before he closes, or you won't have an alarm clock."

I put my hand in his, feeling secure in a way I hadn't known for a long time. He pulled me up, and we walked down the street. I decided I should get it all over with at once.

"I'm pregnant."

This stopped him cold. His face went shock white for a moment, and he looked off into the distance. I couldn't read his expression at all—there wasn't one. As the color filtered back into his features, his gaze locked onto mine. I know I must have sounded irresponsible to him. Here I was, a pregnant woman, living alone for the first time in her life. But that was the thing. It was the first time in *my* life, and I was relishing my independence as much as I was terrified by it.

"That's why he left. I spent most of my life taking care of my sisters and brother. The last thing I wanted was to take care of another child. We had an agreement, and I was fine with it."

"But now you feel differently."

"Yeah." As soon as I'd seen the positive mark on my pregnancy test kit, I knew.

"You're going to need help."

The ice cream man's tinny music began playing again in the distance, a sing-song tune wisping back to us on the sunbaked breeze.

It'd been so long since a person my age looked at me with something besides pity or disgust or fear—or since I'd had a friend of any sort—I didn't know how to feel. But right then, I could see it. His eyes had something hard and determined in them, something I couldn't quite pin down. All I knew was that I liked it.

Five

One day led into another. Two weeks passed, and Arthur didn't come back. I began to relax into my new life. I still threw up every morning. Donna comforted me and told me it would stop after a time. I remembered Mama, and I knew that idea wasn't something to hitch my hopes to. But then I'd go into work and listen to the stories of the customers, pick up new jokes, and pretend I was part of this tightknit town. After work, I'd go for a walk or head upstairs to read. Sometimes Toby made me a cup of cocoa, and we'd swap childhood stories or share about our grumpiest customer of the day. I could do whatever I wanted.

I ushered my customer to the door, holding it open for her. Mrs. Anglebright patted my arm and left with the conciliatory words, "You know dear, you're getting better at this every day."

Someone else might have taken her comments as a slight, but they warmed my insides. This time I'd remembered how she liked her tea—with cream—and didn't like the gravy on her plate, but on the side. Having survived the criticalness of my mother and the control of my husband, her words were a balm.

"See you next Wednesday for dinner?"

"Yes indeed."

Turning to clear away, and gather my more substantial tip, I saw Donna and Nick talking. They passed a serious look between them, Nick glanced at me before giving her a hug and nodding. Donna moved to the counter and started replacing place settings. A heavy feeling filled my gut.

An explicative from a passing man outside the diner window drew my attention. He fought the wind for control of his umbrella, a grimace on his face, as the rain came down in sheets off the awnings over his head.

A few minutes later Donna signaled me to come and sit down across from her in a nearby booth. Making my way to her, I gave her a smile, but my insides were a bundle of nerves. This must be it. Nick didn't think I was doing good enough. I would have to leave, and I had no idea where to go. The comfort I'd had moments before washed away. The idea of returning to my mom and siblings flitted through my mind, but truly, I couldn't think of a worse fate. Don't get me wrong, I missed my brother and sisters—even my mom—but I didn't want to go back to being told what to do every minute of the day. The pressure, the responsibility needed to be Mama's, not mine.

"Is everything okay?" I couldn't contain my anxiety, and I was sure Donna could see it on my face. I was never good at poker.

"Don't worry, now. Nick and I have decided to extend your time here, if you'd like."

I noticed she didn't say hire me on permanently. "Extend?"

"Frankly, he's worried about your husband coming back. And he's worried about what will happen once the baby is born."

I could understand Nick's trepidation. I felt it every time I saw a mom come in with an infant. Every time a toddler threw a spoon on the floor. Every time a screaming kid had to be taken outside and given a talking to. I knew only too well the responsibilities of caring for a baby.

"So?" I didn't want to fill in the blanks for her. I needed to know where I stood and what I was up against.

"We think you should give everything some thought. There are ways of tracking down people. And I'm sure it wouldn't be too hard to find your husband if you know his routes. The police would work in your favor to get child support."

I'd never considered looking for Arthur. The truth was, every day we'd been apart, I got a tiny bit of myself back. I'd started to learn what I did and didn't like. I didn't want to return to the lack of freedom, the lack of mental stimulation, of being trapped in the cab with Arthur. I'd begun to speculate on how I ended up married to someone who clearly didn't love me. The other day, I'd even compiled a list of questions for my mom. I couldn't fathom letting my sixteen-year-old child run off with a man twice her age.

"The thing is, I don't want to find him." I couldn't believe I'd said it out loud. But it was true. I didn't want him, and I didn't want to be tied to his money.

Donna's eyes showed understanding. "I don't know the details, sweetie, but I can imagine it's been hard to live that life."

"It's not the life. I don't mind being on the road, much. Even now, I get itchy feet. I like driving and seeing new places." It was the not getting to choose where we were going part I didn't like.

"Was he cruel to you?"

Was he? He'd never beaten me—which I'd always been grateful for. But if he had, then maybe I'd have a better reason not to go back to him. I still wasn't sure of divorce.... I knew I needed to be there a bit longer, have more time to consider things, before I made a decision. Maybe Nick sensed this?

"He never hit me. But I'm more of a companion than a wife." In most ways, anyway. I pressed my hand against my stomach. "I keep him from being lonely." Arthur had told me so a handful of times. After watching Donna flirt with Nick, and the admiring look on Nick's face as he watched Donna walked away, I knew there was more to marriage than just keeping someone from being lonely.

"What about your folks?"

I'd thought of calling home a few times since Arthur walked out. My mother would worry. She might even insist I go back to him and try to work things out—never mind he'd been the one to abandon *me*. Even if I didn't think she should have used me as a mini-mom, I'd always known she'd do anything to take care of us all. Anything. But something held me back. Not to mention we hadn't spoken for years.

"My father's dead and my mom has enough on her plate keeping the family business together. It wouldn't be right to ask her for help."

"I see."

"When do I have to be out?" I swallowed hard, resolve building. I'd discovered that there was a branch of my bank in Appleton. I could find a ride and withdraw my money. It wouldn't be a lot, but it'd be a start.

Donna's eyes began to tear. "You don't have to leave. Please don't leave."

I rode a pendulum, my life swinging in the balance. "But you said you wanted me to think things over."

"We do. It's not right to live in limbo. You have choices to make. But in the meantime, we'd be happy to have you stay." I didn't understand the desperation in her tone.

The restaurant went still, and I noticed Toby had stopped wiping down tables, but he still held the cloth against the top. He was listening in.

"So I can stay?"

"Both Nick and I think you're working out real good here. But things happen when you don't plan ahead." She glanced at Nick now cleaning the grill. "It's best to think things through."

"Okay. I'll be thinking about things."

Donna smiled and patted my hand. "I'll close up, you go ahead and get some rest."

I collected my dinner from the pass-through and glanced at Toby. He'd gone back to wiping down the booths, but his forehead was creased as if lost in thought.

As I ate dinner in my apartment, I pondered the future. After the baby was born, what would I do with her? I perused the phonebook for day cares. It made me sad to think of my baby being raised in the bedlam of other people's screaming, runny-nosed children. Hadn't my mother done everything in her power to keep all of us together while my dad died? She'd kept us from being handed off to other family members by making me honorary mom. I'd learned to cook and clean. Every now and then my grandmother stepped in to relieve me when I had to go to school—but for the most part, I was on my own while my mother worked in the store.

I think if it had been my choice, if I'd been asked, then maybe I would have taken to it better. But all I'd wanted was to sit at the edge of my father's bed, like my mother had done, and take care of the most important person in my life. Watching my father die from a distance ate at my soul. We'd been so close, and all of a sudden I wasn't allowed to stay in his presence for more than a few minutes a day—if that.

After my father passed, I remember sitting in my room near the floor vent, holding my breath. Arthur had talked to me about leaving, about how it wasn't fair for me to raise the kids, about how I deserved my own future—but I didn't want to run off with him. Watching my father die, taking care of the little ones, stepping into my mom's shoes until she could handle life again wasn't fair. I had a life to live, too. But running away didn't seem right at all. Plus, I was underage.

Arthur said he'd talk my mom into letting me marry him. I got caught up in the romance of the idea. He treated me so good, brought me presents and commiserated with my loss. At the time, I thought that was the answer to my prayers. Looking back, I didn't think God had that in mind, exactly. Through the vent, I could hear murmurs and soft talking. Even though I clearly heard her say no, three days later Arthur had a ring and I had my freedom.

Or so I thought.

My mother wore a sad expression for days. Almost sadder than when my father died. I thought then it was because I was leaving, but now I wasn't so sure. Maybe it was who I was leaving with.

"I'm so happy, Mama. Why can't you be happy for me, too?" I'd packed my suitcase and tried to ignore the sighs emitting from her side of the room.

"It's not as easy as all that. I hope I made the right decision."

The story of Cinderella danced through my mind. I'd found my prince, my means to escape.

"Arthur's a great guy. And he loves me. There's no sense in our waiting two years." I bit my lip, hoping she'd still agree. I'd convinced myself of our love—and there was nothing more sure, or desperate, than a young girl in love with her hero.

My mother came over and took my face in her cool hands. It'd been the first time since my father got sick that she'd really touched me. I could see my form reflected in her wide brown eyes as we stared at each other.

"Are you sure about this, Macy? It's not too late. I can just say no, and we'll make other plans." Her voice didn't sound as sure as her words.

At the time, I didn't understand what she meant by other plans. I assumed she meant waiting until I was older. But now it gave me reason to pause. A lot of things in my life weren't adding up right. And I began to wonder what the missing piece to the puzzle was.

I'd once read that life held surprises around every corner. What the book didn't say was that not all surprises were good ones.

As I served the chicken-fried steak to table six, the front door of the restaurant opened. I heard Donna greet someone and seat them at my station. She came by and nudged me.

"Lady at table five asked specifically for you. See, you're getting regulars!" Her enthusiasm was contagious. I turned around with a huge grin on my face and felt it melt away like an ice cube dropped into a hot mug of tea. Sitting at table five was my mom.

My limbs were leaden as I approached her. Part of me wanted to pretend I had amnesia and simply ask her for her order. I could have pulled it off pretty easily. Frankly, the new blond coloring my mother sported, and my not seeing her for so long, should have kept me from recognizing her on the street. But when you paired that with her all-seeing eyes and the straight set of her shoulders, there was no denying her.

"Well then, I found you." My mother's layered sing-song voice grated over my nerves. She only did that when she was putting on her happy face—the chances she'd try to manipulate me into doing something I wouldn't like had gone up by eighty percent.

"I didn't know you were looking." I pulled out my order pad.

"Arthur called and told me what happened." I couldn't figure out her tone. She sounded accusatory.

"He told you he abandoned me in the middle of Oregon?" There was an edge to my voice I hadn't dared to use with my mother before.

Her eyes went wide for a second.

"He said you'd had a disagreement. He had to get back on his route and thought it was best you stay here."

I couldn't imagine the conversation going the way she put it. I saw her eyes stray to my stomach. At least Arthur had told her that much.

Nick hollered from the kitchen. "Order up, seven."

I handed my mother a menu. "I'll be back for your order in a few minutes."

She grabbed my wrist but let go as I stared her down. "Macy Stone, I didn't ride a bus eight hours for you to ignore me."

Her commanding tone not only got the attention of the whole restaurant, but also pushed all my little girl buttons, and I had to fight the urge to sit down. "I'll be right back. I have customers waiting."

I went to the pass-through and got the order for table seven. Toby came from the kitchen and watched me. The whole place went on alert. I'd heard about tension crackling in a room, but this was the first time I'd ever experienced such a thing. I needed space. I needed to think.

I went back to my mom's table. "If you don't want to order, that's fine. But you'll have to come back later when I'm on break."

"I'll eat. Roast beef sandwich and coffee. I'll need it for the ride back." Again, accusation laced her voice.

"White, rye, or wheat?"

"White."

"Everything on it?"

"You know how I take my sandwiches."

I did know. I'd made plenty of them.

An hour later, I got my break and sat down at her table. I waited for my mother to start talking. I couldn't figure out what she was doing there. I wasn't her problem anymore. I watched as she pushed the last few French fries around her plate with her fork.

"You need to get back together with him, Macy."

"Are you forgetting *he* left me here?"

"He did say that." She stopped, as if I could change what happened. Did she want me to admit I drove him away? "But anyone would have been shocked. You two had an agreement." A flash of something went through her eyes at the word.

"And I never thought to break it." Light began to dawn. "He thinks

I tricked him or something? I didn't do this on purpose, Mom. *You* of all people know how tired I was of taking care of babies."

"Let's not start, okay?" Somehow she always turned it back on me.

"Why are you angry at me? What right do you have?"

"Macy, it was your choice to marry Arthur. I felt plenty guilty about it at the time, but I've learned to live with it. If you want to save your marriage, you'll get rid of the baby."

"An abortion?" If she'd told me to have the baby on the street and give it to a stranger, I couldn't have been more surprised.

"That was Arthur's idea, not mine."

"You have no right to make these kinds of decisions with *my* husband."

"I didn't say I agreed. But what about adoption?"

I leaned in to whisper, not wanting any nosey customers overhearing our conversation more than they already were. "I. Want. My. Baby."

"You just *think* you want a baby."

She loved to read my mind—too bad she didn't have any more talent for it today than she ever did. "I'm not doing it."

Tears came to my mother's eyes. "Macy, do you have any idea what will happen to all of us?"

And now I was stumped. What did keeping my baby—her grandchild no less—have anything to do with them? I watched in morbid curiosity as she dabbed at her eyes and blew her nose. Her lip quivered. "You know how hard it's been to hang on to the station. I've put my lifeblood into that place. I've given up all my dreams to keep it and a roof over our heads." A sob broke from her. "If only your father hadn't died."

"It wasn't his fault, Mom."

Her eyes hardened. "If he'd quit smoking when the doctor told him to, maybe he could have made it. We'll never know, though. I'm doing my best, putting one foot in front of the other. And I've come to accept our relationship is never going to be the same, you and me. But I've got three kids who need a home." She folded her napkin in a perfect square and put in on top of her mostly empty plate.

"What's that got to do with me and Arthur?"

As if a light dawned in her mind, I could see my mother's eyes grasp the issue at hand. I wished she'd enlighten me, too.

"You don't know?" It was more of a statement than a question.

"Know what, Mom? I left home seven years ago and haven't gotten more than a card at Christmas with your name at the bottom. I only hear how you're doing through Arthur."

Tears. More and more of them streamed down her face.

"Oh, no. No." She rocked back and forth like she had the day Dad passed.

Donna came and put a hand on my shoulder, her eyes urging. "Would you like to take your mom to the break room, Macy?"

Looking around at all the politely watchful customers, I nodded and numbly took my shattered mother by the hand. I led her to the break room, where she collapsed on a chair and continued to rock.

"Mom, what is it?" I sank to the floor, holding her hands, trying to get her attention. Compassion for her bubbled forth from the locked-down safe inside.

"He told me you knew. That—" She choked on her words. "—you were happy for the arrangement. I thought you were so sacrificial. But then you stopped writing, and I didn't know if you were angry with me. And when your grandma died, and you didn't come to the funeral, I thought you'd left us all behind."

I sank back against my heels, an ache building in my chest. My grandmother was dead? "When?" I could barely register all that was happening.

"When what?" She wiped at her eyes.

"When did Grandma die?" I almost couldn't ask the question. I hoped I'd misheard her.

"Three years ago."

"All this time? Why didn't you let me know?"

"I told Arthur. I called twice, and he said he'd give you the message. He said he'd left it up to you whether to come or not, and you'd decided not to."

Unexplained phone calls. I'd noticed on occasion Arthur would get calls on his cell he'd ignore. I always assumed it was telemarketers.

"And the letters?" I had to know it all.

She blew her nose. "I wrote to you monthly at first. I never got an answer—only a card at Christmastime. After a while, I gave up."

"Me too." There seemed to be a lot of blame to go around.

Toby stuck his head in the break room, his hand gripping the doorframe. "Everything okay in here?" His eyes locked on my teary ones.

"Fine. We're fine. Thanks." I nodded for him to leave, not wanting any witnesses to how entirely messed up my family had become.

"If you need anything, I'm right out here." His eyes narrowed at my mother and he turned away. I took a steadying breath and turned back to her.

"You wrote to me?" Her voice lifted in hope.

I nodded. "And then I'd give my letters to Arthur to mail at our stops. I never imagined…" I couldn't complete my thoughts at all. For some reason, Arthur had wanted me all to himself. So much so, he'd cut me off from everyone.

"Mom, what does all this have to do with my keeping the baby?"

She swallowed hard. "The money."

"What money?"

"Arthur gave us money when you were first married. He jokingly called it a bride price. He said you knew all about it—that you'd asked him to help us."

"No." I'd never. I was so happy to leave home and the bad memories and feelings behind, I'd never thought about what my leaving would do to them. Only what it was doing for me. "So Arthur gives you money, and you sign me over to him. We agree not to have kids. He takes me away. When I don't hear from you, he tells me it's probably because you never loved me in the first place, and you're glad I'm off your hands since you have so much to take care of now with Daddy gone."

"Oh, no." The crying started up again. I was barely able to take in all that happened. I fought the urge to give her a good shake and tell her to cry later. It was *my* life being manipulated and maligned.

"And when you don't write, I believe him."

"But, I did write." She dabbed at her eyes.

"Arthur always got the mail."

The puzzle pieces fitted together more rapidly now.

"I thought I'd done the right thing. You seemed to love him so much, and he you. I thought you'd do well with Arthur, and we'd be better off financially. I should have known. I should have known."

My mother's sobs grew louder, she was rocking again, but I wasn't really paying attention. I'd been caught up in the lies, following their path of deception. My desperate, bereaved mother being handed the hope she needed to get through. Her belief I'd be better off with Arthur than at home. All the medical bills being taken care of. The family business safe. And me. I was happy in the arms of the man I believed was taking me away from all my worries.

The honesty seeped into me. Bits and pieces of conversation began to filter back into my mind. Things were making more sense now. How upset Arthur was at bills. How he blamed me for not having more money. How he said he didn't owe me clothes, and how I needed to earn my keep.

I was sold to Arthur.

Bile worked its way up to my throat. I excused myself and raced to the bathroom. My lunch and anything else I'd eaten for the day came up. I wretched until I could feel the blood vessels around my eyes breaking. A warm hand caressed my back. If only I could be comforted by her touch.

"I was that way with all you kids."

I couldn't look at her. It was too much to bear. Instead, I stood up and grabbed a paper towel from the roll, wiping the spittle from my mouth.

"Arthur made me think he loved me." My scratchy voice scraped across the rawness in my throat.

"I'm sure he does love you, in his own way." She was trying to placate me, but I didn't need that, I needed truth. I grew desperate for it.

I started to tell her feeding and housing someone does not equate to love. But then, what did I know? Another idea took hold. "How much did Arthur pay for me?"

"Don't make it sound like that." She wrenched her hands together.

"How much?"

"Twenty thousand dollars at first."

I choked back a sob of my own. My life for twenty grand. The fact I couldn't pay back the loan didn't enter my head for a few moments. I touched my stomach. Could I ever sell my child for any price?

I had to know more. "At first?"

"He's sent more over the years. Said even if you wanted to cut things off, we were still your family and he wanted to take care of us."

How gracious of him. "How much altogether?"

"Close to forty thousand."

"Guilt money."

"Maybe he *does* love you, Macy." She said it like she was trying to convince herself as much as me.

"No." I had been a foolish girl, and I'd grown into an ignorant woman letting Arthur control my every move. "And I'm not giving up the baby."

Fear brimmed in her eyes. "He won't put up with it. He told me he's kept track of all the money he's sent, and he'll demand it back if you don't do as he wants."

"He can't legally do that."

"No. But he says he knows a lot of truckers, and he has ties to some of our best customers. In fact, four of our biggest customers came through him. If he tells them to quit coming to us for repairs and gas, we'll lose contracts and everything else in a year."

The truth of what she said sank in. I couldn't wrap my brain around a proper response.

"I'm so sorry, Macy. If I'd thought…" She choked on her tears, and the anger disappeared. I wanted to comfort her, pull her into my arms for a hug to calm her down, like I had tried so many times to do when Daddy was sick. I just wanted to make it better. I still wanted to make it better—but how could I, without giving up something too precious? I tucked my hands under my legs.

My mother calmed down. "Don't decide yet." She patted my arm absently. "We'll call Arthur and tell him you're willing to see him. To discuss it. Don't say no." She sounded so desperate. I had a clear picture of her in my mind, packing up all her things and the kids, maybe even becoming homeless. I knew I couldn't let the kids suffer because of me.

"Okay," I lied.

Later, I walked her back to the bus station, pretending everything would be all right. I waved as the bus pulled out, a fake smile plastered on my face. I had no idea what I was going to do. I just knew giving up my child wasn't an option.

Seven

I lay in bed, unsure what my next steps should be. My mother would call Arthur—to report I wasn't sure what. I was supposed to wait until he arrived, but I didn't know when that would be. I racked my brain, trying to remember our fall schedule. Arthur had been independent for the last three years, but he had regular contracts.

For the life of me, I couldn't remember. Part of me panicked when he walked away—but I'd come to see a larger part was relieved. I'd begun to think I might have sensed something all along.

Reaching under the covers, I touched the baby lump on my tummy. It was more pronounced now, but I hadn't noticed any movement. I pressed, feeling the roundness, the otherness of the person in there. I tried again to imagine selling my child to pay my mortgage. I couldn't fathom it.

My grandma used to pray for me, and with me. My mother never talked about God after my dad got cancer. It was like he'd broken an agreement with her by letting my dad get sick and eventually die. Even before, we weren't regular church people. More like the two time a year folks—Christmas and Easter. Or when Grandma would take me.

I loved going with Grandma. We'd sit together and sing hymns, and I'd hold her hand in mine and play with the large blue veins on the back of her hand, pushing them down just to see them pop back up again. I'd alternate between that and drawing invisible dot-to-dot lines in between her liver spots. She never seemed to mind. Now that I think of it, it probably bugged her. The memory triggered a sense of what it meant to be a parent and to love someone more than yourself.

Grandma would pray in church. I mean, we were all supposed to pray in church with the pastor. But Grandma mumbled and whispered quiet things along with him. Sometimes, after everyone left the building, Grandma would pat my knee—which meant I was to stay in my seat—and she'd go up to the altar and bow her head. She didn't go to her knees because of her arthritis, but I didn't think God minded. I'd watch her. She didn't carry on like some ladies I'd heard. She'd keep her eyes closed and nod, as if she were hearing back something from him. Then she'd come back by our pew and put her wrinkled hand out to mine, her eyes shiny with unshed tears and a gentle smile on her lips. Then we'd go and get my brother and sisters from Sunday school. For some reason, she never made *me* go. I think she sensed I liked being with her.

I think she must have known I wasn't getting the attention I once had. My mother hadn't ever been the cozy type. I'd always gotten cuddles from my father. My mother was the practical one. She'd seen to needs. I only remembered two times we'd ever done anything one-on-one. She was busy trying to "hold us together." For some reason, though, I always felt more like the glue—spread thin wherever she wanted me—than the paper.

I'd begun to see patterns in my life I didn't really like. As I rubbed the bump, I imagined feeling a movement. I knew it was too early. I'd found a book on the shelf about pregnancy and had been committing it to memory—all except the scary parts about what could go wrong. No one needed to know that.

A heavy sense of regret blanketed me. I felt like I should make allowances for my mistakes. Something needed to be said.

"Hey, baby. I owe you an apology. I married a man I shouldn't have." A hot tear slipped down my cheek. For some reason, marrying someone I shouldn't have didn't carry the same gravity when it was just me. But now, with Baby counting on me, everything was different.

I turned on my side and did something I hadn't done for years. I prayed.

Grandma always said to just talk to God like I was talking to her. It didn't feel quite right to address the creator of the world so informally, but I had to start somewhere. I'd read Jesus loved the little children, and he wanted us to come to him with faith like a child. I'd stick with that.

"God, I hate coming to you when my life's a mess. Seems the only time I do. That probably gets old. Would you please protect my baby—any way you can. Thanks. Amen."

I've never been one to pray to God like he was a magic genie in a bottle. I had heard those preachers on TV telling God to do things—how he should heal this person or bless another with lots of money. Although, I didn't know if the last one counted for much. Arthur would always snort when the pastors asked for money and change the channel. I didn't blame him. The whole congregation was better dressed than my school on formal night.

The thing was, I was simple me—pretty insignificant in the world. I obviously didn't make good choices, or my life would be all shiny and safe. I was the last person to give God suggestions on how to fix my mess. I figured he knew best.

Sleep came after many hours. When I woke up, my head was stuffy and my eyes were swollen. I'd been crying in my sleep again. I hadn't cried for years. Once my dad died, I was all cried out. Pregnancy really messed with your body.

How long had I been living an insulated life? It was like my feelings had been turned on again—like the outdoor tap after the last frost. The pipes sputtered and gasped before it all came out in a shuddering rush, pouring out over the dirty concrete, washing it clean. The idea brought more tears to my eyes. I blinked hard, trying to see the clock. I could sleep for twenty more minutes.

Instead of trying, I sat up and raced to the bathroom. The last three days had been different. None of that glowing, feminine feeling for me. No. Now it was a race to see if I could pee before I threw up. If I didn't make it, then I'd wet myself and the floor. I hopped on the toilet to do my best. Instead, yellow bile went down my nightshirt, over my legs, and onto the floor. This brought on another round of tears. How could I do this for the next seven months? Alone?

After I showered and washed out my things in the tub, I decided I needed to ask about having a washing machine and dryer installed in the apartment. I'd been doing my clothes by hand in the tub. It was nothing new for me, but the inside of my apartment looked like the outside of an Italian villa, what with my clothes strung throughout on lines and hangers. The dampness was getting hard to handle. If I wasn't careful, they'd grow mold. I could help pay for the hookups and then find a used set somewhere. When the baby came, I'd definitely not want to do it all by hand. I remembered how dirty my brother would get. No thanks.

The idea sparked another issue I'd put off too long. I needed to get to my money.

Later that day, after the breakfast rush, I wandered to the back corner of the restaurant where Toby was concentrating on wrapping silverware in napkins for the place settings. His head bobbed to the easy-listening station playing "Song Sung Blue" that filtered in from the kitchen radio.

"Toby?" His head kept bobbing, his thoughts must have been miles away. "Hey." I touched his arm to get his attention and he scattered silverware across the floor. His ears turned red as he fumbled to pick them up again and toss them in a bussing station bucket.

"Sorry." I leaned down to help him and our hands brushed. He moved away quickly.

"No problem. It's fine." He sat back down on the bench seat, not making eye contact with me. After counting the wrapped sets and exhaling in frustration, he pulled out another stack of napkins and began again. I hadn't meant to make such a mess of things. Arthur would have shot through the ceiling, but Toby just ignored me.

I wrapped my hair around my finger. He probably wouldn't want to drive me anywhere after that. I was such an idiot.

"Can I help?" I sat across from him, reaching for the silverware.

"No. No, I'm good. It's okay." He gave me a shaky smile and started concentrating on the bundles again. The song switched to "What Kind of Fool" and his head started to bob to the words.

"You like the oldies?"

He looked up, eyes wide, unaware he'd been enjoying the song. "What?"

"Old music? I'm the same way with old movies. I used to watch a ton of television, too. All the reruns."

His eyebrows rose. "I never thought about it. I guess so. My mom listened to all that when I was a kid."

"You don't talk much about your parents." I waited, hoping he'd share, but he didn't. He continued bundling. I decided to help him

46

anyway and started putting a fork, knife, and spoon into the napkin, rolling it tight and securing it with a napkin band.

We worked together for a few minutes before I broached the subject of a ride.

"So, you said you wouldn't mind driving me into Appleton?"

He looked up and gave me a grin, my transgressions apparently forgotten. "Sure. Want to go today?"

Donna stepped over to us. I hadn't even realized she was nearby. "Why don't I loan you my car?" She had an anxious look in her eyes as she glanced at Toby.

"I don't drive." I shrugged as if it didn't make a difference. Arthur said I couldn't concentrate long enough to learn to drive properly.

"You're married to a trucker and you don't drive?" Donna gave me an incredulous look.

"I know how, but he never let me get my license." Toby and Donna passed a look between them. I guessed what they were thinking. I was thinking it, too.

I read a *Reader's Digest* article once in a truck stop in Dallas about a battered wife. I knew it was a classic abuse sign. They didn't give their wife property or freedom. That was bad. I'd never noticed it until now. *That was worse.*

"I'll ask Nick. Wednesday's are slow for lunch and dinner. We can probably handle it." She started back to the kitchen, but I stopped her.

"Could you also ask about getting washer and dryer hookups installed? I'll pay for it."

A pained look crossed her face. "We were always going to do that. Our..." She paused. "...previous tenant used the laundromat. We'll take care of it."

Toby shifted in his shoes and tucked his hands in his pockets, focusing his attention on something outside. Donna returned a minute later. "Nick says it's fine. Both things are fine."

"I don't mind paying for it." They'd done so much already.

"No. It's the right thing." She crossed her arms over her chest in a hug and gave Toby a long look. "You drive careful now, Toby."

I thought I saw Toby's face flush before he led the way outside to his car. He motioned to an old Chevy pickup whose rust and orange paint were competing for control. I climbed in.

"If I find a used washer and dryer, do you think you'd pick it up for me? I'd pay for gas and buy your lunch."

Toby had a serious look in his eyes that softened at my suggestion. "Sure I can. And help you get them moved upstairs, too."

I hadn't thought of that. "Do you think they'll fit?"

Toby pondered this. "Maybe get one of those mini stacking units? They're narrower."

I pulled out my notebook from my purse and wrote it down.

"What have you got there?" He motioned toward the black book.

"It's where I write everything down so I don't forget it. It's my everything book." I'd been carrying an everything book for as long as I could remember. When I was little, my father had given me a small leather book, and I'd drawn pictures inside of things I wanted to remember. Birds in the backyard, a scrawling sketch of our family, photos of the neighbor's puppies and a boy I liked. Every time a new baby arrived, I'd draw them. I still had that notebook in my room back home. As I got older, I switched to words, and my pictures became scarcer. Every now and then, though, I'd still draw something I wanted to remember.

I flipped back a page or two and saw the marquee and the name of the movie that'd been playing that night. I had paid special attention to the light and the way it streaked down the road toward my window. I'd also drawn the metallic napkin holder at the diner in the break room one afternoon. And a sticky bottle of ketchup.

We rode in silence for a while. Arthur usually had talk radio or Golden Oldies playing. I looked for a radio to fill the gaps in conversation and realized he didn't have one. A gaping hole sat in the dash, wires curling and frayed.

"What happened to your stereo?"

He pursed his lips. "Some idiot stole it. Seriously, it was an eight-track. Who steals an eight-track?"

Who knew what made people do what they did? I looked at my everything book again. In the back I had tallies for the money I'd deposited. I should have had about two thousand dollars in the bank. All of it was written in code, in case Arthur found it. Every time I'd made a deposit, I drew a picture of a bird. Finches were tens, blue birds were twenties. Maybe no one else could tell if they were finches or bluebirds—but I knew. I shut the book and examined my life for a bit. I'd been hiding money from my husband for the better part of our marriage. Didn't *that* tell me anything?

"What's with that look?" Toby's voice broke into my thoughts.

"I'm just thinking what a fool I've been about my life." I wasn't used to being so open with people, but being with Toby put me at ease. As much as he seemed to hate talking about himself, he earnestly asked questions about me. Not everyone who asked how you were really wanted to know. In fact, most people didn't. Arthur never did.

"Don't be so hard on yourself."

"You have no idea." I shook my head, hefting mental stones at myself.

"You'd be surprised." His gravelly tone caught me off guard.

I turned and looked at him, but he kept his eyes on the road ahead. His jaw worked as he thought. He did that a lot. It became clear he wasn't going to elaborate on his own. There was a lot about Toby I didn't know. I decided I wanted to. "So you grew up here. Are your folks still around?"

"Yep. My parents live about seven blocks from my house." Again his face went hard. "I keep an eye on them."

"You have your own house?" For some reason, it had never occurred to me. I pictured Toby in a rental of some kind, not as a property owner.

"For a few years now." His mouth clamped closed, and again I'd bumped up against a brick wall. How could someone so unassuming have so many areas of his life locked down?

The cab went quiet again. For some reason, I decided to fill the gap. "Are you dating anyone?"

"No."

I grew tired of being shut down, so I gave up and started looking out the window at the passing landscape. We went by stands of trees and drove over bridges covering creeks and rivers. Farms lined both sides of the road, dotted with brown cows, alpacas, and the occasional horse.

"I used to think I'd like a farm." I said it more to myself than to him, as I figured he wouldn't have much to say anyway.

"I did too. Love animals." His deep voice lightened.

"Me too. We had what my father called a farm—but it was more of a glorified garden on the back of our property. We had chickens, but they were for food. And a dog—but he was as mean as anything. My father kept him chained all day, but let him loose in the shop at night to keep away thieves." He hadn't been cruel, just practical. I'd seen my dad scrub the dog's head with affection and speak kindly to him more than once.

At the same time, none of us were allowed to play with the dog. My father didn't even want us to name him. He wanted him treated as an employee. It was one of the times I could remember being angry with my father. I'd wanted a dog most of my life, and the first time he got one, we weren't allowed to have anything to do with him. If I ever got a place of my own, I'd get one for sure.

"It'd be fun to have some chickens or ducks." He sounded wistful. "I had a dog as a boy, but he was killed by a car. Ran right out in the street. Miss that guy."

"That's sad. I'm sorry."

He glanced at me and his eyes softened. Every time I spoke to him, he seemed surprised to find I cared.

"I don't know if I'd want cows or pigs, though. They smell awful." I remembered camping in trucker lots next to the animal haulers. Animal waste would pour out the holes and pool on the ground. Just remembering the earthy, sour smell made me gag. I envisioned vomiting all over Toby's truck and tried to erase the idea from my mind. *Happy thoughts. Happy thoughts.* It wasn't working.

"Are you okay?"

"I'm a little nauseated. I'll crack the window." I tried to roll it down, but the handle came off in my hand. Toby slowed the truck and pulled over. Taking the handle from me, he reached across my lap and began to roll it down. I became suddenly aware of his proximity. His cologne was soothing to my ill stomach. He glanced up at me, and our gazes locked.

We both became self-conscious at the same time. Toby cleared his voice and leaned back on his own side. "I've been meaning to get that fixed."

"Good idea." My cheeks went hot. I scooted a bit closer to the door and let the fresh air wash over me as he pulled back onto the road.

"I've only had this truck for a couple years. I get so busy at the restaurant, and at my folks' place, I let my own things slide."

"What did you drive before this?"

"A Mazda." Toby clipped his answer, and we were back in brick wall territory. I sighed aloud, maybe a bit more dramatically than I'd meant to—but this was getting old.

"Sorry." He gave me an apologetic look before turning back toward the road.

"It's okay. I just can't say anything right to you." He went from hot to cold faster than anyone I'd ever talked to.

Toby quieted again, but the atmosphere in the truck changed. "It's nothing personal. There's just a lot of stuff I'm going through."

"Did you forget who you were talking to?"

He gave me a sideways smile. "No, you're right. It's just hard to talk about."

"About your folks?"

He took a deep breath, nodding. "I feel like I gave up everything to take care of them, but they don't thank me. Some days…" He stopped.

"Yes?"

"I feel like they're using me up and pretty soon I'll have nothing of me left, you know?"

"I do know. Like they don't even see you anymore, just stuff you need to do for them. Like what you want, who you want to be, who you were, doesn't matter at all."

"Yeah. And there's more. I can't really go into it right now. It's complicated."

I nodded. "I hope I'm around long enough to hear it."

He glanced sharply at me. "You're not leaving?"

"Not if I can help it. But with Arthur coming to town, and some issues with my family, I might not have any choice." I put a protective hand over my stomach and hoped the tone of my voice conveyed my sorrow at the thought of going away.

"We'll make sure you don't have to." The way he said it felt more like an oath than a sentiment.

"Why are you helping me, Toby?"

He gave me a worried look.

"I mean, I really appreciate it, but you must have better things to do than help an abandoned pregnant woman." I tried to lighten what

I'd said with a laugh. It didn't work.

"I…" He paused as if searching for the right words. "I guess it's because I know what it's like to face the unfathomable." He gave me a smile, but something painful hung about his eyes. "As long as I'm around, you don't have to do it alone."

Again, there was a force in his voice that made me feel like anything was possible. It gave me hope.

Eight

At the bank, the teller asked me for my identification. I pulled out my ID and passed it to her. I had memorized my account number long ago and wrote it on the withdrawal slip.

"You'd like to close out your account?"

"I'm moving funds to another bank, one that has a branch where I'm living." I felt like if I didn't explain, she might take offense. I'd never make a good criminal. I'd go to rob a bank and then spend so long apologizing I'd get myself caught.

"I'll get a check drawn up. It'll be a minute or two."

"I'd like cash please." I knew they might put a hold on any large deposit at my new bank, and I wanted the washer/dryer installed as fast as I could get it.

She narrowed her eyes at me and leaned in to whisper. "This is a very large amount. Are you sure it's safe?"

"Absolutely. Please close out my account."

The woman left her window and spoke to the manager. I didn't know why it was turning into such an ordeal. He followed her back to the window.

"I understand you'd like to close your account?" I turned and shrugged at Toby, who'd been standing near the door. I could only imagine how tired he was of waiting. He must have had better things to do than drive me across the county and wait in a bank lobby.

"Yes. What's the problem?"

"It's such a large amount."

Were banks doing so poorly they couldn't come up with two

thousand dollars? "I'm sorry. Could you please tell me my balance?"

The cashier wrote the amount on a slip of paper and passed it to me. My eyes widened. There was thirty thousand dollars in my account. I swallowed hard and loosened the top buttons of my jacket.

"Can I see the computer screen please?" The cashier tipped the monitor so I could see it. The main account number was different, and my account was nested under it. I saw my name next to Arthur's. Something wasn't right.

"It appears you and your husband merged your savings account with your main accounts last week." The lilt at the end of the sentence tipped me off that she was testing me.

My mind and heart raced together, and I swallowed down the fear building inside.

Arthur had discovered my account somehow. He couldn't have known they'd keep the number and tucked it under our other account rather than erasing it altogether. Did he imagine I'd come into the bank and find my account empty? Or perhaps I'd try to do an ATM withdrawal and find my account no longer existed. A temptation rushed over me. I could take all of his money right now and the teller wouldn't look sideways at me. I'd already convinced them I was closing the account. Was this God's answer to my problem? His money would be gone. I'd be set.

But that'd be akin to robbing a bank. Again, not something I could do. Besides, Arthur had proven he was not one to cross. Another idea presented itself. I went with it.

"You're right. It slipped my mind. I'm so glad he's looking out for me." I turned and waved at Toby, who waved back. The teller smiled at him.

"Your husband is very handsome." She nodded toward Toby.

I had to agree. The way his blond hair fell over his brow, the crinkle around his eyes as he smiled, his firm chin and strong shoulders all called to me. He made quite the contrast alongside Arthur with his woolen plaid shirts pulled tight against his middle-aged paunch, and his unruly speckled black and gray hair framing less-than-kind steely eyes.

"Isn't he? Never mind me. I only need to withdraw the amount Arthur transferred over. We've been planning a purchase."

Both the teller and the manager looked relieved. "Oh, of course ma'am. I'll get that for you." She wrote the number down on a slip of paper and went to the vault area. A minute later, she returned with an envelope and a withdrawal slip for twenty-five hundred dollars. A bit more than I remembered, but close enough. I tucked the envelope into my purse and thanked them.

Back in the truck, the shock hadn't worn off yet. Arthur wanted me to fail in the world and have nowhere else to turn, except back to him. He made a stupid mistake, though, keeping my name on the account. He probably had to do that to keep up the illusion I was in agreement with the whole thing. He could be very persuasive.

Toby started the truck and cast a questioning glance my way. "What was that all about?"

"Arthur took my money. The teller thought you were my husband, so I was able to get it back."

"You're kidding." His voice filled with indignation. "How could he do something like that?"

"My guess is, he doesn't want me to be able to survive without him."

"That's not love." Toby's jaw worked as his teeth ground back and forth.

"No. That's not love." Just what love *was*, exactly, I'd been learning by counter-example.

We drove back to town in silence. I guessed I'd given Toby a lot to think about. I know I'd been thinking plenty. People did a lot of things for control. I'd read about the risks they'd take, the lengths they'd go to. I never figured on being married to anyone like that.

Toby pulled up in front of the local bank. It was still an international bank, but a smaller chain. It wasn't as permanent as dumping my money into a totally local one, but this sounded better. Just in case. Of what, I wasn't sure. Living on the road, subconsciously planning to escape, made you search for backdoors.

"Do you want me to go in with you?" Toby reached for the door handle at the same time I did, our hands clasping for just a moment, and my stomach did flip-flops. We both let go like we'd grabbed a frying pan by the handle. I'd been alone for a long time, well before Arthur left me, really. We'd stopped talking, our relationship stalled on misdirection and control.

I couldn't let a passing attraction to Toby change our friendship. Because, that's really what I needed, and that's all we could ever be.

"No, I'm fine. Thanks for the ride." I saw the hurt in his eyes, but I was thinking ahead to the future. Anyone else I got involved in this might be collateral damage—and I didn't want Toby messed up with any of it.

Inside the bank, I opened my account and arranged to order checks. My spirit thrilled with the headiness of independence. My mind wandered back to the large amount in Arthur's checking account. The temptation to go back and transfer the money washed over me. There were any number of books on money laundering in the library. All those mob films made moving millions of dollars to offshore accounts look simple. Mundane. Everyone did it.

Not that Arthur had millions. But still.

I'd have Baby in the states, and we'd sneak out of the apartment one night with only the clothes on our backs—and diapers. Then we'd settle on our own tropical island with only the beach and sand to distract us from our daily routine. I'd invest into a small business and slowly filter anonymous amounts back to my mother to help her pay off her debts. Eventually, one day, we'd all be free. As I imagined the locals chatting with us and helping us improve our place, a blond-haired, bright-faced man entered my vision. He handed me an ice cream and told me how glad he was we'd run off together. Our fingers brushed, and the heat between us built.

I shook myself out of the daydream, shunning the thought, and headed out into the cold. The rain and wind swept up around me, my constant companions in this part of the country. As I reached the diner, the neon OPEN sign flickered off, so I headed down the side alley instead.

I entered by backdoor and headed upstairs to my apartment. I didn't want to talk to Donna or Nick right then—let alone cross paths with Toby. How ironic. I'd finally found a true friend after waiting nearly my whole life, and now I might have to start avoiding him.

Nine

As I closed the lid on my new-to-me washer and dryer set, satisfaction filled me. I'd hired the electrician all on my own. Well, with Toby's recommendation. After Toby and the previous owner moved it upstairs, the electrician came and installed it. It might have sounded silly to someone else, but I'd never hired anyone to do anything. It felt grown-up. When I wrote it down in my everything book, it was as if I'd won a hard run race.

The washer started sloshing my clothes around, and my back tingled in relief. Hunching over the tub to do the laundry had been getting harder and harder. My lump had become a full on baby bump. At Donna's insistence, I made a doctor appointment for prenatal care. Week eighteen loomed right around the corner. I glanced at the calendar by the sink where I'd counted them out with a Sharpie.

Arthur's continued absence lulled me into a false sense of security on some days, and on others, I was edgier than I'd ever been. On those days, Nick, Donna, and Toby gave me a wide berth.

Arthur must know by now I'd secured my money. He must know I didn't need him. Why hadn't he shown up?

The idea of seeing him again filled me with such dread I was tempted to hide in my bed some mornings. I say this figuratively, of course. If I didn't get to the bathroom within two minutes of waking, I'd be vomiting all over my covers and wetting myself. Being pregnant had brought out many strengths I didn't know I had. It was also a demoralizing beginning of my every day. I didn't know what I was supposed to be learning from all this. I wanted it to end. I'd taken to praying as I threw up. This helped take the edge off—but I wondered if God approved of me praying into the toilet.

I headed downstairs and found the restaurant already full.

"Am I late?" I asked Toby as I tied on my apron and grabbed my order pad. He gave me a blank look before scowling at the dining room. Something was definitely on his mind.

"Toby," I said again, "am I late?"

He grumbled something and turned back to me. "No. The mayor has an early morning meeting, and they forgot to tell us. He does that sometimes." Toby picked up several pitchers, filled them with ice water, and hauled them to three separate tables. There was a man at the head wearing a suit, talking to an older blond dressed to the nines. I guessed this was the mayor and maybe a councilwoman.

Nick was hard at it making plates of toast and scrambled eggs. They must have been serving family style. Donna asked if anyone would like juice or coffee. I started handing out silverware settings and delivering platters of food as fast as Nick moved them to the pass-through. Several committee members smiled at me, but the mayor gave me a curious look. I heard him asking Donna about me, and she motioned me over.

"So is this our newest resident?"

I didn't like being put on the spot and inched backward.

"This is Macy. She's a blessing to us."

Blessing? News to me.

"Nice to meet you, Mr. Mayor." I didn't reach for his hand. Something told me I wouldn't have liked for him to touch me.

The mayor grinned. "Roger Beady. Please, call me Roger." He wiped egg from his mouth with a napkin before taking a slug of coffee, but he never offered me his hand. Then he sucked at his teeth before continuing. "What do you think of our town?"

"It's quiet. Peaceful."

"We like it that way. Although some committee members think we should start letting in chain stores." He shot a pointed look at a balding man four seats down. "I think we should maintain the integrity of our small-town feel. Let Appleton get a Walmart or Target. We've got our privately owned shops."

The woman beamed at him. "And during the holidays, it's so pretty downtown. We draw in traffic from all over at Christmas."

The balding man spoke up for the first time. "And that Christmas revenue isn't enough to get us through the rest of the year. You're hiding your head in the sand."

I started to back away, but the mayor put a hand up. "Where did you grow up?"

"Another small town—you wouldn't have heard of it."

"Small towns are the backbone of this country, sweetheart. Tell me, where was it? What did your parents do for a living?" His cologne permeated the air around me, and I stepped back, hoping for fresh air before my stomach caught a whiff.

Donna patted my back. "Leave the girl alone, Roger, so she can get back to work." She sent me a wink. "Nick needs you in the kitchen, Macy. You'd better run along, you know how grumpy he gets when the food sits."

Grateful for the excuse, I pivoted away. As I strode into the kitchen, the world tilted around me, spinning to the side. The heat from the grill mixed with the smell of bacon grease, onions, and raw meat.

The last thing I saw was Toby's worried gaze as he rushed toward me. Then it all went black.

I woke up in a hospital bed. Toby sat by the window, his back to me. The curtain between the two beds was pulled for privacy. I could hear a woman sniffling. My head buzzed, and I ached all over.

"What happened?"

Toby rushed to my bedside and sat down. His eyes were laced with worry, but also relief.

"Low blood sugar."

I nodded. I knew better. I'd missed breakfast because of the mayor and his entourage. "I forgot to eat."

"The doctor says you can't, or you'll put the baby at risk." His warm fingers brushed my hair back from my face and lingered on my cheek. "Not to mention you."

My hand wandered to my stomach, and I comforted the bump. "I didn't mean to."

"He says you've got to increase your calories and put on some weight."

I thought back to that morning and how my pants were getting baggier, not tighter. "Is the baby okay?"

"Yeah, he's fine." Toby's face paled. "I mean, it's fine." He ran a hand through his hair.

I stared at him. I'd never doubted the baby was a girl. From the look in Toby's eyes, I could see I'd been wrong.

"So I should quit calling him Daisy?" I hadn't really been. I didn't have a name at all, but my comment hit home.

"Sorry." He bit his lip.

"It's okay." It really was. Maybe that was God's way of giving me a heads-up. "I didn't know they could tell so soon."

"You're further along than you thought, Macy. You're at least twenty weeks along."

I must have counted wrong. I'd been reading all the baby books, how'd I goof that up?

The nurse came in and handed me a cup of apple juice. She took my blood pressure and then flipped through the paper slip coming out of a machine near my head. I could hear a rapid plunking sound. Shifting to see the monitor better, I felt a pull across my belly—a Velcro strap and circular disk pressed against my skin. "Is that a baby monitor?"

"Yes, that's your baby's heart rate. It's doing fine."

I glanced at all the equipment hooked up to me, and it was like the blood drained from my extremities, leaving me all tingly. The monitor started to race.

"You okay?" Toby moved to take my hand, but that didn't help. The monitor started beeping for a whole other reason then.

"I don't have insurance, do I?"

"Some basic, yes. Don't worry, okay?"

The nurse gave both of us a sweet smile. I could tell from her eyes she'd assumed Toby was the father. Much to my own shame, I pretended he was. His caring tone, the way he checked the monitor and worried over me—that's what my husband should be doing. Reality reared its head all too fast, though, and I was left with an emptiness larger than it was before I let my mind ramble.

"We'll let you leave in a half hour, as long as you feel up to it." The nurse moved to the bed next to me and murmured consoling things. Maybe her story wasn't going to end happily. Maybe mine wasn't either. But for now, I still had my baby, a place to live, and a job.

I calmed down, and my pulse rate slowed a bit. Then Toby started to rub his thumb over the back of my hand, and the monitor picked up again. I tried to pull away, put a friendly distance between us, but he didn't let me.

"Please don't shut me out."

I gave him an *are you serious?* look. "Toby, I'm married. I'm pregnant. As much as I value your friendship, there are lines that can't be crossed."

"But he doesn't deserve you." His hand tightened on mine. "Macy, I—"

I cut him off with a raise of my hand. I didn't want him to divulge anything that would embarrass him later. He didn't deserve the humiliation. "It doesn't matter what he deserves, I made a commitment." I pulled my hand away. "If you want to stay friends with me, then we need to keep it that way. Friends." I wasn't sure where this sudden devotion to my marriage came from. After all, hadn't I been fantasizing about this very thing? Instead of lowering my guard, though, I raised it higher.

Toby's shoulders sagged at my expression. I looked as serious as I could. He needed to believe me, because I was pretty sure Arthur wouldn't take kindly to another man hitting on his wife. Or as I'd come to think of myself, his property.

"So you're going to stay married to someone who doesn't love you or your child?"

"I don't know what I'm going to do right now, Toby. I know it's not for me to make that decision yet." I leaned back against the pillow and closed my eyes. I needed a memo from God on all of this. A little yellow sticky note would suffice.

"So we're friends." He made it sound terminal.

I cracked open my eyes. "I hope so."

And I did. I needed someone in my corner—someone I could really count on—and he showed that in about a hundred ways. I should have confided in Donna and bonded with her. But there was still something in the way of that. She was trying to mother me more than befriend me, and I really needed someone to hear me out. If only there'd been another waitress. On TV there was always the best friend waiting right where the main character needed her. Only, my best friend was written as a male. If only I could call up the director and complain.

As if he could read my thoughts, the betrayal of my desires mixed with selfishness and desperation, Toby moved off the bed and went to look out the window. His shoulders went from being squared to sagging, and he sighed. Torn, I wanted to give him a hug and let him know how special he was to me. How he'd offered me acceptance and friendship at the right time in my life. How he'd made me feel important when all I felt was lost. But it was all wrong.

The nurse came back and checked me over. "You're set." She handed me a stack of papers. "This is some information on prenatal care." Then she handed me three books on pregnancy, infant, and toddler care. "The doctor wants to see you in her office in two weeks. The number is on the paperwork." She handed me a booklet on proper eating habits. "And you need to eat 2,000 calories through several small meals a day. Avoid sugary foods."

I groaned, wishing she knew how much I'd love to comply. I threw up every morning, but that wasn't all. I often even raced to the bathroom in-between serving tables to vomit. Food and I were not on friendly terms. On all the old shows, when someone would turn up pregnant, others would tell them how they glowed, and how wonderful they looked. Their hair and makeup were perfect. And often in real-life interviews the actresses would say how they loved to be pregnant. I knew my mother had a different experience, but I expected mine would be wonderful, magical, what have you.

There wasn't any magic—but there sure was plenty of what have you.

Ten

Thanksgiving was a huge deal at the diner. Much larger than I'd expected. It seemed most of our regulars came in, not because they didn't have a place to go to, but because Nick and Donna offered such a good meal and no family drama. In fact, some families met there for dinner instead of eating at home. I'd imagined seeing only older folks or singles—but that wasn't the case in the least. Apparently, eating on neutral grounds gave the right respite to estranged families.

I hadn't really given much thought to Thanksgiving for myself. After I'd left home, it'd not meant a lot to Arthur and me. Well, really, not to Arthur—and I'd learned not to care. Put another thing on my list of warning signs.

I carried out plate after plate of turkey, mashed potatoes, gravy, cranberry sauce, stuffing, big fluffy rolls, and pumpkin pie until four. Then we closed early. Most folks stopped coming by then. Donna started cleaning the tables as if it were any other day.

"I can't believe so many people came in today." I shook my head as I filled the salt shakers.

"Last year we weren't open." She took a shuddering breath, and I glimpsed a flash of pain in her eyes, but she didn't elaborate. "But we had an awful lot of folks who missed it. They sent notes asking to join us this year."

"So this was by invitation." I swept up crumbs from the floor and shifted the chairs back into their right spots.

"In a manner of speaking. I mean, the whole town's invited, but it's our special customers who came in today." She smiled and gave Nick a warm look. "It's better for us to be here, you know? Serving others."

I'd never thought much about serving others—outside of a job. Strike that. I thought all the time about how I'd already given up so much for everyone else. The bitterness that accompanied it made me want to avoid it all the more. However, having a choice in the matter, as I had today, made everything different.

I took off my apron, readying to head up to my apartment and the solitude there. I cast my thoughts forward and wondered how Baby and I would celebrate holidays. Would I resurrect the meaning and family feel or ignore them? I couldn't imagine not celebrating with my child.

As I headed toward the back, Donna stopped me.

"Where're you going?"

I wasn't sure what she meant and shrugged. "Upstairs, I guess."

"But we haven't had our dinner yet."

I glanced at Toby and noticed he and Nick were putting down a tablecloth over two tables they'd pushed together. Then Toby started moving dishes over from the pass-through. Nick took off his apron and came around with a couple pies.

Donna pulled out a chair for me and motioned me to return. I felt humbled to be included in their celebration. They'd only known me a short time, but I was elevated to the status of extended family.

Toby sat down across from me.

I leaned toward him. "Aren't you eating with your family?"

His eyes darkened at my question. "No. I'll bring them home something."

Nick came around and sat next to Toby as Donna sat next to me, across from him. He put his hands out and took Donna's and Toby's in his while Donna and Toby took mine. Nick said a simple prayer, to which Donna nodded and made approving sounds. I could do nothing but stare at Toby's hand clasping mine and feel the heat and comfort there. When they suddenly released hands, Toby's took longer. I shifted in my chair, heat rising to my cheeks, and took a sip of water.

They started serving the food, passing dishes around. I was pretty sure Baby wanted mashed potatoes and stuffing. I wasn't too sure on the turkey. I guessed I'd find out later. Donna served my plate, piled high with a bit of everything from the table including cranberry sauce (I'd never liked it) and green beans mixed with bacon (a favorite).

As we ate, Donna turned to me with a smile. "Did your family have large celebrations when you were a girl?"

I swallowed the bite of turkey in my mouth with difficulty. I'd never been forthcoming about my past with them. I sort of started and ended with Arthur's leaving. It'd never come up. And now that it had, everything was out of sorts. How much should I share?

Letting out a breath I'd been holding, I spoke honestly. "Before my father died of cancer, we'd have regular celebrations of Christmas and Thanksgiving. Birthdays and such. But once he got sick, that all ended." I sensed their discomfort and Toby's intense gaze. "I tried to carry on for a while on my own, but it didn't seem right without Daddy." My over-explaining seemed to make matters worse.

"You poor thing." Donna handed me a pie and I took a slice, pushing it in between a pile of yams and a puddle of gravy. I really couldn't eat it all, but I didn't want her to feel bad.

"Thanks."

"That's all changed now. You'll have Christmas with us." Donna smoothed out the tablecloth with her long fingers but didn't look at Nick when she made her declaration.

"Now, Donna," Nick started, but then he must have thought better of it.

I jumped in before a family argument broke out. "Listen, I appreciate that, but I've already decided I want to be on my own for Christmas." I hadn't decided any such thing—until then. The thing was, I felt okay about it. Perfectly okay.

"Let's not make any decisions right now," Donna deflected. Nick pursed his mouth and then took another bite of dinner.

I didn't like being dismissed. Arthur did that to me—and certainly my mother had a talent for it. Now that I'd been on my own for a while making my own choices, I was growing accustomed to it and resented being managed, no matter how nice Donna was while doing it.

"Why aren't you with your family tonight, Toby?" I only meant to change the subject, but my question must have hit home in a way I'd never intended.

Toby winced, shifted in his seat, and took a sip of cider. "Holidays used to be excuses for my dad to drink, so my mom canceled the lot when I was about ten." He glanced at Nick before continuing. "I'd come here and have Thanksgiving with Nick and Donna and…" He stopped and cleared his throat. "Anyway, that's why I'm here. I'm always here." The last part of the statement sounded more fatalistic than thankful—but I'd probably misunderstood him.

Nick and Donna had appeared altruistic when they took me in, but I was beginning to see I wasn't their first orphan to be adopted. Before I could ask how many people had lived above the diner—because now I had a clear picture of whoever lived there sharing in their meals and celebrations—the phone rang, and Nick excused himself to get it. The table went quiet while we waited for his return.

"That was old Mrs. Peabody. She'd like her usual tonight." Nick sat back down, giving Donna a soft smile.

I hadn't remembered a Mrs. Peabody ever being mentioned before. "Who?"

Toby spoke up. "She lives in a care home across town. She doesn't like the food they serve, so every holiday Nick and Donna bring her a meal and sit with her while she eats."

Nick and Donna seemed too good to be true. I looked up to see Nick take Donna's hand, her eyes glistening with tears. I started to ask what was wrong, but Toby caught my glance and shook his head slightly.

Holidays were hard on some folks. And I kept getting the impression I wasn't being given all the necessary background on their family yet. But I wasn't one to pry. I had enough trouble of my own.

A wave of exhaustion washed over me, blocking out any more curious thoughts. My usual pregnancy fatigue was mixing with my turkey dinner, and I knew I needed to go lie down. "I'm pretty worn out. If it's okay, I'll take my plate upstairs and finish later."

Donna blinked away her tears. "Of course, dear. Happy Thanksgiving."

I gave each of them a smile and took my plate up to my flat. Kicking off my shoes, I went into the kitchen, covered my plate with plastic wrap and stowed it in the fridge. I headed into the bathroom and grabbed a shower, letting the warm water wash all the cooking smells from my skin. The aroma of fried food lingered no matter how hard I scrubbed. I'd decided it was because the fumes rose up from the restaurant and covered everything in the building. Fortunately,

Baby didn't seem to mind.

There were some aromas I couldn't tolerate. Fish was one. Once it was battered and fried, I was fine, but fresh on the counter or grilled—no way. The other was, surprisingly, bread dough. The sour, yeasty smell made my gut twinge and my mouth water—in the worst way. I brushed a hand over my stomach. Hopefully that'd change, because I sure loved sourdough bread.

After my bath, I turned off all the lights and climbed into my bed. My body ached with tiredness. The feel of the cold sheets and soft mattress beneath me was delicious and soothing. My mind wandered as I drifted, and I wondered what Arthur was doing that night. We'd had all our Thanksgivings in restaurants since our marriage, so tonight hadn't seemed odd at all. I didn't miss fancy centerpieces, dressy clothes, cloth napkins, or formal place settings—I'd never had those to begin with. The regular diner décor of shiny chrome napkin holders and sticky bottles of Heinz ketchup seemed normal to me.

Maybe I'd have to find a restaurant to take Baby to every year. I smiled to myself. Or I might invest in some diner-ware? That was pretty retro. I curled into a ball, lying on my left side because one of the pregnancy books recommended it. I'd gotten through much of the first part of the book, but I'd been deliberately avoiding the labor section. It wasn't as though I didn't know how it all worked. I'd watched my mother go through labor with my sisters and brother. Although, I didn't really remember Bobby's as well as Sarah or Brynn's. The agony my mother suffered with the girls was indelibly etched into my memory. For some reason she wanted me alongside her during labor.

I was about to drop off to sleep when a clear memory wakened me. My father had wanted to remove me from the labor room, but my mother insisted I stay and watch. She'd drawn me close to her, her iron grip encasing my little girl hand. She'd focused on my face and whispered, "This is what it means to be a mother."

I remembered the horrified expression on the nurse's face. "If you keep telling her that, she'll never want children."

"Good."

Was that when it happened? I'd never seen my brother or sisters and me as a burden until then. But after my father got sick, and she'd turned me into a third parent, I wondered. Grandma said babies were a blessing—but my mother had certainly never felt that way. She loved us, in her way, but were we a blessing?

I put a hand to my stomach, and Baby shifted under the weight. Love and hope surged through me. I sure hoped what Grandma said was true. I'd be raising this baby on my own. I'd never tell him his father left us because of him. I'd never say how afraid I was. I'd only ever tell him how much I wanted him. How much I couldn't wait to see him. Right then, I made up my mind to do my best never to make my child feel less.

Eleven

Garage sales were a guilty pleasure. I'd always liked going—even before I had any reason to. Sometimes when we had a several-day layover in a town, I'd grab the paper and walk around different neighborhoods and see the sales. Arthur thought it was silly; there wasn't any place to keep new things. But I would hold those items and wonder about the history of it all. Like an old pair of skates or a scuffed-up chair. How many lives touched those things?

Donna and Nick gave me Friday mornings off, so I decided to take advantage of the free time. The thrift store Toby told me about was nice, but stagnant. I liked the feel of garage sales, the way they changed—and the ways they didn't. I wondered how many times an item had been purchased at a sale, and then moved to another house and saved for another sale.

I was like an archeologist, or sale-ologist. I would mentally tag items and log them in my mind. I'd imagined I could follow them from house to house until they'd finally outlived their usefulness to the world and ended rotting in a heap at the dump.

As I walked from one sale to the next, I was surprised at the number of sales listed in the paper, considering it was the middle of December. But, sometimes folks needed to flush out old things before the influx of new gifts. I found the best collectible music box one year, right before Christmas. It had a ceramic bear dancing with a ballerina. I didn't ever have much jewelry, but I loved the sweet tune it played. I told Arthur about it and even gave him the address of the house it was at—hoping he'd get it for me for Christmas.

He didn't.

At the third house, I found an old suitcase. The locks were rusty, but functioning. It was hard-side, covered in a green plaid material. Something about it called to me. The tag said two dollars. You couldn't beat that. I carried it around the sale, poking at different items. Then I saw something I knew I needed: baby things.

During my past musings, I'd never given baby items a second look. What for? I would never have children. But now, I found myself wondering how many things I could fit into the suitcase. I checked the bottom of the case and found it had wheels. Heading to the table, I picked up several blue and green onesies, all in amazing shape. Blankets, a playpen, a bassinet, and a diaper bag sat in front of me in pristine condition.

The temperature dropped as the sun ducked behind the clouds. I pulled my coat tighter around me, as if to keep the baby warmer. Tucking my hands in my jacket pockets, I calculated everything I'd need in the upcoming year. Glancing at the sky, I hoped the rain would hold off until I could wheel it all home.

"Do you need baby things?" A quiet voice startled me. Behind me stood an older woman with kind eyes.

I smiled. "Yes, I do. Everything looks like it's practically new."

"My daughter was expecting twins. The baby boy didn't make it." She straightened some of the items.

"I'm very sorry for your loss." Worries raced about my own baby.

"Our granddaughter is doing wonderfully, though. She's three." The grandmother picked up a tiny sleeping set and smoothed it with wrinkled hands. "They've had two miscarriages since then. It's too hard emotionally, so they're done."

I couldn't think of anything clever or helpful to say. Oftentimes, the best thing to say after a tragedy was nothing. I lost count of the number of times people told me my father's dying was for the best. I'd been told heaven was richer for his passing. How it must have been a relief after all his suffering to let him go. The Lord needed him home early. Another angel was needed in heaven. Weren't we relieved it was all over?

I'd wanted to scream back *no*.

This wasn't the first time someone had spoken so freely to me about the horrors of pregnancy or great loss. It wasn't the pain that really scared me anymore. Rather, it was the idea the baby might die before I could even hold him. Before he saw my face and knew I loved him.

For some reason, perfect strangers told me the worst stories. And tried to touch my stomach.

"That must be very hard." My hand caressed my bump through my jacket.

"Could you use any of this?" She motioned around us.

I couldn't believe my luck. There was even an infant car seat. I didn't have a car, but it didn't mean we wouldn't be going anywhere. "I can use all of it, but I'm on foot. Can I make several trips?"

"Oh, good heavens, I'll drive it to you. Where do you live?"

"Over the Bridgeville Diner."

"Oh, you're Donna and Nick's new waitress."

I'd begun to see the advantages and disadvantages to living in a place so tightknit. But I didn't feel resentful.

Her eyes were wistful. "Their daughter was a wonderful girl." She went and got a slip of paper and started writing down all the items. "Do you think two hundred dollars would be fair?"

I came up with a much larger number.

She shook her head. "Two hundred is fine." She leaned in and whispered, "They've been trying to sell this for a couple weeks. People can be superstitious about things—I don't entertain such thoughts." She cast a sad look behind her. "They really just want it gone, but to go to someone who needs it. I think that's you." She gave my hand a squeeze and looked askance, wiping at her eyes.

I reached in my purse and pulled out the money, paying her. She headed back into the garage and came out again with her wallet and keys as the first drops of rain began to fall.

"My son-in-law will watch the cash box—besides, he's got to pull in all this stuff. Looks like you made it before the storm. You ready?"

"Thanks. My name is Macy."

"Nora Williams. Very nice to meet you, dear." We loaded the car with every item I could have ever needed. I made a mental note to say a prayer of thanks later when I was alone. If this wasn't answered prayer, I didn't know what was.

As we drove the mile and a half to the restaurant, she filled me in on the town and its history. At least the history of its people. I heard about the current mayor (she didn't care for him) and the past mayor (she did). She'd retired as a teacher from the local grade school about three years ago. Her arthritis flared, making it hard to keep up with papers—and then her daughter needed her.

"And the Stintons live there." She pointed to a large ranch-style house on the corner as we passed. It needed repainting, and the lawn pushed the cracked sidewalk boundaries, bunching up at the edges like a pond of green trying to escape the rocky shores.

"The Stintons?"

"Yes, you work with their son, Toby. Bad business last year. So sad."

I frowned. "What happened to Toby?"

"Nothing happened *to* Toby." She looked sideways at me. "You mean to say, you don't know?"

As I was about to find out, we pulled up near the side door. Toby was there on the stoop, having a cup of coffee on his break. Mrs. Williams went quiet and gave Toby a hesitant wave. I didn't get to find out any more.

I climbed from the car and opened the backdoor as Mrs. Williams flipped up the trunk.

"Toby, you be a gentleman and help Macy upstairs with these things before the sky opens full force on us, won't you?"

Toby stashed his cup on the brick edging outside the door and wiped his hands on his jeans. "Yes, ma'am."

Toby made four effortless trips up and down the stairs. On his third trip, he winked at me. I was strangely jealous of his energy. It would have taken me at least an hour and exhausted me completely to traverse the stairs like he had. After I'd directed him on where to put everything, we took a good look around. What was once a spacious flat for one had quickly become an overcrowded room looking more like a nursery than an apartment. I glanced out the window and watched Mrs. Williams drive away.

"I didn't get to tell her thank you."

"I told her for you." Toby gave me a grin, but my mind wandered elsewhere.

I knew Mrs. Williams had the answers I wanted when it came to my friend.

"Wow, you really made out."

"I have about everything I need." I turned to Toby, who was watching me intently. I couldn't meet his gaze. Being alone with him felt comfortable and set off warning signals in my mind.

"How do you know Mrs. Williams?" I rearranged baby clothes from the suitcase into piles on the table.

"She was my fourth grade teacher."

"Might be hard to live in the same town where you grew up."

"Some days it's easier than others." He studied his feet.

I burned with curiosity about the sad business Mrs. Williams mentioned, but I couldn't bring myself to ask him. I moved to inspecting the car seat and stroller. I had my work cut out for me, that was for sure. What I needed now was a dresser. I wrote it down in my everything book and heard Toby clear his voice.

"I'd better get back." He shifted from one foot to the other, waiting for me to invite him to stay. I didn't. "I guess I'll see you tomorrow."

I nodded. He turned and headed down the stairs, flicking off the light at the end, enclosing the stairwell in darkness. I heard his breath catch, as if he wanted to say something else, but instead he opened the door, letting in kitchen sounds and light. When the door closed, the darkness returned and silence surrounded me.

I unpacked further and found unexpected treasures. My instinct was to hold it up and share my delight—but the empty apartment didn't seem as excited as I was. For the umpteenth time, I wished I could enjoy this experience with someone. That someone should have been my husband.

Twelve

The sun broke through the clouds, enveloping the diner's back stoop in a warm glow. The breeze chilled me, but I turned my face toward the sun, pretending we were nearing spring rather than facing winter. Those steps quickly became my favorite place to eat lunch—as long as the rain stayed away. Nick made an excellent burger. I hoped it would stay with me this time. Baby sure didn't like much of anything I ate. I had another hour of work, and then I'd head to the doctor's office for my first official visit.

Twenty-three weeks along. My pregnancy had gone pretty unremarkably so far. Except for the vomiting multiple times a day, not to mention my blood sugar issue and the fainting episode. Okay, maybe I needed to rethink my situation. Both Nick and Donna had me taking multiple breaks and eating light snacks. Some days that helped, but most evenings I ended up lying across my bed, praying whatever stayed inside after dinner would be enough to keep both the baby and me safe.

My stomach churned a bit, but the hamburger stayed put. I'd tried lighter fare, but there didn't seem to be a pattern to it—so I decided to eat what I wanted. Heading back to my station, I took the next couple's order. They were arguing about something, but I just smiled and handed them their food as if nothing was amiss. Halfway through their meal, they were holding hands and smiling at each other anyway. A mixture of relief and jealousy swirled around me. If only all relationship issues could work out that easily.

Across the restaurant, Donna seated a man at one of my tables.

Glancing at my watch, I figured I could get him through in time for my appointment. Even if I didn't, Donna would spot me. As I handed a menu to the man, my breath caught.

"Arthur?" Even though it was clearly him, I couldn't quite make myself believe it. My legs felt hollowed out and cold.

I saw Toby tense, and Donna gasped before moving back to the kitchen. I imagined Nick was readying his biggest spatula.

"I guess you're doing okay for yourself here, huh?" Arthur shifted in his seat and glanced around.

I didn't know what the others really thought about my marriage. Maybe they believed me desperate and foolish. I'd agree. And quite often, I'd been afraid of his temper, but right then, I was all angry and filled with incredulousness.

"That's all you can say to me?" I stared down at him—him reading the menu as if he'd just stopped in for a lunch break. As if it were perfectly normal to show up after fifteen weeks out of the blue like he'd done.

"You want to join me?" He motioned to the seat across the table.

"No. I don't want anything from you." I couldn't quite believe I'd said it, but the anger pulsed in my temples, pushing my good sense far to the outer reaches. Livid didn't quite describe it.

"Sit down." His tone didn't give any wiggle room for disobedience.

Even though my head didn't take orders from him anymore, my body did and quickly complied. His eyes evaluated me, scanned me like a man checking out a horse he might buy.

"You look healthy enough."

Again, I couldn't seem to keep my mouth closed. "No thanks to you."

He squinted at me. "Don't push me, Macy."

I leaned back against the vinyl seat and sighed. I'd heard baby hormones could make a woman do some crazy things. It was certainly not in my best interest to keep antagonizing Arthur. I bit my tongue. Literally.

Glancing over him, I noticed how haggard he'd become. His hair was more unkempt, his shirt clean, but wrinkled. He looked thinner, too. And that was saying something—because Arthur had never been one to look anything this side of two hundred and fifty.

"You talked to your mother," he stated. "You know my feelings."

"I'm not going to abort my baby."

"My baby." He said it like he'd say *my truck* or *my paycheck*. He never thought anything belonged to me.

"And because you don't want him, it's your right to make me get rid of him?"

"We're not going there." His eyes flashed at me, then fell to my stomach and narrowed. "It's a boy?"

My stomach clenched. I'd never intended to tell him. The less he knew about our son, the better. A strange stirring cascaded over me. Maybe now that he knew the baby was a boy, he'd want to keep it. A miniature Arthur. Something about the idea gave me hope and made me nauseated at the same time.

"You can give it up for adoption, then." Again, a statement made without any expectation I'd object. If the baby were a girl, would no one want it? "Soon we'll get back to normal." He paused. "Cheese melt and side salad."

I'd been blindsided by his reasoning. "You...what?"

"My order." He motioned at the menu. He actually thought that was the end of it. I stood on shaky legs and took the slip to Nick.

"You okay?" He waved his spatula in Arthur's direction.

I shrugged. I didn't know what I was feeling. I nodded toward the order. "He likes it on the crispy side." As if it mattered what Arthur wanted. Maybe it did.

I headed back to the other table, cleared it, and pocketed my tip. Arthur watched me, curiosity in his eyes. As I passed by, he said, "You're pretty good at that."

It was his tone that got me. He sounded surprised I could do something. Didn't he know I was the one who packed his clothes so he didn't look all raggedy and wrinkled? That I bought him special shampoo for his dander? I washed his comb every week and reminded him to pay the bills. I read the map and charted our course. I kept track of the miles and the grocery list.

I shuddered as cold seeped inside my bones. Donna led me away. "You need to eat?"

I looked down at my hands and tucked away their shivers into my apron. "No. I'm good. I have to go to my appointment."

I glanced back over my shoulder, an idea forming. Maybe if Arthur could see his child, he'd change his mind. I wasn't foolish enough to ask him along to the doctor's, but I'd stowed the photo of the ultrasound from the hospital away in my pocket. I pulled it out, taking off the Ziploc baggy and smoothing out the bent corners.

"Order up." After picking up the order, I took a deep breath and set my jaw. Arthur had one more chance.

I put down his food in front of him. He offered me the cursory grunt he gave all waitresses and started to eat. He didn't thank me for making sure the edges were crisp enough, or for bringing his favorite salad dressing and a side of lemon wedges with all the seeds picked out. I slid into the booth and watched him eat for a few seconds.

"I have to go in a minute, but I wanted to show you this." I held out the photo. He didn't even wipe his fingers on a napkin, but took it from me, leaving oily prints on the edges. I should have left the baggy on it.

"What's this?"

"He's your son." I went on to point out the arms, legs, and head. I showed him how they knew we had a son and not a daughter. Arthur gave another grunt.

"What of it?"

"It's a photo of our child. Is that all you can say?"

"Doesn't change a thing."

"You'd still want me to get an abortion?" I said it quietly, shame filling me, not that there was anyone around us to hear. I couldn't believe the man I married was that *callous*.

Again, I got a shrug from him. "Fine. Adopt him out. All I know is I don't want kids, Macy. That was the deal." I could see from his startled expression he hadn't meant to add the last sentence.

"Don't worry. I know." I could barely say the words.

"What do you know?"

"That you paid for me." Ire built, shoving aside my shame.

"You've got it all wrong."

"We got married and you paid off my parents' debts. Seems clear to me."

He took my hand in his. "We needed each other. What's the harm in helping your family?" His thumb rubbed over my knuckles. "I miss you. I want you back." Longing and emotion laced his words.

There sat the Arthur I'd convinced myself I'd loved. The tender, caring man who comforted me in my darkest days. He had to understand. "I can't give him up, Arthur."

"I need you Macy. Look at me. I can't even get the laundry in hand. I'm not eating right. We're a team, you and me. I'm too old to change. I never wanted kids." He swallowed hard. "But I've always wanted you."

"What about my family? Why did you cut off our connection?"

"I didn't want your mother to interfere. You know how she likes to manipulate you and get you to do things for her. She wrote about how she was taking care of your grandma, how she wished you were there to help with the kids, and I couldn't take it. Not again, Macy. You paid your dues. You deserved better."

Arthur's passionate pronouncement brought me up short. Hopefulness built inside. Could it be true? Had he only ever wanted to protect and care for me?

Before I could answer, Donna called from the pass-through, "You've got to get going." She pointed to the clock overhead.

I released a jagged breath, knowing I needed distance to clear my head and make sense of it all. "I have somewhere I need to be. I have to go." Instinct should have alerted me. I didn't tell him where I was going, and I didn't want him to come along. I was no different than most. My heart and head were often at odds, and logic was a distant cousin.

"I'll be in the RV park until tomorrow. Come tonight and give me your answer, Macy." He held my hand against his chest, caressing it. The tenderness in his words and eyes beckoned me. With a mixture of longing and fear, I pulled away and headed to the locker room without looking back.

I sensed Nick and Donna watching me go. I could tell Toby was holding his breath as I passed. I didn't look at any of them. I didn't see anything but the backdoor, fresh air, and escape.

Thirteen

Inside the waiting room of the doctor's office, I was surrounded by young women and the men in their lives. I'd like to say husbands, but there was no way to know. What struck me most, though, was I was the only one alone. Even the youngest of them had someone. I assumed it was her mother, or a close older friend. They were smiling and looking at parenting magazines.

I picked up one, too, and spied the happy family rambling through fall leaves on the cover. Four headlines graced the front, all focusing on baby's firsts. First Thanksgiving, First Christmas, First Friends, First Birthday. I put the magazine back down, picturing my little apartment covered in holiday décor. I hadn't had a tree since I left home—there wasn't room for one in the truck. Although Arthur did let me line the interior of the cab with little colored lights we'd turn on in the evenings when we made camp for the night. I always loved the feeling colored lights gave—cozy.

Christmas was next week. I put my hand on my stomach and vowed to get us a tree.

My eyes strayed to the clasped hands of the couple directly across from me. They had rings on, and he was looking at her with adoration. I told myself I should be happy for them. That didn't work for long. In reality, I was jealous. I was ashamed of it, but it was true. Why couldn't I have married a man who would want not only me, but our child as well? I was struggling with God. My grandmother taught me what a loving Father he was—so why didn't he keep people from hurting each other? Why couldn't I have one thing work out in my favor?

Macy

I sighed aloud, and the couple noticed me and gave me a pitying glance. That was all I needed. The nurse called my name, and relief filled me as I left the waiting room.

"Hi. I'm Doctor Kelly's nurse, Stacy." She wore blue scrubs with bears and kittens on them.

"Nice to meet you."

Stacy had me step on the scale and handed me a specimen cup.

"What's this for?" I started to worry they thought I'd been using drugs. It made sense—my lack of weight gain, my dizzy spells.

"That's to check your blood sugar, to make sure you're doing okay. We'll check it against the sample we took at the hospital."

I didn't remember giving anyone a sample at the hospital. But then again, I was pretty out of it.

Going to the bathroom in a tiny little cup was trickier than I expected. My arm had trouble reaching around my substantial belly. I slipped off the toilet seat once. I looked around, praying they didn't have a camera on me. After I washed up (having lost more than I caught), I put the little cup behind the stainless steel door. As I left the bathroom, Stacy motioned me toward the examination room.

"I've left a robe on the table. Make sure it opens to the front."

I acted like that was a normal routine and smiled and nodded at her until she left the room. She couldn't know the hospital visit last month was the first time in years I'd seen a doctor. After my father died, my mother avoided medical care like a phobia. Something about the smell, or the doctors—whatever it was—reminded her of his death, I think. When Stacy knocked a few minutes later, I sat on the vinyl-clad, tissue-covered exam table trying to keep my thin paper robe closed.

She made small talk while she took my temperature and blood pressure. "Is this your first baby?"

I figured there was a *duh* look on my face but answered her anyway. "Yes."

"Don't you worry. Dr. Kelly is wonderful. And she's got four kids of her own, so she's an expert on both sides."

Strangely, that did make me feel better. I'd never seen a female doctor before. Stacy pulled around some equipment on a portable tray and laid out plastic gloves and a tube of gel. "Dr. Kelly will do an internal and external exam. And then she'll hook you up and we'll

80

take a good look at the baby. Do you want to know the sex?"

"I found out accidentally when I passed out the other day."

Stacy was full of empathy. "I'm so sorry. We'll ask the doctor to confirm the best she can and go from there."

"That's okay. I can prepare better this way."

Stacy stepped out, and moments later the doctor came in. She was a tiny woman, maybe only five foot. If it weren't for the graying hair at her temples and slight wrinkles around her eyes, I'd have guessed she was barely my age. I tried to picture her carrying four babies. I suddenly saw her as a young girl with a basketball under her shirt.

Her hand was out, taking mine before I realized it. Again, she was warm and comforting. "Macy? So nice to meet you. I'm Dr. Kelly. But you can call me Janice if you'd like."

I couldn't imagine calling anyone in authority by their first name. I wasn't raised like that. "Thanks, Dr. Kelly."

"I know you met my associate at the hospital. I hope you don't mind that I'm taking over your care—she's completely booked."

"It's fine."

Having established the ground rules of our relationship, she started the exam.

At that point, I realized how nervous I'd become. I'd started sweating. Everywhere. I tried to scoot down the table to put my feet in the stirrups as she directed me, but the paper had glued itself to my bottom. I froze, unable to move either direction, hoping she wouldn't notice.

"Happens all the time. I wish they'd make the paper a bit more heavy-duty." She gave a chuckle and helped me move back. Without much fanfare, she started my breast exam. I was sore, so against my will, I winced.

"Tenderness should be expected. You're building up your milk supply, getting ready to feed the baby. Perfectly normal." She moved on down my abdomen and started pushing around the baby. Dr. Kelly looked off into space, and I could almost see her mentally restructuring what she was seeing with her hands in her mind. She smiled. "Excellent placement, everything feels great."

Then she slipped on the gloves. "Have you had an internal exam before?"

I gave her question some thought. It seemed like I had. When I was very young. But I couldn't remember what for. "I might have had an infection."

"You'll feel some pushing and prodding, possibly some discomfort. Then I'll slip in a device to keep you open while I make visual inspection. It'll be over before you know it."

It wasn't as bad as I thought it might be. She kept chatting away, and before I knew it, it was over.

"Everything looks healthy. Baby is nice and high." She removed the gloves and helped me scoot back on the table. Part of the tissue paper came with me, stuck to my rump. Although we were on much more intimate terms now, I couldn't bring myself to mention it to her.

Once again, Dr. Kelly pushed past the gown, and I wondered why in the world I was wearing one in the first place. She applied some cold goo to my belly and turned on the ultrasound machine. Within seconds, she honed in on the baby's heartbeat and then started manipulating the knobs on the machine. My baby's form came into view.

"There we are. Stacy told me you were accidentally told the sex of your baby. Do you want to confirm it if we can?"

"Sure." To say I was mesmerized was an understatement. The baby wiggled and moved its arms, saying hi.

Dr. Kelly applied some more pressure and zoomed in. "My associate said you were having a boy, and I can confirm that for you. Sometimes these things are iffy, and sometimes we're so sure of ourselves and then we find out we're very wrong at the birth. But I think having us both make the same call increases the chance you've got a boy on your hands."

I grinned. As much cause as I had to resent men at this stage of my life, I saw it as an opportunity to raise a decent one to offset the ones who weren't. I thought of men I'd known who were good, and my mind shifted quickly to Toby. I pictured him sitting with me during the exam and smiling at the screen, being excited alongside me. I blinked it away.

"Everything looks great. Based on the info you filled out and the baby's size, I set your due date in April."

For some reason—more than feeling the baby and the vomiting

and seeing the baby on the screen—that hit home. I not only felt but, because of the monitor, heard my pulse rate increase. "That's so soon."

Dr. Kelly grinned. "Most women say the opposite. They can't wait to have the pregnancy over and hold their baby."

"Maybe those women have supportive families." I didn't mean to reveal something so personal, and my face went hot as the doctor's eyes filled with understanding.

"I'm sorry. I didn't realize your situation. Do you want to keep the baby?"

My apprehension must have been apparent. I suddenly thought maybe this doctor wasn't the right one for me to see. Maybe she'd think I should have an abortion too. I put a protective hand over my stomach as if to shield the baby from hearing such things.

"Maybe I should go."

"Wait, don't misunderstand me. I wanted to know if you were thinking of adoption, not abortion."

Oh. "It crossed my mind for about an hour. But I can't. I can't give up my baby."

"I totally respect your choice. Here." She reached inside a drawer and pulled out a pamphlet and handed it to me. "This is a support group in our county for single mothers. They also have a pregnancy group. I have two patients who attend, and they love it."

I couldn't explain it, but it seemed worse to be married to a man who didn't want my baby than to be an unwed mother. "I'm not single." My admission physically hurt me.

"Are you living with the father?"

"Not right now."

"Then they'll be there for you. And I'll do whatever I can to help, too, Macy. We want this baby and you happy and healthy all the way through, okay?" Dr. Kelly patted my arm.

The tension in the room faded, and I realized I was the one carrying it. I was the one full of disappointment and fears. "Okay."

Dr. Kelly made a few more measurements and started to move the wand around my stomach, clicking things and frowning.

"Is anything the matter?" I held my breath, worrying about the baby in a way I never had. Palpable fear crept in again. So real I could touch it.

"No, but it appears you only have one ovary—of course, the other could be hiding, they do that. And this one looks smaller than it should be." She glanced at me. "You know, it's amazing that you're pregnant at all."

My mouth dropped open a second before I recovered. "If I wasn't pregnant, would you tell me it'd be unlikely I could ever conceive?"

"Nothing is impossible, obviously, but it'd be unlikely. No worries. We'll be extra sure to take care of you and your little guy. Here's your latest baby photos." Dr. Kelly put a long sheet of four shots on the counter. Then she tucked some tissues into my hand as she left. I stared down at them, perplexed, until I realized I was sticky and gel-covered. I didn't think dry tissues would do the trick.

As I hopped off the table, the tissue paper came with me like a big white tail. I grimaced. The height of humiliation. At least there weren't any witnesses.

I cleaned up and got dressed. As I grabbed the pictures of the ultrasound, I noticed the dates at the top. There was one for the conception date. When I saw the due date, I decided then and there God had a sense of humor.

April 1.

Fourteen

I walked the nine blocks from the doctor's office to the RV park. The sun shone bright and clear, lowering in the west and casting an apricot hue over the sidewalk, but it couldn't cut the cold front rushing in. I pulled my coat closer and walked through the entryway, past the other campers, making a beeline to where I knew Arthur must be—a special section for long-haul trucks to pull into. I recognized a few of the cabs. Some of them were trimmed in Christmas lights—one had the Star of David on the grill.

It was another life getting to know each other out there on the road. More than once, we'd been helped by complete strangers simply because we all shared the same lifestyle. Once, about two years ago, we were on a particularly dangerous portion of coastal road when we lost a tire. I don't mean it blew out, I mean we lost it. Sheared off the bolts, and it went over the edge into the ocean.

We had to pull over in a turnaround. The rain had been coming down in sheets, and I held an umbrella over Arthur's head, helping him look with a flashlight. He was cursing up a storm when I heard another fellow's voice from behind. A trucker had pulled up and offered his help.

As I stood there in the rain, holding the umbrella for both the men, they devised a plan to take Arthur to the closest tire shop and buy a new wheel and tire. Arthur went off with the man as I climbed into the cab and waited. Three hours went by, and then they were back, putting a new wheel on the truck. They shook hands, and the man drove off.

When I asked Arthur if he knew him, he said no, but we'd probably be able to help him out someday. And not a year later, we saw the same truck, pulled over having trouble getting his load covered. If you didn't tarp up in the rain, then you got docked. If it took too long to cover, you'd get docked for that, too. We were on a tight schedule, but Arthur pulled over and helped him cover up in half the time it would have normally taken.

I mentioned how nice he was at the time, but Arthur said it was the code of the road.

As I reached our cab, I found myself unwilling to try the handle. The only home I'd known for the past seven years seemed foreign to me. Instead, I went around to the driver's side and knocked on the door.

"Welcome home." Arthur's voice came from behind me. I hadn't seen him under the sunshade. He motioned toward the lit grill. "Are you hungry?"

There was only one way Arthur could cook, and that was BBQ. The grime on the grill told me he'd been living that way for the past few months without a decent scrubbing. His view was, if it was hot enough to cook meat, it was hot enough to cook the germs.

"No, thanks." Even so, my stomach grumbled in disagreement.

He motioned me to one of our folding chairs, and I sat down, still feeling like a stranger. I knew this creaky chair and the rusty grill and the sunshade—each duct-taped rip and fold. But because I felt like I didn't know Arthur, that discolored everything.

I crossed my arms over my chest as another cutting breeze came up.

"I hear it'll rain again tonight. I have to head to Portland tomorrow and then go on down to do the Texas run."

I nodded, seeing the route on the map in my mind as if it were right in front of me. "Good to do that before snow hits."

Small talk—as if nothing had changed. As if he hadn't abandoned me and our child in the midst of strangers without so much as a dollar or a toothbrush.

"My thoughts exactly." He sat down across from me and began eating his hotdogs. He looked at me sideways. "You sure you're not hungry?"

"I don't have much of an appetite lately."

As if I'd mentioned the baby directly, his eyes narrowed and lost the friendliness they'd held as we spoke about his work. "Before you know it, it'll be over and you'll be back to your old self." His tone accused me.

"The doctor is surprised I'm pregnant, too. She said it shouldn't have happened." That wasn't what the doctor said, of course. The doctor practically called it a miracle, but I knew Arthur had ill feelings toward God, and I figured I shouldn't choose now to make it worse.

"Then it shouldn't happen again."

I went heartsick at his words. Even though he didn't want this baby, I had held out hope that when he saw our boy, he'd change his mind. And there was the thought that I might want more children one day.

Imagine that. Me, wanting more children.

"No, it shouldn't. Which is another reason I want to keep him."

The scowl on his face deepened. "I'd hoped you'd seen sense and changed your mind. Why else did you come by here?"

Before I realized what I was saying, I blurted out, "To gather my things." Cold seeped in past my coat, freezing me from the inside out, as I waited for his response.

"You're my wife."

"And I thought my husband loved me. But if you ever did, there's no way you could ask me to do what you expect me to."

We'd reached a bottleneck. Much faster than I'd expected. The conversation was over, and maybe my marriage, too.

"I won't divorce you." It was a threat more than a statement of devotion or desperation.

Divorce? All the couples I'd admired stuck out in my mind. Had they ever faced something like this? Were they all a farce, pretending to love beyond measure, to cherish, to keep? All those thoughts were buzzing around my head so I didn't notice right away that Arthur got up and pulled things out from under the back wheel-well of the cab. They were my things. My whole life thus far, outside my apartment, appeared to be stowed away in three ragged paper sacks marked Five and Dime. I gave him a questioning look.

"Everything else you used belongs to me. And your money—your secret money? That's mine now, too. It all came from me, anyway. When you discover how hard it is to live on your own, you call me and I'll be back. Until then, you're on your own."

He didn't know I'd already got my money. He hadn't a clue I'd gained more in friends and property during the past three months than I had the whole time we'd been married.

Still, his tone carried a harshness that didn't reach his eyes.

I took a chance. "So that's it? You're leaving me over this?"

"*You're* leaving *me* over this. It's your choice."

He'd always been good at placing blame at my feet for things.

"What kind of choice is that?"

"You tell me." There were tears in his eyes.

Tears? My compassion got the better of me. Perhaps others didn't understand what it was like to be desperate to have someone, anyone, value them. I'd always hoped Arthur was the one to give me a feeling of worth. I mean, didn't I help him? Didn't I give myself to him entirely? He should repay my dedication and love with his love. But that wasn't happening. I reached up and touched his cheek where the tear escaped.

He held my hand there, warm in a gentle grasp. "Don't leave me, Macy. Please. Things will be better once you're back. We can take that vacation we've always wanted. Maybe we'll find a small place on the Atlantic shore, a cabin of our own that we'll retire to some day." I realized Arthur was much closer to retirement than me. And once he was gone—what would I have left?

"Please, Arthur, can't we buy a place now and I'll make us a home? Our child will grow and have a hand in the business one day." My offer was last ditch, and I knew it. I sounded desperate, but didn't care. I had to try.

Hardness creased his mouth and traveled north to his eyes. Everything about him was set against me—against *us*, as I'd begun to think of me and the baby as a unit.

"I need fifteen more years on the road before I can retire. I need you with me, Macy."

He needed me—not the baby. He didn't want me. Didn't love me. He only *needed* me. And maybe four months ago, that would've been enough. But it wasn't now.

I leaned forward and kissed his cheek, the stubble of his graying beard scratching at my face. "If you change your mind, Arthur, we'll be here, waiting for you."

He pushed me back, anger filling out his pupils until all I could see was blackness. I shivered and backed away. I'd seen him angry before, but not like this.

"I'll give you until I get back from my south run, Macy. That's about a two-month turn around. If you don't call me, willing to come back, you know what'll happen with the gas station and your family."

Somehow, I'd forgotten about the conversation with my mom. The pleading look in my mother's eyes. Her begging and me giving in.

"You'll call in your loan?"

He tipped his chin a bit, and I could see the determined look in his eyes. He didn't need to say it.

Fifteen

As I gathered my things in my arms, the handles on the sacks broke, spilling the contents of one on the ground. Kneeling down, I scooped up my bras and panties, shoving them back in before anyone could see. I struggled through the park, past the curious eyes of other truckers' wives, campers, and families. A helpless, homeless feeling tingled in my chest.

I tried to concentrate on my steps, keeping the bags in my arms just so, and my mind focused on the safe haven that awaited me when I got back to the restaurant, back home. The day was uncommonly quiet, and all I could hear was the crinkle of paper grocery bags rustling against my pregnant belly and my plodding footfalls on the gravel of the road. Within a few blocks, I was on the sidewalk, in a residential part of town. I only had six left, but my arms and back ached and, despite the lowering temperatures, sweat trickled down the side of my face. Black dots played on the edge of my vision—a warning sign. It was after dinnertime.

As if to torment me, the aroma of barbeque wafted over the fence of someone's backyard, and I regretted turning down the botulism-tainted hotdog Arthur offered me. I hadn't wanted to give him the satisfaction of seeing me vomit—but I might be giving him what he wanted if I passed out here on the sidewalk surrounded by personal items and no identification.

A truck horn beeped behind me and made me jump. Toby pulled over, climbed out, and rushed to me.

"You look white as Crisco, Macy. What are you doing out here?"

I turned to speak to him, showing him my bags, but I couldn't even mumble a decent response. The world spun, and the last thing I remembered was being lifted into his arms.

When I woke, I smelled chicken noodle soup and was lying on the bed in my apartment. Toby was at the stove, stirring a pan. He glanced over at me, saw me alert, and brought a glass of orange juice outfitted with a straw. He didn't ask me any questions, though I could see a hundred of them flit over his face. Instead, he slipped the straw in between my lips, and I sucked at the sweet, tropical goodness. I closed my eyes and visualized my blood sugar rising like the mercury on a hot day.

Toby helped me lie against the pillows, tucked the blanket around me, and returned to the stove. Glancing around, I could see my tattered grocery bags near the front door.

"Did you carry me up here?"

He glanced back and nodded, then returned to the task at hand. A moment later, he pulled up a dining chair next to me and started to spoon hot chicken noodle soup into my mouth. He blew on it and tested each one before offering it to me.

"It's good." The salty warmth seemed to satisfy my hunger, but I knew it was only my touchy stomach talking. I needed to keep eating.

"Donna's. I pulled out a container from the freezer downstairs. She always makes a ton to keep on hand for the cold days. You add the noodles as it cooks." He offered me the spoon again, and I took it, feeling very much like a little girl chided for getting her shoes wet in a puddle.

"Thank you, Toby."

A telltale crease formed between his eyebrows. I had gotten to know his worried face and could pretty much bet on what he was going to say.

"I don't want you walking around town without me. You call and I'll drive you wherever you need to go." If Arthur said that to me, it'd sound possessive. The way Toby said it sounded more like a promise of protection.

I sat up a bit and put my hand on his, to pause the shoveling of soup into my mouth. That was a huge mistake. We were locked in a staring contest, his eyes full of concern, looking deeply into mine, mine noticing how kind and gentle his were. After the hatred in Arthur's,

Toby's gaze drew me. The electrical energy passing between my hand and his arm crackled in my blood. Time stopped. I swallowed hard, let go, and looked away.

"No." There was double meaning in what I tried to tell him. I didn't want to hurt the one person I could truly call a friend in my life.

He put the soup on the chair and went back to the kitchen, cleaning up the mess he'd made cooking. "I don't know why not. I mean, what were you doing out there?" Toby said *out there* like I'd been in the wilderness alone, not a few blocks over on the edge of suburbia.

"I was telling Arthur good-bye."

Toby turned, eyes filled with hope. I put up a hand again.

"Before you start, it's because he's on his way to Texas. I'm hoping he'll be back and then he'll take the baby and me and settle us somewhere."

"But he doesn't want the baby."

"He could change his mind. I can't think that my whole marriage…" But I stopped. Why did I defend a man who abandoned me in the middle of nowhere, who took—or thought he took—every last penny I'd saved, and who was threatening my family if I didn't get rid of my child?

Why did I keep making excuses for him?

"I'm not sure what your marriage was supposed to be, Macy. I do know what it's not. He doesn't love you. He couldn't, or he wouldn't treat you the way he does. You deserve better."

My anger built. At myself mostly, but as Toby closed the distance between us, fear got the better of me. Fear and baby hormones.

"You don't know what I deserve, Toby. You don't know me." This stopped him in his tracks as if he'd hit a force field. And maybe he had. "What could you possibly know about me that makes you think you'd know what I deserve?" I yelled at him, unable to stop. "I can take care of myself. You can just keep your opinions to yourself." I could see from Toby's eyes that he didn't believe any of it. He'd rescued me from myself too many times.

"I know it because no one deserves it." He went to the kitchen table, grabbing his truck keys. "The heat's off on the stove. There's bread and butter set out."

Toby's footsteps slammed down the stairs, and the door shut with a resounding finality. The echo of my own regretful sniffles confirmed my guilt, and I knew I'd done serious damage to our friendship. I'd been wrong. I was really yelling at Arthur—the man who promised to take care of me and protect me.

For the baby's sake, I continued eating the soup and then got up to grab the bread and butter. It was so tasty, I had to have more. I ate another slice. It was the first time I'd eaten anything in weeks that hadn't set off my nausea. Bread was safe again—thank goodness. Maybe I could get by on homemade chicken noodle soup and fresh bread for the rest of my pregnancy. I'd be okay with that.

After my feet began to feel more solid under me, I dumped out the bags of my things on the kitchen table. Besides underclothes, there were a few dresses, some overalls, makeup, and hair care things. My toothbrush rattled out on the table, the bristles intertwined with hair and dust. I threw it away. The last thing that fell out was my old everything book. I hadn't known I was missing it until I saw it.

I flipped through the pages, sure Arthur had read it. There were coffee stains here and there, and I wasn't much of a coffee drinker. Every page held mundane details along with hopes and dreams. I read through it to make sure my own words hadn't betrayed me. I'd never said a word about wanting a baby. Arthur must know I didn't plan this.

Yet he blamed me.

I stared out at the street and watched a family walk by, the mom and dad holding hands with their daughter, who couldn't be more than four. Every now and then, she jumped up and they'd swing her high. I couldn't hear the laughter, but I could see the smiles on their faces. My spirit wrenched with sadness and regret. I looked away.

After folding my things and stowing them in the cubbies of the armoire, I sat back down with my now-cold bowl of soup. It was dark outside, and I had yet to turn on a light in my apartment. The bulbs on the movie theatre filtered through—now red and green in honor of Christmas. It was enough.

I went into autopilot, clearing away the food, cleaning the counter. After I changed for bed, I lay down and pulled my purse toward me before switching on the little light near my. It cast a golden hue over my hands, warming me. Inside my purse, I found the sonogram pictures. I rubbed my fingers gently over Baby's tiny head and smiled.

Macy

Nothing that happened today really changed anything. Arthur still didn't want us and I was still alone. But seeing the photo reminded me I wasn't as alone as I used to be.

"Okay, Baby. It's you and me. You all right with that?" As if in answer, the baby gave me a kick. As I fell asleep, I thought of boy names. Ones with power and promise. Names of a man who would never buy a wife and leave her family homeless.

Names that called to mind a kind man who would befriend and care for a perfect stranger. And feed her soup.

Sixteen

I woke to the sound of knocking on my apartment door. I climbed from the bed to answer it but didn't get the chance. Instead, I raced to the bathroom to perform my daily wake-up call. The knocks persisted as I cleaned up and made my way down the steps.

"Who is it?"

"It's Donna. You okay? Toby said you passed out again yesterday." Toby.

"Yes, I'm fine. I'm a bit slow getting going. Am I late?"

"No, but I wondered if we could talk a few minutes?"

Fear raced over me. Maybe they'd gotten tired of my deadweight around the restaurant. "Sure, could you give me a few minutes?" If I was going to be fired, I wanted to do it fully clothed with clean teeth.

"I'll be back in fifteen. Sound okay?"

I agreed and headed back up the stairs to pick up the apartment and wash up for work. As I ate breakfast, she knocked again.

"Come on in, Donna," I called down to her.

Donna came upstairs with several bags of baby clothes. "I was at the thrift store the other day, and I…" She stopped when she saw all the things in the apartment. "Oh, I didn't realize you'd gone shopping." Her tone suggested I shouldn't have gone without her.

"I went to some garage sales a couple weeks ago and got everything I needed. Unless you have some older boy's things. Although I don't really have much storage space right now."

Donna's hands picked over the baby's things. "Most of these are brand new."

"Mrs. Williams' family was having a sale. I needed boy things. It worked out really well." I could tell from Donna's pale face she understood why.

I took a peek inside the bags Donna brought and saw most of the items inside were new, too. Along with baby items, there was a bag of maternity clothes, all my size. I was getting to the point where I couldn't get by with popping the top button on my jeans. Some food must have been staying with me.

"I can sure use those." I pointed to the pants and tops.

"Good." She held them up in front of me. "Your color's not the same, but I think they'll work. She never got to wear them." Donna's voice went quiet.

"Who, Donna?" I'd been putting things together in my mind. How Donna's daughter was gone. How this apartment sat ready for a woman my age and size to move on in. The pregnancy book on the shelf.

"My girl. Danny. She was pregnant." She fingered the shirt in her hands. "We made a lot of the outfits together—you can't imagine how awful some of the maternity things are these days. Nothing comfortable, you know."

"Where's Danny?" I didn't want to ask, but I'd been feeling like I was living in someone else's shoes for a while now.

"She's dead. Killed in a car accident."

It wasn't what I expected to hear. Donna's eyes were red with unshed tears. "She was about five months along. Losing them both like that—" She stopped and put a hand over her eyes.

"I'm so sorry, Donna." I put my arms around her and let her cry. After a bit, I handed her a tissue and waited for her to compose herself.

"You can't change the past. If something good can come out of tragedy, then that's a blessing. You take these things, okay?" Donna got up and headed down the stairs. "We open in twenty minutes."

"I'll be there. And thanks."

Donna waved at me and closed the door behind her.

That must have been what Toby and Mrs. Williams were alluding to all those times. What heartbreak for Donna and Nick. I'd only been a mother for a few months, and only seen my baby in black and white snippets, but I knew what I'd given up to keep him. And what I'd give up to save him.

Donna didn't mention a husband, or the father of the baby, so there must not have been one on the scene. I sure hadn't seen evidence of one in the apartment.

Looking around, I started to see through another young woman's eyes. I wore her clothes and slept in her bed. A renewed sense of responsibility strengthened me. I wasn't having this baby just for me. I was doing it for Nick and Donna, too.

I put the bags of clothes aside, loaded my dishes in the sink, and traced the butterfly design on the cups. Did Danny pick them out, or were they second-hand items just put together for this place? Remembering the butterflies on the light switch cover in the bathroom, I sensed a theme. A theme planned by another hopeful girl. Another single girl.

Because that, for all effects, was what I was.

As I entered the restaurant, Toby gave me a slight smile and went back to chopping and mixing for the morning rush. Nick nodded at me, and Donna gave me a warm pat on the back as she moved to change the CLOSED sign to OPEN.

Outside, the rain drizzled and the sun did its best to push warmth and light through the thickening clouds. A short line of people trickled in and took their seats. I gave them my best smile and started to pour the coffee.

"You've got a regular," Donna whispered in my ear and motioned toward one of my booths. In it sat a sweet-looking little lady with white hair, pushing off her coat to reveal a hand-knitted sweater. Her hands shuddered as they picked up the menu. I didn't know why she bothered, as she ordered the same thing every morning. She used to go to Donna's booth and had done so for years. She was one of the hardest customers I'd had in my few months of waitressing. But whenever I made her happy, it felt better than helping a hundred other easy ones.

"Good morning, Mrs. Tate. Tea today?" I already had the hot water pot in my hand, and basket of her favorite blends tucked in the crook of my arm, but asked out of courtesy.

Mrs. Tate stared at the menu, pursing her lips together. I watched, mesmerized as her mouth wrinkles folded together like someone was pulling an invisible string on flesh colored cloth.

"I think I would like some tea, yes." She flipped the page of the menu. I filled her cup and put the teas down.

"I'd prefer a pot today, please. I'm expecting a guest." *Tricky.* I grabbed a pot, filled it and put it on the table. I moved the jam selection over, because I knew that'd be next. She liked raspberry and marmalade.

I found myself staring at her, and she looked up at me expectantly and perturbed. "A second place setting?"

"Of course. Sorry." *Rats.* I grabbed a place setting and brought it back to the table as an older man sat down across from her. He gave her a warm smile, and her eyes shone back at him. Shone? Mrs. Tate?

"Good morning." I placed the setting in front of him, and he took a menu.

"Should I give you a few minutes?"

"No dear. Mr. Tate knows what he wants. Eggs over easy, whole wheat toast, a side of fruit. I'll have the fruit plate and a dish of cottage cheese with sourdough toast." She glanced at the jam basket, her eyes narrowing as she found it lacking. "He likes blackberry."

I made a dash to the counter and grabbed packets of blackberry jam, returning just as he put the menu down and began to pour hot water over his teabag. I stood stunned. Mrs. Tate had never mentioned a husband—although to be honest, she never said much of anything at all to me, except complaints.

"You have the cook make his eggs just right, dear. And his toast, not too brown."

I adjusted the order and turned away, still in a stunned state. I put the slip on the pass-through wheel. Nick grabbed it and started on their meals. Donna rushed by to pick up an order.

"Did you know she was married?" I asked Donna from behind my hand.

"Sure I did. But he only comes in once a year with her—on their anniversary, the day before Christmas Eve."

My mind was still whirling as I took three other customers' orders and then Nick yelled that table four was ready. The Tates' table. I still hadn't decided what would keep an older married couple apart for all those mornings. My mind created many scenarios, one of which had Mr. Tate being a cat-burglar and since he worked nights, he couldn't get up early and have breakfast with his wife. As I stole a glance at Mr.

Tate, his long lanky form, I giggled and tried to picture him ducking in and out of the shadows before returning home to Mrs. Tate with a bag of loot.

Shaking myself out of it, I remembered some fresh flowers Donna had brought from the local florist's shop, sitting on the table in our break area. Her friend let her have the older ones for a discount. I rushed back and snipped some, putting them in a smaller vase.

As I carried out their order, I put the vase on the table between them. "Happy anniversary."

Both the Tates looked up at me with appreciation in their eyes. Mr. Tate spoke. "How did you know our flower was the lily?"

They had a flower. As Mr. Tate took his wife's hand in his, I began to see Mrs. Tate in a new light. She blushed.

"What are your plans for the rest of the day?" I'd gone from hesitant to curious.

Mrs. Tate opened up like the white and pink flowers in the vase before them. "We plan to take in an afternoon showing at the theatre. And then we'll go for a drive into Appleton and have dinner at the Italian restaurant there."

Mr. Tate gave her a warm smile. "It's our place. That's where I proposed fifty-six years ago. Of course, it was a Hungarian restaurant then."

She laughed. "Yes, it's changed hands many times through our marriage. We never know what kind of food we'll have on our anniversary, only where we'll be."

Against my previous judgment where I'd seen her as a challenge to overcome, I found myself genuinely liking Mrs. Tate. "Would you like some more hot water?"

She nodded and smiled. I still didn't know why she ate alone every morning, or why she was grumpy (maybe that was why), but today she was happy, and that gave Mrs. Tate a whole new look in my eyes.

People were complicated and, as I was learning firsthand in my own life, not always as they seemed.

The next few hours went by in a mad dash. As soon as I stopped for a break, my feet started pounding to the tempo of the headache squeezing my brain. I needed to eat something substantial. I washed up in the bathroom and left to grab lunch when I saw Toby sitting at the break table, biscuits and gravy with a side of fruit waiting for me. It made no sense at all, because the gravy was a bit oily—but my stomach not only craved it, it kept it down.

Toby didn't talk to me much, except to ask me to pass him the salt. Attentive, he knew what I wanted before I could think of it. I had a small glass of orange juice and a cup of strong tea along with my food. In the past few months, he'd shown more concern for my wants than anyone besides my grandma. I could handle him caring for me, but I couldn't take the silence.

"This morning sure was busy," I offered.

"Yep." I watched as he took a bite of hash and a swallow of coffee. His eyes traveled to the newspaper on the table, and he flipped it open.

"So this is how it's going to be between us, then?"

Toby's eyes narrowed at me around the corner of his paper. "Isn't that what you want?"

"I want—" I stopped. What I wanted wasn't fair. At all. "I'm sorry. I was out of line yesterday."

His eyes softened. "Yes you were." He paused. "If we're going to stay friends, you're going to have to get used to me doing things for you. That's the kind of guy I am and I'm going to be honest with you. Can you live with that?"

I opened my mouth to speak, but Donna walked in and sat down at the table before I could respond. It was for the best, because I was about to betray everything I'd believed in for my whole life. There was no point in denying it. The last thing I wanted to be with Toby was just friends.

Seventeen

That night, I lay awake a long time in bed, staring at the small live Christmas tree I'd purchased from the grocery store. Even though the space under it was small, the lack of presents left me feeling empty. I kept the mini-light set turned on and let my eyes go out of focus so the colors would blur and double in size. Baby kicked me here and there, but he wasn't what was keeping me awake. I was, for the hundredth time, upset with God. Why had my life taken such a turn?

"Grandma, I wish you were here. I'm so confused." My voice cracked, and when I heard the emotion there, I began to cry. I so missed her.

Even though we'd been out of touch, words of wisdom would often trickle into my consciousness when I least expected it. The things I remembered most were stories about how she stuck by my grandfather through hardships and joys. I used to dream I'd find someone like him. Someone who cared for me more than he cared for himself. When Arthur proposed to me, I thought I'd found him.

Anger billowed around me. Anger at myself for not seeing the truth of the matter, and then at my mother for not protecting me. Nothing made sense in my head. And if it wasn't my mother's fault, then it was God's. He let me get married.

My conscience twinged a bit at the accusation. My mind shifted again, and I became mad at my father for dying, at my mother again for being too trusting, at Arthur for being selfish. For Toby not entering my life earlier.

I could have played the blame game all night. As I closed my eyes and wished for sleep, I saw the arrows connecting from one person to another, from one mistake to the next and it ending with me cuddled on a dead woman's daybed, praying for daylight.

Somewhere in the night, I must have fallen asleep, because my alarm went off and I was in the bathroom throwing up before I was fully awake. Every day, it got a bit harder—throwing up, getting dressed, and serving people. I really loved my job, but my body still ached from the day before. A rush of chills raced over my skin, so I decided to grab my shower before eating.

That was perhaps not the best idea. The hot water hit and made me very dizzy. Spots raced before my eyes, and I fell against the side of the tub, bruising my elbow. I carefully climbed from the tub and realized I'd gotten a huge welt on my knee, too. I tried to dry off without falling over and headed to the kitchen for some juice. I needed a boost, fast. I felt myself fading, my brain shutting down.

I glugged juice straight from the carton and grabbed a bite of leftover ham sandwich from the previous night. My legs turned to noodles, and I flopped down hard on the chair near the table, towel wrapped around me. Shivers cascaded over my skin, and I put my head on my arms, willing the food to be digested into tiny energy-boosting particles, picked up by my bloodstream and shunted to my cells. I breathed in and out, slowly, counting until the world came into focus.

As the sun's rays filtered in through my window, the buzz in my head cleared and strength returned. I stood and took a couple small steps before discovering the puddle-path of my escape from the shower—like a slug trail. I took off my towel and began to mop up the mess and caught sight of myself in the full-length mirror I'd bought weeks ago. I had been compelled to make sketches in my everything book of my ever enlarging stomach—me and my new roommate.

In retrospect, seeing my underweight, swelling, bruised body was not in my best interest. I clenched my eyes closed and focused on sopping up the puddle. Before long, I gave in to curiosity and glimpsed myself on all fours, mopping the floor in the nude, and my sobs turned to laughter.

"Oh, Baby, I hope I know what I'm doing here. You're going to have to be very patient with me."

He kicked.

I wasn't alone. Even if I was mad at God—for what exactly, I hadn't decided—I had him and I had Baby.

An hour later, I helped Donna prep for breakfast and acted like everything was fine. Toby couldn't keep his anxious eyes off of me. It was apparent I wasn't doing so hot. But to everyone's credit, they didn't say a thing. They must have sensed my brittleness.

I'd shoved the incident at lunch yesterday out of my mind. Today was a fresh start. I could be friends with Toby and nothing had to come of it. And after Baby was born, I'd give it one more try with Arthur.

My thoughts brought me up short, and I nearly dropped the plate I carried. Donna steadied my arm, and I flinched in pain.

"Oh heavens, what did you do to yourself?" She lifted my sleeve, and I could see the bruise from earlier had spread up my bicep. I should have taken time to ice it, but I wasn't thinking right.

I sensed a pattern.

"I slipped a tiny bit in the tub. I'm fine."

"And her knee, too." Toby stared at my leg and then into my eyes accusingly. "Did you forget to eat again?" The emphasis he put on *again* stirred my ire.

"No, I vomited all over myself and needed to shower off before I ate." I walked away to serve my table, not sure what was more humiliating—throwing up all over myself or announcing it to the whole diner.

After serving breakfast, I headed back to use the bathroom, and when I came out a meal once again waited for me. This time it was a ham and cheese omelet. Toby didn't join me, but I knew it was from him. It was exactly the way he'd seen me order it for myself. I ate alone and cleared the table. Donna called me over and told me to go upstairs and rest. But I knew if I went, I'd lay there, worry, and think myself to death. So instead I opted for a walk to clear my head. I promised to be back for the dinner rush. She didn't comment but gave me a sad look.

They were probably thinking how irresponsible and stupid I was. And I couldn't really put their fears to rest. I mean, I didn't exactly make choice decisions.

The fresh air did what it needed to. As I turned a corner, I found myself in front of the library and headed inside. Staying up late reading would be a much better hobby than lying in bed and crying myself to sleep.

After I filled out my library card application and used my new address again—this never got old for me—I started searching for some books. The choices of new releases overwhelmed me. Instead, I opted for a classic, *Oliver Twist*, and a couple from the "Fresh and Fun" shelf. I didn't know what was fresh or fun about books, but I figured if the librarian worked so hard on a sales technique to get people to check out new releases, I'd bite.

Before I headed back downstairs, something drew me to the microfiche machine. I used one a few times in high school for reports I had to do. I always liked the whir-click sound they made as they flipped and searched through items. I walked to the woman at the information desk.

"Excuse me, do you have the local paper for the past couple years on microfiche?"

She smiled with her mouth and eyes in a way that told me I'd made it worth her while to be there that day.

"Oh yes. I'll get that for you right now."

I told myself I was only curious about the town's happenings. But as the fan came to life, blowing the familiar warm plastic smell up into my face, I knew I had an ulterior motive.

I moved through one article after another, going back, back, through one month of announcements, then the next. And I saw it. Danny's obituary. I zoomed in on the article, clicking, clicking until there she was in black, white, and gray pixels. I didn't mind. I could easily imagine her hair and eye color. Because she looked like me.

Eighteen

I wasn't sure what I expected to see when I found Danny's obituary. But that she looked like me, was about my age, my height, even a similar nose, shocked me. I knew we couldn't be related, and yet she had the same lost and alone look in her eyes I'd always had. As I suspected, she wasn't married.

I know Donna and Nick didn't ever mistreat their daughter—I could tell by the way they'd been treating me, and how they acted toward each other when they didn't think anyone was watching. So why did she have that look? In a second photo, not as close up, she stood with her parents at a party. Over to the side, there was a young man under the shade of a tree, but I couldn't make out his face. Could Danny have already been pregnant in the photo? Maybe shadow-man was the father.

Curiosity burned through me. Yet as I continued my research, I found no mention of the accident except a blurb on the Public Safety blotter about a wreck a week prior to Danny's obituary. That had to have been it, but they didn't give names or deaths. Everything was all very technical, and it listed the location rather than who was in it. As if one thing mattered more than the other.

My frustration grew, and then a thought occurred. Maybe she didn't get into an accident in town. Maybe I'd find the information in Appleton's papers. I made a mental note to do that next. I could also start asking around town. It might cause unhappy feelings, though, if Nick or Donna heard about it. But I didn't feel right coming out and asking them. They'd already been hurt enough.

The clock in the library sounded off three soft bells, and I realized I'd been sitting there perusing the town's history for much too long. I had to get back and help with dinner prep and an early close. After all, it was Christmas Eve, and the town promised to close up tight in time for church services and family dinners. I returned the microfiche to the librarian and thanked her before heading out with my few selections.

My books weighed heavily in the crook of my arm and forced me to carry them on each side. My elbow was much sorer than it had been that morning. Tonight I would put some crackers and peanut butter in the bathroom to keep it from happening again. The idea of storing food in there made my upper lip curl, but I needed to eat before I tried to take a shower. Or bath. Maybe from now on I'd take a bath.

I tried to picture myself at eight months pregnant climbing from the claw-foot tub, and all I could see was me, shiny and round, slipping again and breaking my neck. Not to mention being found nude. I crossed the idea of baths off my list and entered the diner in time to hear Donna and Nick arguing about something. They stopped as soon as they saw me, and the hair on the back of my neck stood up as if to confirm that yes, they were talking about me. I glanced around but didn't see Toby anywhere.

"Sorry I'm late." I gave them a smile that told them not to worry, I didn't hear a thing.

As I passed by to grab my apron, I did my best not to listen. But I heard Toby's name and my own. When I came out and started checking the ketchup bottles, I noticed once again Toby wasn't anywhere in sight. The unsettled feeling I had when I first arrived increased.

"Where's Toby?"

"I'm not sure." Donna gave me a pained look that was supposed to pass for a smile and handed me a towel. "Could you wipe those back few tables? I don't think he'll be back."

Fear—real, ragged fear—shivered through me. "Back? You mean ever?"

"Oh, no. Just not today. Don't worry, I'm sure everything is fine. He's got some problems at home, and we let him go early to help his mom get ready for Christmas."

Guilt and relief battled inside. If I could force myself to stop the attraction to Toby, I would. For some reason, I kept forgetting Toby took care of his family. Another mystery I hadn't quite figured out.

As I wiped down the booth, I took a good look at Donna and Nick. Neither of them had red hair—so maybe Danny didn't either. Maybe it was dark brown. I started to imagine what it would have been like to grow up there in the diner. Coming in for a snack after school let out for the day. Sitting at the bar with the locals, listening to gossip and laughing at stories.

Much better than my childhood, by far. I grew up pumping gas for backwoodsmen and truckers. I heard stories, too, but none I should repeat. I took care of a menacing dog and fed chickens while I pretended my father wasn't dying in the back of the house. I went to school and acted like my life was great, studied hard, and at night dreamed of what it would be like to escape one day. Not all dreams that came true had happy endings.

The early dinner rush came in, but it was more of a slow creek than a fast river. Folks were probably at home putting the finishing touches on their turkey or ham, wrapping presents and buttoning coats to leave for church.

Before I let the loneliness take over, I caught Nick cooking and singing carols and throwing the occasional flirty glances at his wife. They loved and respected each other. No one had been sick or dying in Danny's life. She didn't appear to have family hardships, but she still got herself into a mess.

I didn't want my baby growing up with more issues than he had to—and if he ever found out, even by accident, that his father not only didn't want him, but wanted him dead, that'd scar him for life. That's when I made my decision. Or maybe it was a prayer—a prayer I wouldn't have to return to Arthur and his anger.

I didn't know if that was something I should pray. I changed my prayer that God would work things out the best he could. As I glanced around at the diner, wishing I'd made different choices, I realized running away from your life didn't really work. It all caught up with you again.

Christmas morning arrived like any other day. I halfway expected to be invited to Toby's house, or to Nick and Donna's, but no one offered anything except Christmas wishes. That was okay. Even if they'd asked, I would have declined. I wanted to be independent, just as much as I wanted to belong to a family. As I held a conflicted pity party, a knock came on my apartment door followed by retreating footsteps after I didn't answer. I waited until I heard the bell ring over the door and headed down to take a peek.

Outside my door lay a package and a box of food. I carried both upstairs, putting them on the table. I put the present under my little tree and looked in the box to find pancakes and sausage for breakfast. To the side was a foil-wrapped cherry pie, and underneath sat a turkey dinner, complete with sides of mashed potatoes and cranberry sauce.

I opened the note and read it, tears filling my eyes. It was all from Toby.

As I ate my breakfast, I stared at the package and wondered what was inside it. I hadn't had a Christmas present for years—unless you count things like T-shirts and hats with gas station or trucking logos Arthur had collected over the years and re-gifted to me.

Memories of our first Christmas flitted through my mind. We had stopped for the night at a national park, and it had snowed, so the windows were covered in white dust. I woke up excited and gave Arthur his present, a leather log book and new flannel shirt. He unwrapped them and told me thanks and asked what was for breakfast.

I'd tried not to feel hurt. Christmas had always been a big event at my house—until my father got sick. I'd still put up a tree and had the kids help me decorate. We'd given one another presents—mostly handmade ones, like scarves and hats. My mother retreated into herself and shut off all sources of happiness—it'd been hard to get her to participate at all. My father still tried. She had let us in the last Christmas with him, to sing songs and share our gifts. But he'd started coughing and turned gray, scaring us all, so she ushered us out and warned us to keep quiet.

Later, that first Christmas, Arthur went for a walk and came back with a black leather book and pen set he'd picked up at a mini-mart. He seemed embarrassed as he admitted he'd forgotten it was Christmas and hoped I liked my gift. I loved it, because until then my everything books had been spiral bound or plastic covers at best.

I convinced myself of his romantic intentions, how he cared for me and went out of his way to show me. I shook my head in wonder and amazement at my immature ideals. My low expectations.

I reached for Toby's gift, testing the contents with my fingers. It was clothes—probably for the baby. As I unwrapped the paper, keeping a scrap for my everything book, I uncovered a red, long sleeved T-shirt, just my size. As I held it up to myself, I read the writing over the middle of the shirt: BABY'S FIRST CHRISTMAS.

I cried until it felt like there wasn't any liquid left in my body. Toby knew what the baby meant to me. We didn't have to have long conversations about Baby's worth, about my chances of ever conceiving again, about how hard this pregnancy was for me—he just knew.

And I hadn't gotten him anything.

I searched my mind for things Toby might need. I'd been on the receiving end of his friendship all this time and hadn't offered him anything in return. Not that friendships were about getting stuff—but he'd done plenty of giving.

As I took bites of breakfast, an idea built in my mind. I grinned. It was perfect.

Toby entered the break room, hanging his apron on the hook. I pretended to be engrossed in my magazine. He picked up a box, covered in Christmas wrapping, flipping over the tag, reading his name.

"What's this?"

I shrugged and went back to my magazine, fighting a smile.

As he unwrapped it he laughed. "You're kidding. Where did you find this?" He held up an eight-track player in like-new condition—well, as like-new as could be.

"I have my ways." I'd seen it at the thrift store when searching for some other items I needed. I motioned under the paper in the box. He dug deeper and pulled out four yellowed eight-track tapes.

"That's crazy." He shuffled through them. "I don't have any of these."

"There's more at the thrift store. But she said they were selling out fast."

"Ha. Probably to the guy that ripped me off." He tucked his gift back in the box.

"You could set up a sting operation." I chuckled.

He glanced up at me, and his smile softened. "This is about the best gift I've ever gotten."

"Really?" I suddenly wished I would have picked up some more albums.

Toby came around the table, leaned down, and hugged me. "Really," he whispered. His arms were warm but strong. He smelled like soap and musky aftershave and fresh bread. I caught myself melting into his embrace, accepting his comfort. It'd been so long since anyone had held me.

Someone cleared their voice. Toby froze, then he let me go and his ears went red. Nick stood in the door, waving his spatula.

"Got five new orders out here, could use some help." He gave me a pointed, pained look, and went back into the kitchen. Shame raced over me. I expected to see much the same look on Toby's face. Instead, after stashing his present in his locker, he looked back just long enough to give me a victorious smile.

Nineteen

Weeks passed, and January neared its end. I kept catching myself watching the calendar in fear of Arthur's return. I'd grown mechanical in my daily routine. I got up, vomited, went to work, vomited, came home, and vomited before bed. Sometimes Baby tossed in a couple extra vomits here and there to keep me on my toes. In the back of my mind was the ever-nagging sensation that maybe Arthur was right about all of this. I hadn't wanted kids, maybe I'd be horrible at being a parent. But just as I was beginning to feel the baby inside was more of a parasite making me ill than an actual person, he'd give me a swift kick and remind me we were a team. And I loved him.

As I ate lunch in the break room, pondering my life, Toby came back and joined me. This had turned into the part of the day I looked forward to, when we could share ideas. He'd started opening up about how hard it was to be grow up with an alcoholic as a parent. How hard it was to cover for him and try to make everything perfect for his mom. Somehow, instead of her protecting Toby, he'd ended up protecting her. Not the healthiest of relationships.

I pretended to be content with the situation of us just being friends. But lately, I'd been picturing the future in my head—vacations at the beach, going to the zoo, park trips, and play dates—and always at the hazy edge, there was Toby. Waiting.

"Can you tell me something?" Toby's voice startled me, and I nearly dropped my fork of mashed potatoes. His eyes were dark and heavy. They seemed to take in my every feature as he waited for me to respond.

"What?" I gripped my napkin, worried.

"Do you love Arthur?" That was Toby. Straightforward—no holds barred.

"It's complicated." I didn't meet his eyes.

"I've watched *Dr. Phil*. I know about women who stay married to abusive husbands past the point of reason. You know what happens to them?"

"Seriously—*Dr. Phil*?" I started to move away from the table, but he stilled me with a touch. His hand wasn't forceful or rough like Arthur's. His was gentle, hopeful, protective.

I sat back down.

His eyes filled with emotion. "You must know I care about you, Macy. Please don't let yourself be taken advantage of. Don't let yourself or the baby get hurt."

In all my life, outside of my grandmother, no one had ever expressed such concern so deeply for me. My tear-filled eyes stared back into his. I wished I could come clean and tell him *everything* I was going through, but it felt private and hard and impossible.

"I don't want to leave." I nearly choked on the words.

"Then don't go back to him."

"It's not that easy."

"I know it doesn't seem like it. But you have a job and a place to stay—that's half the battle for most abused wives."

I sighed. I'd been pretending we could go along this way forever. But we couldn't. And I needed to make a decision. Soon.

"It's not me. I need to protect…" I stopped, not knowing how far to take our conversation. "There's part of Arthur that's good. The part I fell in love with. Then there's a whole other part that is manipulative. He's afraid I'm going to leave him forever. I think he's always been afraid of that—which is the only reason I can figure he's kept such a tight hold over me." I shook my head. "The funny thing is, when he's kind, he's amazing. I've seen him help strangers. He helped my family." The more I spoke, I realized I was trying to convince myself just as hard as I was trying to convince Toby.

Toby pointed to my ring. "I doubt that was altruistic."

Arthur couldn't have wheedled his way into my family's good graces to cart me off one day. He'd have to be an amazingly talented con man to do so. I didn't think he was that smart.

Toby's eyes narrowed. "I think he saw an opportunity not to be alone anymore and took it."

"You're right. I'm sure that was part of it." Hadn't I done the same thing in a way? With Arthur, I'd seen an opportunity to escape. I closed my eyes, realizing the fluctuation of my desires, the feebleness of my mind, and the weakness of my spirit. The verse in James my grandma would quote about being double-minded and tossed about in the sea raced through my head. I wish I had more than sand to stand on.

"Macy, even if you don't care about your well-being or happiness, you need to care about your son's."

Nothing Toby could have said would have cut me deeper.

"I'm thinking of my son and my mother and my sisters and brother. I'm thinking of you and of Arthur."

He took my hand in his. "But tell me—what do *you* want?"

I didn't want to think about what I wanted, because it didn't seem possible. I couldn't afford to think about it. But I made the mistake of looking up into Toby's eyes, his earnest, caring face and it all spilled out. "I want to have a regular life in a rambling ranch house with a husband, a couple kids, and a cuddly dog and a big flower garden in the backyard." There was more. I wanted to be loved and to love. I wanted to share my heart with someone, my dreams, my hopes. I didn't dare divulge the rest.

Hope flashed in his eyes, and I immediately regretted my words.

"But I didn't marry that person. I married Arthur." I patted his hand and removed my other one from his grasp. "Thanks for trying to help me, Toby. There are things that have been done that can't be undone."

"I can protect you."

The very idea conjured up dangers I wasn't aware of until then. Arthur might do Toby harm. I didn't think I could handle that. "You can't." My words were firm and I saw he'd heard me this time. He sat back, hurt etched across his features and looked away from me.

The phone rang. Donna called out to me, and I picked up the back extension. I expected it to be Arthur, but it wasn't.

"Macy?"

"Mom? What's wrong?"

"We lost one of our contracts today. It's not a huge one, but they told me they'd heard we were having trouble and needed to find a dependable stop."

Arthur. "I'll take care of it, Mom."

"What are you going to do?" She was breathless on the phone, her panic contagious.

"I'm going to get ahold of him and explain things once again. It'll be okay."

When I hung up, I found I was alone in the back room. The only thing waiting for me was my cold meal—and I no longer wanted to eat anything. I went upstairs to my apartment, picked up the phone, and dialed his familiar number.

"Stone."

"Arthur? My mom just called."

"Getting the message?" The coldness in his voice still surprised me. Did the man I married exist outside my imagination at all?

I swallowed hard. "Listen, can't we talk about this? We used to care about each other." The words tasted bitter in my mouth.

"You used to love me."

"I don't even think I know you anymore, Arthur. Maybe I never did. I don't want my family to be stripped of everything they own."

Arthur went quiet. I could hear the road noise coming over the speaker and the thrum of the tires under the rig against the cement freeway. He must have been going through southern California now.

"Arthur?"

"You're right, Macy. I don't want to hurt anyone. But what are we going to do? I need us to go back to where we were."

"But that wasn't any good either, Arthur. You kept me from my family. You need to let go."

"Nothing good ever came of me letting go of anything. I've got investments all over the country. Do you know how I did that? Living lean. Sleeping in my truck. Then I found someone trustworthy to share my life with, and she betrayed me."

"I didn't get pregnant on purpose, Arthur."

"I'm not talking about you."

The blood in my ears rushed.

"I knew your mom a long time before I met your dad, did you know that, Macy?"

My stomach turned, and I saw golden sparkles before my eyes as my legs went out from under me. My rump hit the chair hard, jolting me out of my shock.

"But when I was out carving us a future, she married your dad. I didn't come around for fifteen years, but then I started bringing my truck by their place. I thought I could handle it, being around them. And you were there. You made that easier for me, Macy. You lifted my burden. You hung on every word. You made me feel important."

"Arthur..." I started, but I didn't know what to say. My stomach roiled. *No, Baby, not now.* I pushed gently on my tummy and hoped he'd listen for once. The last thing I wanted to do was throw up.

"Macy, you were better than her. She used you, just like she used me. As soon as I saw that, I knew I had to get you away before she broke you. It worked. She got what she wanted, and I got you. Now you want to go change everything."

"But..." I stopped again, still not knowing what to say.

He cleared his voice. "You want to have the baby?"

"Yes." Hope filled me.

"Have it and give it to your mom. She'll do fine by it. She owes you. Then you come back to me, Macy. I need you."

"But I want the baby."

The noise on the line went still. I couldn't even hear him breathe. Then the most startling, cold voice filled the ear piece.

"I've been very patient about this, Macy. You come back to me without the baby, or it'll all go. The shop, their house, all of it. You understand? You're mine."

I'd often imagined the romance of hearing someone saying I was theirs. It was nothing like that.

Shivers raced through my body. Once again, I found myself lying. "Okay."

"Good. Good. Any hospital bills, you let me know about them. And I'll set up an educational fund for the boy. Everything's going to work out for the best. It's all going to be okay." Relief flooded his voice...but it drowned me.

My apartment shifted around me, warped and warbled like looking at the world through the bottom of a canning jar. The colors shifted into the gray creeping in at the corners of my vision. The linoleum on the floor bent up to meet my head in a resounding slap.

My last thought of the day? There sure were a lot of dust bunnies under the daybed.

Twenty

I had always considered myself to be pretty resilient. But in no way, shape, or form would I be going to work today. As I held ice to my blackened eye, I went over the ridiculous list that had become my life as I knew it. My father? Dead. My husband, once in love with my mother, had married me as a consolation prize. My mother? In dire straits, about to lose her life's work and home. My siblings? About to be homeless. Me? Pregnant and abandoned. My best friend? In love with me and unapproachable because of said love. My head throbbed.

And once again, I needed to throw up.

Luckily I was sitting on the side of the tub as I iced my face and needed only to lean over to lose the little breakfast I had ingested a half-hour ago. Pressure pounded in my head, pulsing through the bruise. If Baby gained any weight at all, it'd be a freaking miracle. He seemed to hate everything. Not fair to blame the baby I suppose, but *someone* needed to take the blame for all of this.

As if in perfect timing, I caught my reflection in the mirror and nodded at myself. *Yep.*

Someone knocked on my apartment door. Donna opened it and called up the stairwell.

"Macy, you didn't come to work, so I'm checking on you. Are you okay?"

"Come on up, Donna." The act of rolling my eyes at her timing shot daggers of pain through my head. I held my position at the side of the tub, ice pack numbing my injury.

Donna followed my voice to the bathroom. The look of horror on her face said it all. "Oh you poor thing. That's it. We need to put some of those no slip tiles in your tub."

"It wasn't the tub, Donna. I passed out and hit the floor."

"Low blood sugar again?"

"That and a phone call from my husband. Anyway, I'll be fine, but I think I need a couple days to recuperate." I lifted the ice pack and beheld the terror in her eyes once again. "And some heavy foundation from the drug store, I suppose."

"Sweetie, what do you think about moving?"

"I'm probably going to have to. How did you know?" I'd kept everything pretty close and couldn't imagine how she'd found out.

"I mean in with me and Nick. You need someone keeping tabs on you. We have a spare room."

"Danny's old room?" The resounding echo of a prison door slamming shut clanged in my imagination.

She sighed. "Yes. Danny's old room. It's not decorated anymore. She'd moved completely out by the time she…" Donna stopped. "It's got new paint and a full-sized bed. We'll still keep this place for you. It's just until the baby comes."

"I can't." I shook my head and regretted it, feeling what I was sure were sloshing fluids around my brain pulsing against my injured eye.

"You *have* to." The tone in her voice put me on edge. I'd had enough of everyone telling me what to do.

"I need to rest, okay?"

Donna, as if sensing she'd gone too far, nodded and headed down the stairs. "Do you want me to send Toby up with lunch?"

That was the last thing I needed. "No. Absolutely not. Thanks though."

Two hours and a much needed nap later, I had a small lunch of leftover potpie. Even leftover potpie by Nick beat anything I could make. Tears flooded my eyes. I would have to leave here, I knew it now. I didn't want to, but when the Arthur-bomb went off, everyone nearest me would be hurt.

I lifted the phone to call my mom.

"I talked to Arthur."

"And?"

"You didn't tell me you knew Arthur before you married Dad."

"Oh."

"Yeah. Did you know I'm the consolation prize?" I wanted to hurt her.

It worked. "He said that? I had hoped—" She broke off, and I could hear her sniffling. Just like I couldn't blame the baby, I really couldn't blame her either.

I swallowed down the guilt. "Look. So many people have done wrong here, we can't lay blame anywhere but on me. And I'm going to take care of it all." I wrapped the springy phone cord tightly around my fingers.

"How?"

I sank down on the daybed. "I'm coming home in another month. I'll have the baby there."

"How's that going to solve everything?"

"I'm not sure yet. But I'm praying."

"Macy, praying never did much for your father."

I exhaled, trying to keep my emotions in check. "I'm not asking for guarantees from God, but I'm praying he's going to work this mess out." And for the first time, I knew it to be true. Faith rose up inside me—from where, I had no idea. But I put the credit at my grandmother's feet.

So did my mom, except hers sounded more like blame. "Your grandmother did this to you. I hope you have more than prayers working for you by the time you get here." Cynical didn't quite cover the tone. Bitter and cynical. Bynical? Citter? I shook my head to clear it of silliness, and felt the same pounding regret. I had to quit doing that.

"I'm going to go. I'll call again in a few weeks, okay?"

"You know, I'm glad for one thing, Macy."

"What's that?"

"We're talking again. I've missed you."

"Bye, Mom." I think she expected a gushing response. My whole life she'd made me responsible for things I wasn't ready for—it wasn't something I could easily forget. Or forgive.

I'd hung up before she tried to delve too deeply into that. I still wasn't sure who was the most to blame there. Me, for trusting Arthur was mailing my letters and then not calling to be sure they got there, or her for not insisting she talk to me? I mean, if Baby ever moved away and cut off all lines of communication, I'd haul myself to wherever he was and demand to know why.

"We're sticking together. Got that, Baby?" I leaned over and stared at the bump the best I could. My twenty-nine week pregnancy was getting in the way a bit more every day. I cuddled back up on the bed and lost a few more hours of the day.

When I woke for dinner, darkness had filled my apartment, and the marquee lights were once again flashing. I wandered to the kitchen and pulled open the fridge door to find half a hamburger and some cold fries. Not the highest in nutrition, but I'd be throwing it up in a half hour anyway, and then I'd eat the chicken salad sandwich. Toby made the sandwich. There was something mystical about his knowing what would set well in my stomach more than I did.

There was a knock on the downstairs door. I ignored it. There were only two people it could be, and I didn't want to see either one. I pretended to be asleep. I got very quiet, anyway, and held my breath. I heard their footsteps move off, and then the far off jingle of the bell over the diner door. Someone was locking up for the night.

I took two bites of the burger before the nausea hit. I made it the ten steps to the bathroom and vomited. I took a shower and got my pajamas back on before reaching for the chicken salad.

Baby and I were getting the routine down.

Twenty-One

After donning my hoodie to hide the bruise and sneaking out the backdoor, I headed to the drugstore for a heavier foundation. I had to return to work tomorrow, and there was no way I was going to show up looking like I'd hit the broadside of a barn with my face.

On the way back, I heard footsteps behind me. It was Mrs. Williams. As she passed me by, I ducked my head. To no avail.

"Oh, Macy, dear, is it you?"

I looked up and caught her widened eyes as they locked on my face.

"Oh good heavens. He didn't do it again, did he?"

I frowned. "Who didn't do what, Mrs. Williams?"

"Toby of course. Did you have an accident? Did he go on a bender? I knew that boy couldn't stay off the drink."

My head, still fuzzy from being up so early, couldn't grasp what she was saying. "I fell, Mrs. Williams. Toby had nothing to do with this."

"Oh, good. Forget I said anything. Take care, dear."

Pretty sure Mrs. Williams never said anything without meaning to, I had to wonder at her motive. And what did she mean about Toby being a drinker? I'd never seen him drink anything stronger than Nick's dark roast coffee.

By the time I got back to my place, my pulse pounded under my face from walking too fast. I headed up the stairs before anyone else could see me and pulled off my hoodie to start working on my makeup.

Applying it hurt like crazy, but it took down the purple to a slight gray someone could confuse for a shadow. Or so I hoped. As I nibbled a piece of dry toast, preparing for the next round of sick, I let my mind wander. Toby. Accident. Drinking. Danny.

No. It couldn't be. I mean, why would they let Toby work there if he'd killed Danny? It didn't make sense. They wouldn't be able to stand being around him—I know I couldn't. I thought back to the photo of Danny and the boy over to the side. He was about Toby's size. No. Toby would have said something. Someone would have.

I headed downstairs to grab lunch and check in with Donna and Nick. I knew they must be worried. As I came around the corner, nearing the kitchen, I heard them talking.

"I think we need to insist on her moving in with us."

"We can't. She's an adult." Nick's voice grated, sounding fatigued. "We've been over this. I really like the kid, but she's not *our* kid, okay? If she needs help, she needs to go home."

"No. We can't let her leave. Can't you see? This is our chance."

Nick sighed. "Sweetie, we lost our chance last year. Danny's gone. She's not coming back."

"But God sent Macy here. She's Danny's size, the pregnancy, everything. Can't you see it? And she's all alone. Like Danny."

Nick slammed his hand against the table. "Danny was not alone. We told her we'd take care of her. We fixed the apartment for her; we did everything we could, Donna."

"No. If we had, she wouldn't be dead." Donna sobbed.

I couldn't help myself. I kept listening, kept putting puzzle pieces together. I held my breath, embarrassed to be there but hoping they'd reveal more.

"That wasn't our doing!"

"She shouldn't have been walking alone on the road. Toby wouldn't have picked her up." She gasped. "And he wouldn't have driven them both into the tree. And his poor father."

"That's enough."

I knew that tone. It was the same one Dad would use when Mom or I pushed him to the limit. I tiptoed back to the apartment door, opened and closed it with a loud thud, then came around the corner, acting the best I could like life was fine.

Donna turned away, wiping her eyes, and went to the front door to flip the sign to OPEN. Nick nodded to me, then turned to the grill. His back tensed, and his shoulders shuddered. He moved swiftly past me and out the side door to the alley. It'd been years since I'd seen a man cry. I knew I would never forget the anguish on Nick's face, the haunting pain in his eyes.

Toby came in through the front door and waved to Donna. She didn't look at him, didn't speak. He gave me a grim smile and moved through the kitchen. "Where's Nick?"

I wasn't sure what to say. My brain dared my mouth to ask him about Danny and the accident, but I didn't take the bait. "Nick had to step out." I bit my lip to prevent anything else escaping.

Toby stuck his hands in his pockets. "I'll start prepping then." He began getting out the vegetables for chopping, readying them for the omelets to come. The restaurant door opened, and Donna greeted the customers with a warm tone, but the smile was gone from her eyes. I didn't know how she was coping. If I'd lost my child and grandchild less than a year ago, I'd be a mess. Part of me wanted to send her out to Nick. The rest of me knew it'd be better to pretend I didn't know what was happening. And for the most part, that was true.

A couple came in and sat down in one of my booths, so I headed over to take their order. I went to the pass and glanced down at the scrawl on my pad. Somehow, without really looking at them, I'd written down a bowl of oatmeal, toast, eggs over easy, and a fruit plate. I glanced back at the two who were now laughing and pouring creams and sugars into their coffees, wondering who'd asked for what.

I guess I'd find out in about fifteen minutes.

Had Toby really done it? And if it were really an accident, why were they blaming him?

"Everything okay with Donna?" He looked over his shoulder at me as I clipped the first order of the day onto the wheel.

"I don't know. She and Nick had some words this morning." I watched as Toby took the order and started cooking the eggs, prepped the fruit plate, and scooped up oatmeal into a bowl. He did it so easily.

"You can cook?"

"Sure. I've filled in more than a few times. He does get sick now and then, have doctor appointments and the like." He smirked at me. "You didn't know I could cook?" He grabbed the next order off the wheel—I hadn't even seen Donna put it up. She was greeting a large group, and I realized the mayor had decided to come in again.

Toby grimaced. "Just what we need."

I had to agree. "I'll go check on Nick." I headed out the side door to the alley, but Nick wasn't anywhere in sight. I stepped out onto the sidewalk and looked both ways. If Nick were around, I sure couldn't see him.

I went back in and shrugged at Toby. "He's not out there."

"What were they arguing about?" He flipped some pancakes and leveled his eyes to mine.

I tried to act nonchalant. "Something about Danny."

I watched him for a reaction—and did I ever get one. Toby's eyes filled with hurt, then worry. He chewed his lip and went back to flipping pancakes. Despite his opening up more and more about his family and childhood, he'd never told me anything about Danny. If I thought he was going to divulge anything to me now, I'd been a fool.

The mayor must have had something bigger on his mind than selling the town to me this time, because he only asked for the check. He gave Toby a stony look but barely gave me a glance—or a tip.

Later, Nick came back in and started cooking like he'd been there all day. No one asked for an explanation, and he offered none. Toby went back to clearing dishes, much to my back's relief. Waiting tables *or* bussing—I could handle one or the other in my condition. But not both.

As evening arrived, things slowed, and then at eight Donna flipped the CLOSED sign. I'd never seen a day go by without Nick flirting with Donna. I'd never seen them act like strangers. Nick moved through his end of day duties—cleaning the kitchen and starting the commercial washer—without saying a word. Donna tossed her apron into the dirty bin in the break room and left through the front door.

"I'll leave you two to close up." Nick tossed his spatula in the sink and left through the back.

As I locked the front door, I turned to Toby, who was also acting as if nothing at all had happened. I couldn't stand it any longer. As I was about to ask, though, a wave of nausea hit, and I raced past Toby to the bathroom. When I came out, a meal of mashed potatoes and meatloaf waited in take-out containers on the break room table. The lights were off out front and the side door locked. I carried my meal upstairs, shutting my apartment door behind me, flipping the latch.

The grating noise echoed through the stairwell. It hit me then. The very thing I craved five months ago had begun to wear on me.

Being independent wasn't everything I'd hoped it would be.

Twenty-Two

Some day off I was having. I sat in my kitchen, head pounding from stress and fatigue, my everything book clutched in my hand. Another call from my mother sent me into alarm mode. Three more regular customers had canceled their fleet contracts at my family's garage. She had to lay off two men. That left her and Bobby to run things. And the younger two to care for the house and store. Bobby was next oldest at eighteen, then Sarah, sixteen, and Brynn was only twelve. I tried to imagine Bobby orchestrating meals and bath times, helping with homework and tucking the girls into bed. I couldn't. He didn't strike me as the responsible type. More than likely, Mom would pull Bobby into the garage to help and put Sarah in charge of the household. She was sixteen—so young.

I ground my teeth at the idea of my mother laying such responsibility onto Sarah's shoulders. Or little Brynn. She was the age I'd been when everything in our lives fell apart—when Daddy got sick.

Sarah. She should be attending prom and getting over crushes. She should be studying for college exams and dreaming of a future, not running things for Mom. *Sixteen.*

My breath caught. *I'd been sixteen when I married Arthur.* I'd been so old and responsible. So ready to grow up. I shook my head from side to side, slowly at first, then more rapidly, more in time with my racing heart.

"No. No. No." I clutched the book harder in my hands—the book I'd so carefully taken notes in, the book in which I'd written down my hopes, my savings. My own plans mocked me. A gasp and a sob escaped, like the release of the steam valve on the radiator, and everything I'd held back in my whole life rushed out in spurts of cries and heated anger.

I flipped open the diary and read past my tears, wiping them away when the words blurred. Dreams I'd had, plans I made. And then that stopped when Daddy got sick. I wrote about Daddy dying and my mother commanding my obedience. The babies needing someone. Me, trapped. Me, crushed.

I tore out page after page and crumpled them in my fist. I threw them across the kitchen, and I lobbed them at the window. They deflected off with tiny plinks and skitters. Mom keeping me from Daddy. Arthur keeping me from my family. Everyone always keeping me, pressuring me, manipulating me.

No more. No more.

"I won't have it!" I screamed. I looked up at the ceiling, to the place where God hovered, and the words tore a raw path from my throat. "I won't have it, you hear me?"

I winced then, waiting for the wrath of God to descend. I'd never screamed before—never let myself feel the depth of the pain I carried with me. And I'd especially never screamed at God. Grandma taught me better.

Grandma was gone.

"Why?" I shuddered, sobbing, sinking to the cold linoleum floor. "Why'd she have to die with her thinking I didn't miss her, didn't love her? Why'd you have to let Arthur do all of this?"

I knew though. Deep down. I'd been a willing participant. And my mother, in her desperate hope, had been willing, too.

My stomach contracted and roiled inside. "No you don't. Not this time." I spoke with a seriousness, a force like I really believed if I told my stomach (my baby) no, it'd listen this time.

Hardly. I had to move, had to get to the toilet. My leg had gone to sleep, with a deep amputated feeling. It wouldn't hold me if I stood on it. Dropping to all fours, I crawled as quickly as I could over the pages of notebook, over my dead dreams and forgotten wishes toward the bathroom.

I almost made it, too.

I couldn't face it. I scrunched my eyes closed against the mess I knew was there. Rather like when I grew up and clenched my eyes against my own reality. I peeked through the haze and saw sticky bits of crumpled paper floating in a pool of what had been lunch. My energy spent, I had no idea what to do next. I wished for a loving mom to come and clean me up, wipe up the mess and cuddle me in her arms. I longed for her to tell me everything would be okay. No one came. There was just me and the baby.

"God, I don't even know where to start. I know I don't have a right to ask a thing of you, but please help me and"—I looked down at myself—"clean this mess up."

As I mopped up my sick and threw away my pages of dreams and fears, something inside me grew stronger. A stirring in my spirit and a resolve built. Somehow I knew he'd heard me.

Grandma always said God listened, but I never knew she meant to *me*. She was so strong, so steadfast—I figured everyone listened to her. But this—this was different. This was tangible.

A warmth ran through me. I'd only sensed it once before, when I was a kid and Jesus had become real for me. But not long after, Daddy got sick, and all thoughts of a loving God left me.

Here he was again.

I hadn't done a thing to gain his attention, except I'd been offering mine more and more lately—even though it'd been at desperate times of leaning over the toilet or trying to get dressed. Grandma always said the relationship between me and God was a two-way street.

The phone rang. Then again. It could only be my mother, with more bad news. Shutting it out the best I could, I gathered some handy wipes and sanitized the floor before heading into the bathroom. The ringing stopped as I turned on the hot water.

An hour later, I sat once again at the table—having had two baths already today—and listened to the sound of my own breathing.

Okay. That was depressing. I had to get out of there. One glance out the window, and I knew what to do. I grabbed my purse, popped a hard candy into my mouth to stave off the nausea, and headed out. Fifteen minutes later, I stood in line with an ever-growing crowd of Sunday matinee hopefuls, ready to watch a couple back-to-back Hitchcock flicks.

Nearly everyone in line had someone to chat with, but I didn't mind. I'd wanted to go there ever since I'd moved in over the diner—and today was the perfect day to lighten my spirits. I sighed aloud, content.

"Didn't know you were a Hitchcock fan." The familiar timbre of his voice near my ear sent tingles over my neck. My stomach flipped at the sound, but it wasn't nausea. I turned around to face him.

"Toby." I was equally glad to see him and hesitant, not sure how this would play out.

"I called a bit ago to ask you to come, but you didn't answer. And here you are." His voice held a light tone, but he carried a wariness in his eyes. After the disagreement in the break room I could understand why. We were in unfamiliar territory.

"I love Hitchcock." It was nice to be certain about something.

"Another thing we have in common." He smiled.

"I also love popcorn," I offered.

That sent a twinkle to his eyes. "That clinches it. As long as you eat it with Milk Duds tossed in."

At that moment, the baby shifted and kicked. "Oh!"

Toby mistook the startled look in my eyes and held me by the arm. "Are you okay? Do you need to go lie down?"

I laughed. "No. Apparently Baby wants Milk Duds. I haven't a clue why, I won't get to keep them down long enough to enjoy them—but what the heck? Why not try?"

He didn't let go of me but let his heated palm slide down my arm and took my hand in his. I didn't know that something like just holding his hand could feel so natural and right. My skin tingled. I didn't feel trapped. At least not by anything I could see. My spirit shuddered in response, and I knew it was a mistake. I took a step back, released his fingers and tucked my hands in my pockets.

He pursed his lips together and gave me a half-smile.

The line started to move. "Can we at least sit by each other?"

Every cell of my body shouted yes. "I guess that'd be fun." I tried to keep my tone level and disinterested. A pleased look laced his glance, and as we reached the ticket window, he paid for me. Ushering me inside, I was comforted by the aroma of popcorn, melting butter, fifty years of aging red velvet carpets, and trampled candy wrappers. We bought our snacks, and he put his hand at the small of my back, leading us to our seats. I felt like we'd done this a hundred times.

I'd come to be alone in the midst of a crowd and bury my sorrows in junk food and old movies, but it hadn't turned out that way. I glanced at Toby. His face showed hopeful victory. I took a sip of pop and it burned down my throat.

How could the same day I'd grown closer to God be the same day I realized that what had been building with Toby was all kinds of wrong?

I'd failed at so many things today, I'd lost track.

Twenty-Three

As *Rear Window* and *To Catch a Thief* played, hours slipped by unnoticed. I'd devoured popcorn mixed with Milk Duds and two hotdogs. They'd all stayed down. Maybe the trick was to feed Baby junk food? The idea garnered a giggle.

"What's so funny?" Toby whispered. I waved him off, not wanting to miss the final scene. Cary Grant gathered Grace Kelly in his arms and told her he wasn't the lone wolf he thought he was. And Grace Kelly, proposed marriage in a way only she could get away with by kissing Cary Grant soundly and telling him her mother would love his villa.

I watched the scene end, the credits roll, and felt uneasy when the lights came on. It had been all too simple to pretend my life was uncomplicated during a double feature. As I glanced down at the ring on my finger and ever expanding baby bump, conviction ran through me.

Toby put his hand out to me, and I gave him the empty popcorn container. That wasn't what he had in mind. He gave me a smile, but disappointment hung about his eyes. People shuffled out ahead of us, and I ducked back, trying to remain inconspicuous. As if living out my worst fears, I heard Mayor Beady call out to me.

"Good to see you here, active in the community. Isn't our theatre grand?" He tipped his head, pretending to look around when really his focus was on Toby. "I didn't know you two were friends." He was in full-on mayor mode now. "Of course, you would be, being co-workers and all. Tell me, Macy, when will your husband be joining you?" Judgment and condemnation resonated in his voice.

Toby's jaw ground, and his eyes riveted to the popcorn container in his hands.

A flush of heat raced over my face. I didn't like being put on the spot, and I especially didn't like the mayor. He had something up his sleeve. No matter what he talked about, there was always an angle to his speech I couldn't quite measure.

"I'm afraid he won't be." I didn't elaborate.

"Well, now. That's too bad." He chuckled entirely without humor. "You two have a nice evening then."

The little peace I'd gained over the past four hours washed away in the wake of uneasiness left behind by the mayor.

"Let's walk." Toby put out his arm rather defiantly, and I took it for the same reason. Once outside, we walked in a direction I had yet to take. We moved through a more residential part of town. I could tell he had a destination in mind, but he said nothing of it.

Instead he offered me advice. "Try not to let him get to you."

I glanced sideways at Toby. "He seems to dislike you." *And me.*

"Lot of folks do." He shrugged.

My eyes were glued to his face, trying to read him and his tone, so I didn't see the raised crack in the sidewalk. Toby caught me just in time.

"Easy now. Are you okay?"

"Yes. Thanks." Why would so many people dislike Toby? Could it be true he'd killed Danny by drinking and driving? I was about to broach the subject when we stopped. I glanced around and spied a craftsman-style house, painted brown with green shutters and cream accents. It was the most beautiful place I'd seen in a long time. There were multi-paned windows, flower boxes, and a cobblestone path leading up to the front porch. It reminded me of homes I'd seen on the cover of design magazines.

"How beautiful."

"I hoped you'd like it." Toby let out a slow breath. "Want to see inside?"

I resisted the pull on my arm. "I don't think they'd like us looking in the windows."

"We're going inside, not just looking through the glass." He pulled a little more, but I moved back. Is this why the town disliked him—was he a thief?

"Toby, we can't go inside." My eyes darted up and down the street to make sure there were no witnesses.

He smiled. "Sure we can. I own it."

I still hesitated, baffled, but the evidence seemed in his favor as he drew out a set of keys and unlocked the deadbolt. As we passed through the front door, I was taken aback by the hardwood maple floors, the throw rugs, and the mica lamp shade over the dining area. Little touches all over the house showed artisanship, love, and tender care. He ushered me through, like a realtor might—but I saw passion and pride in his eyes as he explained why he chose one material over another.

We went through four bedrooms, two baths with claw-foot tubs (although, I wasn't sure if I liked *them* so much anymore), an office, family room, and living room. The kitchen, though, astounded me. I caressed the cabinets, reveling in the smooth warmth of the honey-toned wood. My hands brushed over the cool, solid marble countertops, and I sighed.

"You like it?" There was a hopefulness in his tone. He reminded me of my brother, Bobby, after fixing one of his first small engines. He wanted me to enjoy every nuance, the hum of the motor, the wheeling parts, even the smell of the oil.

"It's beautiful." There were a couple cups in the sink and an empty package of cookies on the counter. The place was furnished. "Does someone live here?"

"I hide here sometimes." He tossed the wrapper in the garbage.

"Did you build this house?" I wandered away from the kitchen, away from the dream, to the safety and openness of the family room.

"Built and designed. I used to be an architect."

I looked quickly to see if he was teasing. He wasn't. "Then why—"

"Why am I working at the diner?"

"Yes. This place is gorgeous. You have such talent."

His eyes glowed for a moment, and then an edge entered in. "Just like you, I guess, Macy. Sometimes you don't get to choose your fate, it chooses you."

I didn't argue with him.

Toby motioned for me to move on. "Look out back."

I did. Through the backdoor, I saw a cute yard and dormant garden.

A huge craggy oak, leaves long gone with winter cold, stood central, arms wide as if waiting for a young child to climb its limbs and take it captive.

A picture of Baby, much older, jeans rolled up, scrambling up the trunk, filled my mind. My breath caught, and I jerked away as if I'd touched a hot stove. I clenched my eyes closed to shake the image, but it remained suspended, real enough to touch. I opened them again into Toby's.

"I've seen it too." The gravity in his voice startled me. "What's his name, Macy?" Toby put a gentle hand against my stomach, holding his breath as if he were waiting for me to tell him the future.

My soul ached. Baby's name flashed clear in my mind, because at that very moment, my imagination was calling him in from the yard for dinnertime. "Michael," I said in a whisper of hope.

Toby's eyes filled with tears, mixing with joy. It was like all the movies and TV shows I'd ever seen where the husband was overwhelmed with happiness hearing he was going to be a father for the first time. Then he picked up the wife and drew her into an intimate embrace and she molded against him, burying her face in the warmth of the crook of his neck.

Except Toby wasn't my husband, and just before his lips met mine, I pushed out of his arms and slid away, shaking my head, tears dripping down my face.

"Please, no."

He was crushed. I know it because I was crushed, too. I turned away and wiped at my eyes with my sleeve, and he handed me a tissue.

My voice shook when I said, "It's not fair to either of us to pretend."

"Who says I'm pretending?"

I avoided his gaze, knowing it mirrored the pain in my own. There was truth and longing in his eyes, but I couldn't look at it. It'd make it too real.

I took a shuddering breath and hoped he didn't notice it. I had to change the subject to something more neutral. "Why don't you live here, Toby?" He acted like he wasn't sure what I meant, so I ran a finger over a wooden shelf and showed him the dust.

"I have to take care of my parents."

"At the house Mrs. Williams showed me? Why can't they live here with you?"

His eyes narrowed and a hardness entered. "What did she tell you?"

"We were driving past your parents' home, the ranch-style a few blocks from the diner, and she mentioned they lived there." For some reason, I didn't want to force his hand. If he was going to give me information, I wanted it to be voluntary.

"I understand helping them out, but why do you have to live there all the time?"

His shoulders relaxed, and he seemed to search for an explanation. "My dad was in a bad accident last year. He's hard for my mom to handle, so I help her get him in and out of the tub, move him to his chair, and watch him when she goes out."

"Can't you live here and do that?"

"No." I heard a familiar bitterness in his tone that I knew too well.

We walked back onto the front porch, and he locked the door. The deadbolt's *click* locked something else away, too—an unfulfilled promise I'd hold in my memory forever. We meandered back through the darkening streets, neither one of us in any hurry for the night to end, until we arrived at the side door to the diner.

"See you in the morning, Macy." He leaned in to kiss me but must have seen the resolve in my eyes and stopped.

"See you in the morning." By the time I unlocked the door, he'd already turned away, the gravel grinding under his heels. I watched him tuck his hands into his pockets, his shoulders slumping, carrying his burden with him as I must carry my own.

I wondered, and not for the first time, what life would have held for me if I'd waited for God instead of forcing his hand and taking the desperate plunge off a cliff I had no hope of rescaling.

Twenty-Four

The next day, every word shared with Toby sounded stiff and forced. It was like when you meet a new friend at school and share a bit too much of yourself too quickly one day and regret it the next. Although, in this case, neither of us would be gossiping at the lunch table about the other. Somehow, deep down, I knew I could trust Toby. With anything.

As I moved through the day, taking orders and delivering meals, I couldn't shake the image of Michael climbing that oak from my mind. I'd given him black hair and bright green eyes. Why I didn't picture him with my own red hair, I didn't have a clue.

The phone rang, and Nick called me to the back room. I could see from the tense look in his eyes as I took the phone from him that it was trouble.

"This is Macy."

A small voice, sobbing, met my ears. "Mama's sick."

Even through the years of not hearing her voice, even given the changes to it, I recognized my sister's tones. "Sarah? What do you mean?"

"She took in the mail yesterday and then went to bed and hasn't gotten up again. She just lays there. Bobby says to leave her be, but something's not right, Macy."

Sarah sounded so young, even for sixteen. She'd must have been more sheltered, more protected than I had been. I tried not to be jealous.

"Take the phone to her for me, okay?"

136

I heard shuffling and rustling. Sarah's voice called, "The phone is at her ear."

"Mom? You can't do this again. You need to be there for the kids. Bobby's not going to pick up where I left off, and Sarah can't do it. It's not fair to lay that on Brynn."

I had a clear image of my mother. It was from seven years ago, right after my father died. I thought she would take over the household again. It had been the one clear hope in my father's death I'd held on to. But it didn't happen. Not until I got engaged.

"He's canceled another contract. We can't make the payments on fuel. We'll be empty in two weeks. It's all over, Macy." The accusation in her voice made it past the deep sadness wheedling through the phone.

I glanced out of the back room, through the pass, and locked eyes with Toby. I didn't know what I'd been hoping in my subconscious. Maybe that Arthur would relent. Maybe that I'd be able to divorce him for all his lies and manipulation and then I could stay here and live happily ever after.

"I'll call him, Mama." I hadn't called her that in years. "Then I'll come home and help." The latter choked me, and I envisioned a silk scarf being pulled tightly around my neck. Toby's eyes narrowed and his shoulders slumped. He moved away, shaking his head.

"You promise, Macy?" She sobbed some more.

"Yes. I'm calling him right now. And then I'll buy a bus ticket and come home."

I heard sniffles, and Sarah came back on the line. "Mama's getting up, Macy. She's going to take a shower. Is it true? You're coming home?" Sarah sounded relieved. I would have been, too.

I hadn't seen my sister in over seven years. Somehow, she'd been pressed into my memory and forever stamped a young girl. Silly. I knew she must be as tall as me by now.

"I don't know when, exactly, but in the next week or so. I'll call when I get my ticket."

After I hung up, a heaviness blanketed me. My heart had been put into a box, and a steel padlock applied. No one would ever be able to give me the key.

Nick and Donna watched me in apprehension, but I didn't dare tell them what had transpired. I couldn't trust my voice.

After I delivered four more orders, Donna turned the sign to CLOSED. My feet ached a straight line up into my back. Nearly eight months of pregnancy had gone past. I had about a month and a half left and still no idea what I should do next.

Toby watched me from the kitchen as he cleaned the grill. Everything felt so final. So over. As I walked past the break table, I found my dinner waiting in a familiar take-out box. My stomach growled in anticipation of whatever concoction he'd packed for me that night. Tears ran down my cheeks as I ran my fingers over the warm lid. Inside lay something he thought I needed. And, strangely, he was nearly always right. I didn't often vomit the dinners Toby chose for me.

I glanced over my shoulder and saw him scrubbing the countertops and putting away the last of the food for tomorrow. Nick and Donna hollered a good night, and he nodded to them. I think he must have known I was watching him, committing him to my memory, but he didn't look at me.

Heading up the stairs, my back ached, and I wondered how many more times I would be able to climb them. Leaving was the best thing. These stairs were sure to become a problem as I ended my ninth month. And there'd be more space for me and the baby at my mom's house. Hopefully.

No. No matter how I turned it, I felt like I was about to be incarcerated and locked away in a prison not of my own making. Considering I'd been in one I'd designed by my own hands, I was curious what the difference could be.

Before I could ponder that any further, I sat down to inspect the box. Dinner was roast chicken, green salad, and a fresh roll. He'd packaged a cookie inside a wrapper. As I turned it over, I saw he'd put "Michael" and a happy face on it. With shaky hands, I unfolded the wrapper, removed the cookie, and then folded it again. Then I carefully took out a plastic bag and inserted it inside, writing the date on the outside. I slipped it into my everything book. When I got a memory book for Michael, I'd put that in there. Even if Toby wouldn't be around as Michael grew up, I wanted him to know that there was a man who loved him and wanted him.

After dinner, I bathed and climbed into bed. I stared at the phone, knowing I needed to call Arthur, knowing I was breaking my promise to my mother. But I couldn't face it yet. Tomorrow would come soon enough. I switched off my lamp and wished the marquee lights were flashing in my room. Instead, darkness greeted my exhaustion, and I fell to sleep quickly.

Pounding on a door, a slam beneath my apartment, and yells burrowed into my dream. I woke coughing, seeing red and yellow lights flashing across my ceiling. I didn't remember the marquee having that pattern. I choked, and then again as a burning sensation stole my breath away. I tried to get my bearings, wondering where I was and if Nick had burned a burger on the grill. Smoke. Lots of smoke filled my apartment and scorched my nostrils. I gulped for air and then my brain awakened entirely and I screamed for help past my gagging throat. I crawled across the floor of my apartment, trying to orientate myself. I grabbed my purse as I moved past the kitchen table, inching toward the stairs.

"Help!" I covered my face with my nightshirt, trying to filter the air for a better breath. I couldn't see down the stairs and had no idea if it was safe to go that way. "Help!"

"Macy, let me in!" Toby screamed, but I couldn't manage the stairs, everything was going spotty before my eyes. I heard pounding, then splintering wood and feet slamming up the stairs.

"I've got you, I've got you." He murmured against my head as he carried me back down. A sudden hilarity struck me in how he'd now carried me both up and down these stairs, but the laugh came out more like hysteria as my eyes glanced back up through the haze and I realized I would lose everything I had.

"It's okay, it's okay." His pressed his lips against my ear and we entered the restaurant, while flames licked the ceiling.

Firefighters raced inside to help carry me out. Black smoke and acrid air surrounded us as we exited. The flashing red lights from the ambulance and fire truck lit our way over a path strewn with water hoses and debris.

An oxygen mask snapped over my nose, and the sudden purity of the air hissing into my lungs triggered a coughing fit. Hands massaged my back, and a paramedic lifted the mask as I vomited—this time it had nothing to do with the baby and everything to do with the fiery feeling in my chest as I tried to breathe. They gave my mouth a quick swipe with a moist towel, and the mask went back over my nose.

"Thank God you're all right." I looked up into Donna's eyes and watched her expression shift as she saw the hoses and water, men stomping through the front door carrying axes and hearing whacks on the interior walls. With every chop, she jolted as if she was the one being hit. Nick came around the side of the ambulance, and his shoulders sagged with relief when he saw me lying there.

For a moment we were all in awe of the dance the firefighters did with one another, shifting hoses, shoving debris. And then it was over. They came out, and Nick asked the chief for a report.

"A fire started at the grill. Best we can tell in all this mess. We'll know more after our investigation."

"Can it be saved?"

The firefighter took off his helmet, and I saw Mayor Beady. He gave me and then Toby a look-over. "Got your girl out, did you, Toby?"

Toby moved from my side and stood up to the mayor. "That's right. You guys were more worried about the restaurant than saving her life."

Donna stepped in between them. "I'm sure that's not the case, is it, Mayor?"

"Certainly not. We had to get things under control before we could risk anyone's life going up after her. There's a bigger picture here, boy."

If I hadn't been so incapacitated, I would have hit him square in the face.

Toby stiffened. "There's always a bigger picture when you want to look for it. If you were more than glorified volunteers, you would have headed straight up to get her." He glanced down at me and then back at the restaurant. "Is it okay to go inside and see if we can salvage Macy's things?"

"The electricity is shut off, so I'd wait until there's daylight. The smoke and water damage is done, no use risking your life over what will still be there tomorrow." Nick's voice sounded distant and broken.

Toby's fists clenched and unclenched. I removed the breathing mask against the wishes of the EMT, pushing his hands away from my face and off my arms.

"I'm fine. Please." I was trapped by the mask, by Toby's anger, by the mayor's indifference, by the damp and cold.

"Macy, think of the baby." Toby's anger shifted immediately to worry, and he moved to put the mask back on.

I looked up at him. "I am. I'm fine." Everything in me wanted to climb back up the stairs and rescue whatever was left. When I looked into Donna's eyes, I saw the same desire. The apartment didn't only hold my dreams, but also Danny's.

An hour later I'd been shuffled to Nick and Donna's house. I showered, and she gave me a clean T-shirt to sleep in. As I cuddled down under the flannel sheets of their guestroom, I realized I was once again sleeping in Danny's bed. Just like the water glasses in the apartment, butterflies graced the ceiling of the room, and delicate tulips were painted around the edges of the windows. I imagined I could smell their spring fragrance rather than the smoke still clinging to my hair. I clicked off the bedside lamp and prayed for unconsciousness.

Sleep came in starts and when I awoke it was nearing noon. I wondered what would happen next. Part of me thought to call my mother, but to tell her I had been delayed because of a fire would only add to her stress.

"God, what do I do now?"

A knock on the door broke into my prayer. "Macy, dear, are you awake?"

"Yes, Donna. Come in."

Donna poked her head around the doorframe and gave me a sad smile. From the dark gray circles under her eyes, it didn't appear she'd slept much either.

"I wanted to see if you were up to going over this afternoon and checking on what we might find salvageable."

Here she was, giving again. "Donna, don't worry about me. Worry about the restaurant."

"Oh, we're insured. We'll rebuild and repaint. The kitchen needs to be replaced, and we lost an inner wall, but it's smoke damage everywhere else. I'm so thankful the flames didn't burn through the ceiling and get to you. I was so afraid when I heard the alarm being

Macy

called in."

"How did you hear it?"

"Nick listens to the police scanner in the evening. He loves to be up on the news, and has a CB. When the weather turns, he's on the emergency crew that helps folks in the area." Her eyes dimmed. "He was right behind the EMTs and firemen on the scene when Danny died."

I sat up in bed, eager to know more. The mystery never left me for long. "What happened, Donna?"

She came all the way into the room and sat on the foot of the bed. "She'd been having a hard time and was out with friends. I think at a bar."

"Even though she was pregnant?" I hadn't meant to sound accusatory, but Donna didn't let on if she took it that way.

"I begged her to move home, but she wouldn't."

"Where was the father?" Part of me thought Toby was the baby's father—I hadn't realized my thoughts until then.

"He'd passed on through. I don't even know if she knew where he was from. If she knew, she never told us. He stayed in town long enough to earn her favor and then when he heard she was pregnant, he left."

Awash in relief, I barely heard the next part of the story until I heard Toby's name.

"What was that about Toby?"

"He was driving her home. He'd been at the bar and offered her a ride. He shouldn't have been driving anywhere."

The blood in my body felt like someone had dunked me in a tank of liquid nitrogen. I couldn't move, couldn't breathe for a moment. "He was drunk?"

"That's what the police said. He confessed, you know, to all of it. Served nine months in jail. Lost his job. He used to be a successful architect in this area. But after that, no one would hire him."

I couldn't find words. My brain couldn't parse what she was telling me.

"It was too much for his poor father. He had a stroke, you know."

Thus, Toby living at home, working in a diner. "How come he only got nine months?"

"First offense, well-known in the community. His mother begged for him to be able to come home and help with his father. He's still on probation."

"Why...?" My brain whirred to a stop.

"Why did we hire him after what he did?" Donna smoothed the bedspread out by my feet.

"Yes." I couldn't fathom having Toby around the place every day as a constant reminder of what he'd done and who was missing.

"Nick and I were counseled by our pastor to forgive him. He needed work, and we needed a busboy. Toby used to work for us when he was in school. He knew the routine." Donna stared out the window for several seconds before turning back to me, tears and a slight smile on her face. "Nick got on the idea first, and after a while, I warmed to it. It helped me see he wasn't bad, you know? He just made a horrible mistake."

The forgiveness they'd offered Toby was unfathomable. I hadn't even begun to think about the ramifications for Toby's life, and what this new revelation meant to me.

Donna rose from my bed and moved toward the door. "I'll let you get yourself together. There's toast and eggs on the dining table when you come out. I put some clothes and new toiletries that should suit you in the bathroom." She motioned to the adjoining room and left me with my thoughts. I was back practically where I started—about to use donated items, letting Donna and Nick rescue me from my predicament. Before my brain could wrap around it all, the nausea hit, and I raced to the toilet and threw up.

After brushing my teeth I showered again, trying to wash the last bit of the smoke and grime from my hair. As I stepped from the shower, I found more grit in the tub that had washed off. I touched it, feeling the gravelly bits near the drain, wondering what part of the restaurant it used to be. My towel, fresh last night, smelled of leftover smoke, so I grabbed another.

I got dressed, looked into the full-length mirror in the bathroom, and fingered the top and pants. I knew these clothes. They were the ones Danny had worn to the picnic in the photo I'd found at the library. Despite the warmth from the shower, goose bumps broke out over my arms. Except for the hair color, mine being red and hers being brown,

Macy

I'd taken over Danny's life, stepping into her shoes. As I exited the bathroom, I found my bed made, and on the dresser were makeup, hairbrushes, and costume jewelry. A jacket was tossed at the foot, waiting for me. In the back of my mind, I realized Donna had me right where she wanted me. I didn't mean to be ungrateful, but it was true.

The closed-in feeling I'd had last night returned. It was as if I were trapped under the mask, the suffocating heaviness, everyone making decisions for me all over again. Because it was clear as far as Donna was concerned, I'd come home.

Twenty-Five

As I walked up toward the restaurant, trailing after Donna, a crowd joined us. There were regulars everywhere, holding brooms and pulling garbage cans on wagons. It looked to me like the whole town had come out to help.

Toby was there, already covered in soot, putting things in plastic garbage sacks and piling them in the back of his truck. I could see little baby outfits pressing through the stretched white bags.

I watched him lug another bag across the street and saw people stepping past him without offering to help. The animosity I'd once believed to have been in my imagination was clearer than ever.

A man wearing fire gear moved into Toby's path. Toby attempted to step around him, but the man shifted in his way again. He wasn't anyone I recognized, but it was clear Toby knew him.

"Ross, get out of my way." Toby sighed in exasperation. I stepped closer but stayed out of his sight-line. This was his best childhood friend, Ross?

"Destruction and mayhem follow you, don't they?"

"Please move. I'm pretty done in and still have a lot more to do. You'd be more useful helping than getting in my way." He stepped around Ross and tossed the sack on the pile.

"Stealing stuff now? First you kill Danny, then you set this place on fire, and now you're thieving." His lip curled back in anger and disgust. How could someone who held such esteem in Toby's memories be so hateful? My hand flew to my mouth to keep me from shouting at him. How Toby could keep himself from striking him, I didn't have a clue. Then Ross told me.

"Go on. Take a swing at me, why don't you? Land your sorry self right back in jail where you belong."

Toby wiped the grime from his cheek with the back of his hand. Even from where I was, some ten feet away, I could see the anger blazing in his eyes. "Excuse me. I've got things to take care of." Toby turned away, but Ross grabbed his T-shirt at the neck, spun him back, swung, and his fist connected with Toby's chin.

Toby lay splayed out on the ground at Ross's feet, blood dripping from a split in his lip. I raced over, unable to stay out of it any longer, and got in the way. Donna called me back, but I ignored her.

"Leave him alone." I leaned over him, protecting Toby with my pregnant body. "I thought you were his best friend."

Ross glared down at me. "You're mixed up with him? Better watch yourself. His girls turn up dead." He spun on his heel and stomped away before I could think of a clever response.

"You shouldn't have gotten in the middle of it." Toby's voice sounded gravely with pent-up emotion.

"And let you punch him out and break probation?"

Toby's gaze locked on mine, and his face washed over with shame and disappointment. "So you know now."

I looked him in the eyes. "Is it true?"

"I confessed." He shrugged his shoulders and sat up, brushing the street grit from his palms.

"But is it true?"

He tipped his head left then right, stretching his neck muscles. "That's what they say." He stood up and wiped at the blood trickling down his chin. I pulled a tissue from my purse and helped him. His eyes still hadn't left mine, and I could tell there was more to the story than anyone had told me yet. But I wasn't going to get the rest from Toby.

He pulled out a handkerchief and pressed it to his lip. "Are you ready to go upstairs? I got out most of your and the baby's clothes, but I might have missed something." He reached his other hand inside his coat and pulled out a Ziploc. "Here, I found this."

Inside the bag was my everything book. I rubbed my thumbs over the plastic. "Thank you." My voice sounded shaky, not more than a whisper.

"Come on." He tucked the bloody cloth in his pocket and took my hand.

I wasn't sure if I was ready or not, but I nodded. Toby led me through the throngs of people scrubbing down walls, mopping, and washing dishes. The wall behind the stove had split from the heat and the ceiling blackened. The backdoor had been chopped through. Charcoal streaks and smudges lined my stairwell. The distinct aroma of a fall campfire mixed with melted plastic hung in the air.

On the kitchen table sat my Christmas tree. I'd intended to repot it and one day, plant it in our yard. Then every year, I'd decorate it and remember my first Christmas with Baby, the goodness of the people who'd helped us, and be thankful of how far we'd come. As I fingered the soot-laden needles, I knew that dream, with all my others, were over. I didn't take it with me.

My windows were all open, and a damp breeze shifted the papers strewn across the floor from a book stomped apart by fireman boots. The wardrobe stood open. The only things left were a few empty hangers. He'd emptied the bathroom, too. Baby toys in a bucket, books, car seat, and the stroller were the only items left. I lifted the bedspread and gave it a sniff, then coughed. Smoke permeated every fiber.

"Smoke damage is a messy thing. Everything can look okay and still be ruined. I don't think you want to keep the stroller and car seat. We'll find another set for you some place."

I agreed. My cute little haven wouldn't be livable again any time soon. Really, did it matter? I would be gone in a week. I wasn't sure how everything had turned so quickly. Footsteps sounded in the stairwell, and we both turned to see Nick coming in.

"Did Toby get your things out?"

I nodded. "Everything that's worth saving. Do they know what happened?"

"A short in the stove somehow. Doesn't seem right, though. We kept it real clean. It should have been able to be on all night and never cause a fire like that." He glanced at Toby. "You cleaned it and turned it off, didn't you, Toby?"

The atmosphere shifted in the apartment. "Of course I did, Nick. I always do it."

Toby had been upset last night. Had he missed something?

"You haven't been drinking again, have you? Could you have forgotten, like the night of the accident?"

Toby stood taller than I'd ever seen him. "No. I'm not drinking. And I didn't forget."

"Okay then." His voice sounded assured, but I could see doubt and an old ache lingering in his eyes.

"That's it then." Toby shook his head. "No worries. I'll make my way somewhere else." He pushed past Nick and stomped down the stairs.

Nick, devastated, turned to me. "I didn't mean to accuse him."

"You didn't have to. The rest of the town did it for you." Justified rage swirled through my mind. I moved past Nick and turned with a last thought. "I haven't had a chance to tell you, yet, but I'm leaving town at the end of the week. Sorry you'll lose your busboy and waitress at the same time, Nick. I know the timing is bad."

I wasn't really sorry, though. A rush of protectiveness and a pride in Toby I hadn't known I carried made me want to hurt Nick for not standing with him. Nick nodded, so I knew he'd heard, but he didn't respond. I moved on, wanting to rid myself of the defeated look in his eyes.

I caught up with Toby at his truck. I started to speak, but he cut me off.

"I'm going to take your things to the launderers, and we'll see if they'll wash out. Smoke can be tricky."

"Yes. Smoke." I gave him a leveling look he ignored. "I appreciate it. I'll go with you."

"No, you'd better stay. I don't think I'd be very good company today."

I ignored him. I'd worked so hard for the life I'd carved out above the diner, I wasn't about to let my things get out of my sight. Plus something told me I should stick with Toby today. And the last place I wanted to be was around these people who didn't seem to trust either one of us.

"There's nothing for me here. I'm going." I certainly wasn't going to hang out in Danny's room at Nick and Donna's place.

I moved past him and climbed into the truck.

Toby started the engine, and we pulled away, past the glances and some glares of the townspeople who were now arriving en masse to help with the cleanup. Word sure got around fast.

"I'm not sure you want to be seen with me, Macy."

"It doesn't matter." I couldn't bring myself to tell him I was leaving. Right then, it felt like I was leaving *him*. He'd lost his job, and his low standing in town had sunk ever lower. To lose his closest friend, maybe his only friend? Life didn't feel fair at that moment. Not a bit.

At the laundromat, we untied bags and sorted things in the back of his truck. I didn't want to sort all the smelly clothes inside and ruin their business.

"You know, this stuff is pretty bad. I better go ask if it's okay." I wandered inside and found the manager at her desk. She had frizzy, dyed-black hair pulled up into a bun and smacked her gum to the rhythm of the Muzak playing overhead as she read a magazine.

"Excuse me. I lived over the diner that caught on fire last night, and my clothes all need to be washed because of smoke damage. Is it okay if I do them here?"

She peered at me over her magazine. "Sure honey. Sad thing about the diner. Nick and Donna been through so much, you know?" She came over to the counter. "You the cute little waitress they have over there?"

"I suppose so." I liked her instantly. Not because she said I was cute, but she didn't seem to be judging me.

"Smoke's nasty stuff. You'll have to use powered detergent and then wash them through at least two times. Dry cleaning's best, but ours is closed for a few days—owners went out of town on vacation." She smacked her gum. "My name's Cheryl."

"Macy."

"Got enough change?"

That was a good question. I realized I didn't have any cash at all.

"I've got her covered." Toby's voice carried over my shoulder.

Cheryl's eyes lit up. "Why Toby, I haven't seen you in here in ages. How are things going with your father?"

"Rough some days. Mom is going downhill a bit now, too." I stared at him, but he kept his eyes on Cheryl.

"Hard times. Hard times. I need to stop by and see your mom."

My like of Cheryl increased tenfold when I saw the affection she had for Toby reflected in her eyes.

"I know Mom would really like that. She gets lonesome with only Dad for company—he sleeps most of the day now."

Cheryl gave Toby a measuring look. "I'll do that." Then she glanced back to me as if remembering I was there. "Use the bigger machines, maximum water on hot. That's the best way to wash out all the smoky smell."

"Thanks." Toby followed me back out, and we started hauling in loads of smoked clothes. A sudden desire to eat kielbasa raced over me. I glanced up and caught sight of a food vender across the street. The silver, portable kitchen on wheels beckoned me, and my stomach growled. I hadn't eaten a thing since a piece of toast and bite of eggs that afternoon.

"Michael's hungry?" Toby teased, and I blushed knowing he'd heard my stomach.

I nodded, and a warm sensation filled me at how sweetly he spoke of my child. We were, once again, sharing an intimacy I'd longed for with my husband.

"We'll get these loads going, and I'll go grab us some dinner. What sounds good?"

"Polish sausage?" I grimaced at my words, but he laughed.

"Anything for you and Michael."

A shiver ran up my side where he was standing. I watched him load my clothes with care and shake out Michael's things. I couldn't picture him in jail, or being drunk, or hanging out with Danny. I knew something wasn't right, but I didn't know if I'd ever get the answers.

As he jogged over to the food truck, I watched him through the window, desperate for images that might stick with me the next few years. I suddenly felt like a woman about to die, or saying good-bye to her loved ones for the last time before a trip.

That's when I knew.

I'd always been one to learn by bad example—which could be very counterproductive. But now I could very clearly see what love wasn't. Love wasn't tricking someone into marrying you. It wasn't forcing someone to cut off ties to their family. It wasn't using someone for a companion and taking away their freedoms. It wasn't even marrying as a means of escape.

Love was helping someone and not expecting anything back. It was being there, in the darkest hours, just to hold a hand. It was carrying someone up the stairs and making them eat when they'd passed out. It was making someone dinner every night, thinking of their best. It was waking up early and hauling out sooty, smelly clothes and dragging them to the laundromat and not expecting a word of thanks.

Love was sacrifice.

I wondered if I'd been anywhere near the friend Toby had been to me.

I kept my eyes on him, memorizing the way he interacted with others in the line, the way he joked and laughed with the man taking his order, and the careful way he carried our food back, as if it weren't just hotdogs and drinks, but a fine meal. He'd lost his job today. To look at him, you'd never know.

Toby came back inside and sat down next to me at the table and handed me my food. His sparkling eyes locked with mine. "Everything okay?"

I swallowed hard, not wanting to tell him yet. We'd enjoy a last meal and some nice conversation first. Then I'd crush his hopes. "Sure. Thanks for lunch. Seems like you're always doing so much for me."

He chewed his bite of hotdog. "That's what friends do, Macy." I couldn't help but hear the implied emphasis on the word *friends*. I wondered if he knew how much more than friends we'd become in my own mind.

"But I don't seem to do anything for you."

He put down his hotdog on the table and took my hand in his. "That's not the point of friendship." He my fingers with his. "And it's also not true. You're the first person in this place not to ignore me or think the worst about me. You showed up when I thought I'd go crazy needing someone to talk to." He took a deep breath. "You were an answer to prayer for me."

"Toby—"

"Listen, Macy. I know you're going to hear a lot of things about me, but you need to know..." He stopped, looking around to make sure we wouldn't be overheard. "They aren't true."

I squeezed his hand. "I know. I never thought they could be, Toby. I don't know what happened that night with Danny, but I don't believe for a minute you're guilty."

He swallowed hard. "Why not?" It was as if everything hung on my answer.

"It's not in your character. It's not who you are. It's not anyone you could ever be." I couldn't put my finger on it, but I knew it was true. "Why do you let them believe it?"

Satisfied, Toby pulled his hand away and took another bite of his dinner, thinking. After waiting for what seemed like hours, he sighed. "I have to."

If I'd learned anything about Toby, it was when to quit pushing for answers, no matter how badly I wanted to figure things out. Tonight, though, I didn't stop. I needed to know. There wouldn't be a later.

"Who are you protecting, Toby?"

His eyes blazed, but he didn't answer. Shutting off in succession, the dryers stopped, and the laundromat went still. He handed me a tube of quarters, and I plugged the machines and started them again. When I turned he was giving me a strange look.

"What is it?"

"I can't help it, Macy. I can't let you go."

Twenty-Six

"How did you know I was leaving?" Grief I'd never experienced before weighted me down. The time for pretending was gone.

"I can tell. You should be more upset about living with Donna and Nick, about losing your place. Instead, you're resigned."

We pulled the clothes from the dryers and dumped them on the folding tables.

He stopped me with a hand. "Tell me I'm wrong."

I continued folding my clothes, acting as if my world weren't coming apart before me. The reality of leaving settled in, sank into me with devastating pressure. "I'll probably be gone by Friday. And there's nothing I can do to change it." I hoped he heard the implied desire I had to do otherwise.

"Why not? We can run away from here. Start over someplace else. Change our names. I have money set aside."

I shook my head. "You need to stay and take care of your father."

Toby's face went ashen. "I know. He won't last much longer, I don't think."

I'd never heard him be so pragmatic. "That doesn't make you sad?" Thoughts of my own father wasting away of cancer, my anguish at not being able to see him anymore, ran through my head.

"For some reasons, but not the ones you'd expect." He held up a blue and green striped pair of footed jammies, and his eyes softened. "Michael's red hair is going to look great against these, you know?"

"He's got black hair." I hadn't meant to sound so certain.

"I hate to disagree." He moved closer to me, entering my personal space, and cupped my cheek before twisting a lock of my hair gently between his fingers. "He's going to have green eyes and red hair, like his mama." His words were a caress, and suddenly I could see Michael the way Toby did. All thoughts of his likeness to Arthur rinsed away. Toby's hands on my face, his nearness, set off warning signals.

"Don't you love your father?" My voice shook, and I tried to push him away, but my arms became trapped between our chests.

"Love? Yes, I expect so. Respect? That's another matter entirely." He stepped closer, closing the gap even more. I imagined the feel of his warm lips against mine—and I knew without a doubt what would happen next. I wanted it to happen. My heart raced in anticipation as my eyes flicked from his eyes to his mouth and back again. His eyes darkened, and I could smell his cologne and the sweetness of his breath as it mingled with mine.

And then I was slipping out of his grasp, nearly running out to the truck, putting space between us as fast as I could. I looked down and saw my ringed hand cradling my oversized belly. This was wrong. All the way wrong.

His stomping feet came up behind me.

"Macy, what is it?"

I couldn't catch my breath, and my eyes kept darting to his mouth. I looked away.

"We can't kiss, can't be together."

"He's not honored your wedding vows, Macy." Toby's voice was harsh and desperate. I knew the feeling. "He didn't love or cherish you. He didn't protect you." He reached out to me, but I backed away.

"I can't let you be that guy, Toby."

I saw my words hit home. He knew I was right.

"Arthur not honoring me doesn't mean I should break them, too. I made them before God, Toby. And I meant them. You can't break a vow to the Lord." I knew these were my grandmother's words more than mine, but her voice was starting to sound like me—or maybe it was the other way around. I wouldn't divulge the rest. I knew I'd never forget that kiss if it'd happened—and I couldn't survive that way, remembering Toby and living without him. And I had to live without him.

Anger filled his eyes. At me, but I think mostly at Arthur for finding me before he did.

"Even if it means giving up your happiness?"

"Even then."

I couldn't explain my family's desperate situation. Besides, the very idea that Arthur had purchased me (and I'd let him) still filled me with shame. I doubted I could ever tell another soul. We stood, staring at each other for a minute, and then he looked up to heaven. I imagined what he might be saying to God. Then he looked away, down the street at the trees blowing, the darkening skies readying for a storm.

"I'll help you finish up your laundry." He went back inside. I picked up his discarded food and bunched our wrappers and napkins up, letting them fall one at a time into the garbage can.

We spent the next hour in silence. What more could be said? After the last load was folded, we put everything into fresh bags and started to load it in the truck. I let him finish and I went and climbed in, waiting, and then we drove to Nick and Donna's house. Several hours had passed since I'd left, but it felt like weeks. It was dark, and the porch light was on. A spattering of rain blew down, and large drops hit the roof of his truck and crackled against the garbage bags in the back.

Toby unloaded everything to the porch before he turned to go. I followed him back to his truck, away from the house and the possible listening ears inside. This was my moment.

"Toby, I don't know what happened between you and your father, but I hope you can make it right. And I hope the person you're covering for comes forward and releases you from the punishment you carry around with you. You deserve to be happy."

He chewed on the inside of his cheek for a moment. "That's not going to happen, Macy."

"So you'll live your life taking the blame for something you never did?"

He crossed his arms and gave me a measuring look. "You'll live your life married to a man who keeps you like property."

"It's not the same thing!" Toby was more right than he knew, but I couldn't admit it.

"Why isn't it?"

"I'm honoring the agreement I made to God."

"I'm honoring my parents—that's in God's Word, too, isn't it?"

Those little puzzle pieces tossing around in my head began clicking together again. "Your dad?"

Toby kicked at the dirt. "There's not much of him left, Macy. And when that's gone, so am I."

"Was he driving?" I whispered, afraid to say anything loud enough for someone else to overhear.

"He had been in the bar that night. Heck, he was in the bar every night. I would go home and eat dinner and then head out and get him and bring him home. But I had to work late. So by the time I got there, he'd left. I followed the path I thought he'd take, thinking to catch up and stop him. But instead, I came upon the accident. I guess he'd given Danny a ride home. Why she got in the car with him, I'll never know."

He choked back a sob, and I saw the memories of that night flash over his features. "She'd been thrown from the car, her neck broke. And my dad had hit his head but was alive. He wouldn't let me call for help until I'd promised to cover for him. He kept screaming that it'd kill my mom." He shook his head. "I was so scared. I know it doesn't make sense. I just had to take care of it," he swallowed back his emotion. "So, I drove back a bit and ditched my car up an old logging road. Then I ran back and moved Dad to the backseat. He was unconscious by then. I called 9-1-1 and reported the accident. When the firemen came, they smelled the alcohol from an open container, and I told them I'd been driving. I wouldn't let them test me."

"So they'd think you were guilty."

He nodded.

"Toby, why?" I couldn't believe what I was hearing.

"Because it was my fault! If I hadn't been late, Danny wouldn't have gone with him, I would have driven them both home. She'd be alive. The baby..." He sobbed.

"Was he the father?"

"I suspected so." So much for a traveling man. "I'd seen them together drinking at the bar before. Lots of times. I'd seen them kissing. I couldn't do that to my mom—let all that come out. Our town is so tightknit. If anyone knew... I told them I'd been driving us home and seen Danny on the road and picked her up."

"And your dad's stroke?"

"The doctors aren't sure. They think that might have happened from the accident. Or the alcoholism."

"Or the guilt from killing Danny and his child?"

"Could be." He kept his eyes trained on the ground at his feet.

"Does your mom know now?"

He shifted his weight from one foot to the other. "She knows I didn't drink—at least not like that. What hurts is I really hoped she'd step in and say something. Like tell me it didn't matter and I didn't need to cover for Dad. Or at least be on my side, even if it was in secret." He shook his head. "Stupid right?"

"No. Not at all."

Our moms had let us down. In different ways, but they'd both failed to protect us. And now we were paying for it. But in my mind, Toby didn't have to. He didn't have to suffer under the town's condemnation.

"You've got to come clean! You can't do this Toby." I moved toward him, reaching out, afraid for him and what he'd done. "You've given up everything for him—he doesn't deserve it."

Something keen sparkled in his eyes. "We've got more in common than you thought, don't we?"

Again, I could say nothing to dispute it.

Toby came toward me, and I backed up a foot. Temptation lingered in the invisible barrier between us.

"You said I deserved to be happy. So do you. I'm going to ask you one last time, Macy."

"No," I whispered.

"When he passes, I'll be free to go my way and start over someplace else. I won't stay here. You'll come with me. I'll build another house, and it'll have a huge oak or maple in the backyard, and we'll watch Michael climb it together." His voice shuddered and a tear rolled down his cheek.

I shook my head.

"Then when Dad dies, I'll come find you. I'll take you away from Arthur and your mom and everything." What he said sounded *so* familiar. That's what got me in trouble in the first place, hoping someone would rescue me. Believing someone could.

My head shook with a bit less conviction. Crossing my arms over my belly, I wished like anything life was different.

"We're done then."

Macy

I nodded, and the tears in my own eyes spilled over the edges and coursed down my face.

He came to me, taking my hand. I couldn't have resisted him, and I think he knew it. He didn't overstep, though, he just held my hand in the most tender way. And I knew this was good-bye.

"I hope someday you'll find someone else who will love you for who you are, Macy, not for what you can do for them." Toby leaned and kissed my cheek. I took a deep breath, committing his scent to memory. "Don't forget me."

"Never." I couldn't.

My tears ran freely as I watched him drive away, taking the last bit of my hope with him. I turned around and pulled the bags up higher on the porch. Tomorrow I'd box and mail them to my mother's house. Tomorrow I'd pack my things and buy a one-way ticket home. My old life waited there, frozen in time, beckoning me to step into my old shoes and cast off these new freedoms I'd been enjoying. Tomorrow.

Twenty-Seven

The jarring screech of the packing tape echoed in Danny's room as I boxed our things for shipping. The sour tape smell lingered with the slightly smoky aroma still hanging on despite the thorough washing our clothes had gone through. For some reason it reminded me of Christmas. Except I knew when I got to my destination, those boxes wouldn't hold any glorious surprises. Instead, they'd carry bittersweet memories of a freedom I would never taste again.

A knock on the bedroom door brought me out of my gloomy reverie.

"You about ready to go?" Donna motioned to the clock on the bedside table. "The bus leaves in an hour." Her eyes held a hard resolve. I'd spent the better part of the morning arguing with Donna about leaving. I'd won, but, as with every victory, it came with a cost.

"Yes, my things are all packed. Here's the money for shipping. Thanks for taking these to the post office for me." I handed a white envelope to Donna. It held more than the cost would come to, but I owed it to them. They'd done so much for me—no matter what their motives were.

"Nick told you we'd take care of it. You keep it. I think you're going to need it." The worried tone didn't improve my mood any.

Instead of arguing, I tucked the envelope back in my pocket. It crossed my mind to leave it tucked under a book somewhere in Danny's room, but I knew Nick or Donna would probably cut open one of the boxes and mail it back to me.

I took one last look around the room and grabbed my suitcase, following Donna from the room. Nick stood in the living room, waiting for us, looking at a loss, tucking and untucking his hands from his pockets.

"All set then?"

I nodded. "Thanks again for everything."

Nick shrugged his big shoulders at me. "Will Toby be meeting us at the station?" His tone told me he hoped not. I wished he'd give Toby the benefit of the doubt.

"No. We said our good-byes." I frowned at him. "You don't know the whole story of that night. No matter what the police said. And you have to know he didn't start the fire, accidentally or on purpose."

Nick's eyebrows creased together. "There's no need to be worrying about any of that." He reached for my case, took it, and headed out the door.

I glanced at Donna, waiting for her to follow, but she didn't.

"I'm staying here. I don't like good-byes much." She gave me a sad smile. "I'm sure glad we got to know you. If you ever need a job, there's one for you here." Donna pulled me into her boney embrace and gave me a real hug—not one of those stiff kinds where you feel held at a distance instead of loved. Part of me wished I could stay—if not for me, then for her.

"I'll write now and then."

Donna nodded, turned away into the kitchen, and started to do the dishes. I could clearly see there weren't any in the sink, but she'd started to wash the clean ones from the rack. I took one last look at the living room, the pictures of Danny as a girl—the candid shots, the school photos. Part of me wanted to tell Donna the truth, that Danny wasn't worthy of this shrine they'd created for her. But the rest of me knew it wasn't about Danny at all. It was for them. And from my view, I truly was the last one to judge anyone.

Anyone at all.

The bus idled at the station as I bought my ticket, filling the area with the fumy stench of diesel exhaust. I saw the driver and a station assistant loading luggage into the undercarriage storage. I tagged my suitcase as I waited for my turn. After buying my ticket to Spokane, I approached Nick, who'd been standing next to the wall, watching me.

"Here." He held out a brown paper sack lined with ice packs.

"Sandwiches, a couple juice boxes, and some bottles of water. Don't let your blood sugar drop."

I felt a bit like a little girl going off on her first trip to camp. "Thanks." I tucked the bag under my arm and shifted my backpack to counter balance Baby.

"You take care now." I expected Nick, a man of few words, to leave. Instead, he pulled me into a tight embrace, one laced with fatherly love, tapping the empty spot in my soul. The aura of chicken-fried steak enveloped me, and I knew I'd never enter a diner again without remembering that moment.

He whispered over my head, "You need anything, anything at all, you call and I'll come get you." His voice cracked, and he gave me a quick squeeze, turned without looking back, and left the station.

I pulled my coat tighter around my shoulders and waited to board the bus with the rest of the passengers. Twelve of us stood outside the silver liner, like kids waiting to take a ride on a field trip. Some of them looked like they'd been traveling a long time, others were fresh and pressed like me, just starting out. I gave a young woman a kind smile, seeing she was on her own, too.

She looked away. So much for kindred spirits.

"Load up. Service to Portland, Hood River, and then on to Spokane. Welcome aboard."

I headed toward the back of the bus, taking a window seat. I put my backpack in the seat next to me to discourage anyone who might want to sit there. As I glanced out the window, I spied a familiar orange truck parked at the corner. The light reflected off the windshield, so I couldn't see if anyone was inside. Part of me hoped he'd be there, but the rest of me shunned the idea. I remembered back to a *Little House on the Prairie* episode, where Laura and Almonzo fought over something foolish, and she was leaving town. The romantic part happened a few miles down the road as he chased the coach down, begged her to come back, and proposed marriage.

Foolish daydreams and fantasies had wasted enough of my time. Life wasn't like that. I'd been lied to for the better part of my childhood as I watched afternoon reruns. Real happy endings were rare. And the last thing I should be fantasizing about was Toby chasing down the bus and proposing to *me*, a married woman.

Macy

I still hadn't figured out what I was going to do with Baby. I prayed the Lord would work out a way I could keep him with me and keep my mom and siblings safe. I even prayed things would somehow, strangely enough, work out with Arthur. But how it could be escaped my imagination entirely. I couldn't see any scenario that would put Arthur and me back on an even footing. That would make me fall in love with him all over again—or would wipe out the awfulness I'd discovered.

How the women in foreign countries still endured arranged marriages was beyond me. Love had to count for something. Love had to enter in somewhere. I'd read historical romances where the woman would join her husband on the plains and some tragedy would bring them together and help them realize they loved each other after all. Just like in TV land—happy endings all around. A cool breeze shot through the cabin of the bus, and I pulled my coat even tighter.

Everyone took their seats, and the bus rumbled into gear, pulling away from the station. The sound, the shimmy of the floor beneath my feet, connected in my mind and I imagined I was in our truck, hauling across the country with Arthur on the way to one stop or another. All diesel engines had a similar vibration and sound to them. And aroma. Baby squirmed, and I tried to ignore the picture forming in my head of me vomiting in the portable potty.

I'd never minded the freedom of the road, or traveling from place to place. The newness of it all sucked me in when we were first married. I'd never left the Spokane Valley area as a kid—except once on a trip to Seattle. Everything thrilled me, from the other friendly truckers to the out-of-the-way gas stations and eating out every meal. The latter lost its appeal after the first month with Arthur. I started asking to drop by grocery stores and bought snacks for in the cab and food we could cook on the grill. When we weren't pressed for time, I'd even taught myself to cook in a Dutch oven.

Once, on a layover, I'd found a used bookstore. Arthur tolerated my buying a book here or there to keep me occupied, as long as I left them at the next town before buying another. This time, I took my used pile of four to trade them in on more exciting fare. I'd wandered through the musty store, soaking up the titles, absorbing the aroma of book glue and dust from a hundred households all blending together.

I returned with two fictional pieces and two cookbooks. One of which instructed the chef on how to cook on an auto-engine. It was a bit like Crock-Pot recipes for your car. You'd wrap up all the ingredients in a foil packet, sealed tight, and place it safely against the motor where the heat would cook it slowly over a matter of miles. Brilliant to me—silly to Arthur.

Occasionally Arthur would invite another driver and his wife over for dinner when we'd stay at campgrounds, and we'd get to know other couples. The first time it happened, I'd set the picnic table up like a real dining table. Jack's wife gave me many compliments, and I thought I'd made a new friend. Hours later, on the way to the showers, I overheard her talking to her husband about how Arthur had no business taking such a young wife. I told myself she was jealous—and I think I believed that until I'd started deciphering the small talk, the shooting glances and the pity some women would give me.

Most of the men, Jack included, didn't see an issue. I began to think it was every man's fantasy to marry a younger woman. One day changed my mind, though. We were pulled over by a police officer for having a taillight out. He questioned Arthur for quite a while, asking for his Class A license and load paperwork. He talked to Arthur, but he kept his eyes on me.

Arthur took him to be interested in me, and the rant I heard for the next hour about a man's wife not being safe from the law anymore would be revisited from time to time. But I knew different. The officer had looked at my ring finger, asked how I was and if I liked riding the road. He didn't *want* me, he was worried about me.

Over time, we crossed paths with Jack and Cindy more often, and she came to accept me and our marriage. But I could never forget the cut of her words. It had been the first time I wondered if my life wasn't quite right. The policeman was the second.

The bus shifted gears, bringing me back to the present, and we pulled down the street. I hadn't called Arthur and told him I was leaving. For some reason, I wanted to be back on my home turf before approaching him again. For all I knew, he'd already called my mother and they'd settled my future. I tried to imagine going back to that life—sleeping on a twin mattress, washing the few clothes I had at roadside stops, eating at diners or off our grill. Keeping as little as

Macy

possible with us to help with gas mileage.

I looked down at the cotton pants I wore, the flowery top, and tried to imagine the overalls and unkempt hair. I wouldn't go there again. I needed to keep something of myself this time. If he didn't like the clothes, he could get rid of some of his own. And I'd bring plenty of books. I wasn't willing to give up myself entirely to him—not ever again.

There wasn't a moment I could put my finger on where I'd lost myself—but I sure knew when I'd found me: the day I'd taken the pregnancy test.

The bus shifted gears. "We're on our way, Baby." I patted the bump, and he kicked back. I tried to keep my eyes glued to my gut as we moved down the next street, but failed. Despite my own good sense, I watched the corner, my eyes on Toby's truck as the bus passed by.

I didn't know what upset me more—that the truck was empty, or that I hoped he'd be there in it.

Twenty-Eight

I tried a second time to be friendly to the younger woman but failed. Instead, she plugged her earphones into her MP3 player, and then she pulled out a tablet PC and plugged it into the bus's seat console—things I never knew existed until now. Every once in a while, she'd lift her phone and text someone. She sat back, cocooned in a world of her own, unapproachable and content.

I didn't have any electronic devices. It hadn't occurred to me to want one. Arthur had a cell phone, but who would I call? Never mind a computer I could use. Arthur had one, but I wasn't allowed to touch it. Business use only. I'd hopped on one here and there in the library of towns we'd passed through while waiting for our rig repairs, or for a new load to be ready.

I pulled out my everything book and made a note to look into a tablet like the girl had. Baby would need to know how to use those things, and it was time I had an outlet, too. I was sure my brother and sisters knew how to use them. I hoped so, anyway.

I glanced sideways at the girl once again. Would having those gadgets give me an escape like she had, or an advantage in our age?

Looking out the window, I watched the speeding landscape pass by in a blur. Spring was beginning to be realized in this part of the country. Here and there, snowy patches hid in the shadows of the hill—but the leaf buds on the trees told a different story.

I hadn't lived in snow country for a long time. Arthur took great pains to avoid wintery routes. Going home to the Spokane Valley would be a shock. Then again, they didn't get loads of snow like some parts of the country. I closed my eyes and pictured Michael and me building snowmen together or making snow angels. He gave me a kick, and it made me wonder if we were linked mentally.

My thoughts went unbidden to a corner of my mind that still, strangely enough, hoped Arthur would be there next to us, building snow creatures. To say I was conflicted didn't begin to describe my emotions.

What would happen if Arthur should change his mind and want the both of us? I certainly couldn't raise Baby in the truck traveling from one side of the country to the other. I pictured me holding him, feeding him, changing smelly diapers in the front of the cab. He shifted to an older, busy toddler in my mind, pulling on levers and pushing buttons. Arthur impatient and screaming—taking a swing at me. I flinched and opened my eyes. Out of breath, I looked around quickly and then at my watch. I'd been asleep for three hours. The teen gave me a slanted eye glance and went back to her computer. Had I screamed aloud?

My mind came fully awake, and I realized two things: one, I was very hungry and two, I needed to go to the bathroom. Glancing back, I saw the toilet—which seemed so close when I sat down—was more than half the bus-length away. I unbuckled my seatbelt and stood. This was no easy feat, because the seats, although comfortable to sit in, were very close to the next row and Baby threw off my equilibrium. I grabbed the seats to balance myself. Cocoon girl gave me another cursory glance then submerged back into her own world.

I shifted along the rows, bumping one side, then the other as the driver took twists and turns on the highway running parallel to Snake River.

A grandmotherly woman reached out and placed her deep brown hand on my fair one, giving it a gentle pat. "Careful now."

Her mocha brown eyes were full of affection and concern. For some reason her kind words cause tears to spring to my eyes. Her tone, the tilt of her head, reminded me of my grandmother. As much as I tried to blink them away, I couldn't. I gave her a watery smile and kept traversing the rubber walkway back to the bathroom cubicle. I passed five more rows and a few more strangers who didn't look up at all.

When I arrived, the door sign said OCCUPIED. I start to sit down, but the bus took another curve, sharper this time, and I tumbled into the nearest seat as the door unlatched. Out stepped a well-dressed businessman, adjusting his tie.

"Are you okay?" He didn't put out his hand to help me stand.

"I'm fine," I lied. The armrest had dug its way into my left hip, and it throbbed to the thrum of the road under us.

He wandered back to his seat with ease. He must take this route often.

I used the seat in front of me to pull myself back up and headed into the bathroom. The roominess of it surprised me. The rest room was rigged to be wheelchair accessible—although how someone pushing a wheelchair up the slim, bouncing aisle could make it that far was beyond me. If a pregnant woman couldn't make a straight shot to the potty, it'd be impossible for someone in a chair to do it.

I closed the door behind me, shutting out the noise of the cab and shutting in the zip-hum of the tires on the road and the engine burring along. Lowering my pants, I sat down and started to go. Another curve hit. I gave a yelp and grabbed the handle bar nearest me—but this did little to help. I caught a glimpse of myself in the brushed metal door, hanging off the edge of the seat, whites rimming my eyes.

No one should see themselves sitting on the toilet. Ever.

I tried to remove the image from my memory—the wild eyes, pants around my ankles, expression panicked—but was unsuccessful. If there was a punch card limit for the number of times to be humiliated, I'd reached the maximum. I wanted more than a stupid free drink though.

I clenched my eyes closed to concentrate. "Just go, just go, just go," I chanted through my gritted teeth, my fists still clenching the grab bar. The bus thumped over a bump in the road, and the solution in the toilet splashed up at me. This wasn't happening.

Someone knocked on the bathroom door. *Seriously?*

"Uh, hang on a minute," I hollered to the door. I knew I'd need much longer and a nice long stretch of straight road if I were to ever get off that seat. As if on command, the bus leveled out and all seemed peaceful. I finished up quickly and decided I never wanted to try that again—but I knew I would have to. We had another five hours to go, and there was no way Baby was going to let up on the bladder pressure.

As I exited the bathroom, Cocoon Girl was waiting outside the door. For a moment I wondered if she was checking on me, because she certainly knew it was me in there—where else would I be? But her eyes didn't show any curiosity as she pushed past me and locked the door. I shrugged and ricocheted back to my seat. By the time I sat down, I was panting like I'd traversed a mountain range and my stomach and groin muscles were in spasm. Was it it those Braxton Hicks contractions I'd read about? Too much stress and strain. I should have sat closer to the back of the bus, but I'd been worried about motion sickness. Ha.

I pulled out my lunch snack from my carry-on bag and started eating my sandwich. The ebb in my blood sugar's tide turned. The familiar taste drew my mind to when the restaurant might be open again. I swallowed hard as I thought of my apartment. It was the first place I'd ever had that was really mine. For a few months, anyway.

The images and dreams of raising Baby over the restaurant, and in Bridgeville, were tied to my hopes. I knew they weren't right anymore, but casting them off created an ache of helplessness in my throat that burned up into my ears. How could I let go of yet another dream and resign myself to this bleak future?

After lunch, I settled back in for a quick nap that turned into a long, dreamless sleep.

"Spokane. Last stop."

I jerked awake in my seat. Somehow I'd arrived. I peered out the dark tinted windows and saw a mostly empty parking lot below me edged with glowing orange lamp posts. The bus sat on an incline above the station. A train horn sounded, and I heard the rush of the Amtrak as it pulled into the station. My itchy feet fantasied about getting a ticket to some anonymous town and starting all over again. Baby kicked me, and I pictured us both homeless in the alley of a big city, hiding from muggers. I changed my mind.

Gathering my things, I noticed Cocoon Girl had left already. The grandma and I were the last of the passengers on board. She moved ahead, stopping by my row. "You got folks meeting you, sweetie?"

"No. I've a bit to go yet. I'm hoping for a taxi." Really, my only true thought had been spending the night in the station and calling my brother in the morning, because I couldn't fathom spending the extra cash on a taxi ride out to the boonies.

"Where you headed?"

"Elk River."

"My boy is picking me up, and we're going just north of there. We can drop you off." Her statement, full of conviction, made the decision for me. The swell of rebellion shifted through me, but I knew she meant to be kind. I shouldn't take rides from strangers—but I really just wanted to be home.

Ironic.

"Maybe you should ask your son first?" I gave her an easy out, making sure she meant it.

"Oh, he doesn't mind, trust me. He's a good boy and listens to his mama." She gave me a wink, and the warmth in her eyes belied any imagined dangers. I nodded and followed her off the bus. As we walked into the terminal, I heard the rattle of the baggage wagon behind us.

"I'm going to get us a pull-cart, we can put your suitcases on it, too." I motioned toward the baggage wagon.

"Oh, no need. My son can take care of all of those. There he is." She waved to an enormous, disgruntled-looking man in his fifties grousing near the front of the station. The hesitant feeling I had earlier came rushing back. Then she called out, "Randy! My boy, Randy!"

Randy's face shifted to joy as he took in the sight of his mother. His eyes rushed with tears, and he lumbered quickly toward us. He must have been six-and-a-half feet tall, and easily three-hundred pounds.

"Mama! Thought your bus wasn't ever going to get here." He picked her up in a bear-hug squeeze and gave her a spin. "Mama, welcome home. Welcome home." He must have noticed me standing awkwardly by, because he locked his eyes on me and gave me a half-smile as he put her carefully down.

"Hi." The hustle of the station drowned out my voice. His eyes strayed to my blooming stomach before glancing back up. I pulled on my shirt as if to hide Baby.

"This here's my friend," she said, and for the first time I realized we had yet to exchange names.

"Macy. Macy Stone. Nice to meet you Randy." I put out my hand, and his enveloped mine with a warmth reminding me of a heated towel. It was rough from hard work, but so gentle I could barely feel the grip. He was near reverent. How was it the touch of a perfect stranger could leave me feeling cherished, where my own husband never could?

"Nice to meet you, Macy. Mama never goes anywhere without making a friend." His eyes filled with love every time he glanced at her. I couldn't help but like him.

"I told Macy we'd drop her by her place in Elk River. That's okay, right?"

If it wasn't, I couldn't see any evidence of it in his glance.

"You bet. We live about seven miles north of Elk River, out in the hills. Let's get your bags loaded."

We headed to the luggage carousel, and he pulled off his mother's many bags. I motioned to mine, and he placed them at my feet. "Let me pull the truck up to the door. I'll be back for you and yours." He loaded himself down with her luggage—a suitcase under each arm, an overnight case, a backpack and a duffle bag, before heading out through the terminal.

As Randy passed out of earshot, she leaned toward me and held out her hand. "My name's Clara Jones. My Ralph died, and I've moved home to be with my son. His wife is like a long lost daughter, and my grandbabies are fine people." I figure this was information I must need for the road so Randy didn't think he's giving a ride to a complete stranger.

I shook her hand. "Nice to meet you, Clara."

"Are you headed home or visiting, Ms. Macy?" Her eyes twinkled, but as she saw the expression on my face, the twinkle faded.

I had trouble speaking. All I could get out was one word. "Home." There was no warmth, no excitement. Instead, dread gripped every part of me.

"I see. You take this." She pulled out a business card with a cute little flower up in the corner. It had her name and cell number. "If you need anything, you give me a call." She put it in my hand and closed my fingers around it with a gentle push.

I was taken aback by a retired grandmother who carried business cards and handed them out to hopeless strangers she'd met in the bus station. Just as I was about to break down in tears, Randy came back in and gathered my cases under his arms.

"You ladies ready to go?" His booming voice echoed in the now-empty station, all the other passengers having filed out like ants hot on the trail of a nearby picnic.

My bladder, forgotten for the time being, twinged in complaint. "I need to make a stop. I'll be out in a moment." I raced to the bathroom. My body rejoiced in the still floor of the stall. I relieved myself and headed to the sink. As soon as I relaxed, my shoulders began to shake, and all the emotion I'd held on to for the entire trip came choking out in quiet sobs.

Within an hour, I'd know what I was up against. Arthur could already be at my mother's. I could only imagine what plan they'd hatched to deal with me and my unexpected rebellion. Just once, I wanted to know what it was like to make my own choices.

A voice echoed in my head, reminding me Arthur *was* my choice, but I shoved it away. I'd been manipulated, cajoled, given false hope, and my desperate sixteen-year-old self had grasped it.

My conscience prickled me. Didn't I listen to the news and scoff when someone blamed their childhood or age for their problems? I sniffled and blew my nose loudly into a wad of cheap toilet paper. A female janitor came into the rest room and started replacing the rolls. Apparently pregnant females crying their eyes out made little impression on her. She left without ever making eye contact with me.

I pushed the auto-taps over and over, trying to get enough water out to wash my face. I grabbed some of the towels and dried off against their harsh surface. The dampness clung, and my skin stung from a thousand tiny wood-fiber scratches from the crunchy towels. After taking a steadying breath, I fixed my running mascara and took a long look at myself in the warped metal mirror. I was haggard and road weary—and towel burned. Was there any way in the world to get out of doing this?

Not that I could tell.

Twenty-Nine

"So how long have you been away from Elk River, Macy?" Randy tossed the question over to me as he drove us through the pitch-black country outside Spokane.

"Maybe she doesn't want to talk about it." Clara shifted between the two of us, leaning forward as if to shield me. Her instincts were uncanny.

"Nearly seven years now." I figured I owed Randy some conversation, seeing as he was giving me a ride.

"Who are your folks?"

I took a steadying breath, trying to sound light and interesting. "They own Robinsons' Gas and Groceries in Elk River. My mom owns it now. My dad passed away about eight years ago."

"I've stopped in there and had my truck worked on. Your brother's name Bobby?"

"Yes, that's him." I guess I shouldn't be surprised someone who lived seven miles up the road from my mom would know my brother. I'd forgotten I'd entered the static life again.

"He's a gifted mechanic."

I tried to imagine Bobby in charge of the shop, but in my head all I could see was a boy in greasy coveralls pooled around oversized work boots, carrying a wrench much too large for his hands working on small engines. He'd obviously gotten to follow his dreams.

"He's fixed this truck a couple times. Charges fair, too." The admiration in his voice spoke volumes and pride filled me. As much as I tried to follow the conversation, though, my brain was stuck in a time warp. We were driving past road signs, down highways, and over bridges I'd been familiar with—and yet they all seemed a bit different in the dark. We crossed over the Elk River bridge, and I was startled by the changes.

"This is new." The beams were larger, the road wider than when I was a girl. This new one sported a bike lane.

"The old bridge needed to be replaced after the flood a couple years back. Debris ruined some of the side supports. Brought jobs to the area for a while."

I hadn't heard of any flooding, but then again, Arthur kept us on a tight schedule to earn his bonuses. The only news filtering through to me was from talk radio we tuned in now and then or discarded local newspapers in restaurants. Tiny Elk River flooding was hardly worthy of national attention.

The headlights flashed over the directional sign ahead. I'd be home in eight miles. I went numb with dread.

Clara patted my hand as if she could sense my trepidation. "Going home after such a long time away is going to be hard." Her serious tone carried conviction and empathy. I tilted my head her way but couldn't read her features in the dim light of the dashboard.

Randy broke the tension. "You're going to be okay, Mama."

Clara sighed. "I don't quite know what I'm going to do with myself. What if no one remembers me or needs me? Worse, what if they do need me and I can't do the job?"

I wasn't the only one having an attack of doubt.

"Now, Mama, you know Sheryl wants you around. And the grandkids can't wait for you to share all your recipes with them. Don't get me started on the women's group at church. They can't hardly contain themselves. Nearly every blue-haired lady came up to me last Sunday at church and asked me when you were going to be home."

Clara clucked her tongue in mock disapproval, holding back laughter at his description. "Shame on you." She slapped his arm. "I think I'm going to break in real easy like. I don't want folks to think I'm going to let them saddle me with all their cast-off projects. You know how they do to widows and stay-at-home moms." She pushed up at the back of her hair. "Tell you what, Macy, you give me a call once in a while. We prodigal daughters have to stick together."

"I'm not sure how long I'll be in Elk River. My husband is coming to meet me there." The tone of my voice made it sound more like a prison sentence than the longing of a woman to see her husband after so many months. Randy missed it—but the echo lingered in my head. So did guilt. Lots of guilt.

"I'm sure he's excited to see you." Randy chuckled. "Hard for a man to be separated from his wife—especially when she's expecting."

I didn't respond. Clara squeezed my fingers, and I wondered if Clara was short for clairvoyant.

"Your mother will be glad to see you." Clara's voice lilted with a ring of optimism.

"Probably." I tried to imagine not seeing my son for nearly seven years and then have him come home. *I'd* be overjoyed. I tried to change the subject. "Sounds like you have a lot of grandchildren."

"Oh yes. I have four grandchildren from Randy and another three from my daughter Mary. Although, they don't live around here anymore. Mary and her husband, Terrance, live in Hawaii. He's in the service."

"Do you get to visit them?"

"I've gone three times now. Wish it was more often, but I'll take what I can get."

"Mary wants you to come for Christmas this year." Randy's statement held a secret significance.

"Oh, I couldn't do that. I want to have Christmas with you and the kids. No. Maybe next year. This year I want to settle in and get my routine." Her voice cracked at the end, and she turned my way. "First Christmas since my husband died, you know. And here's Easter right around the corner. Two weeks away."

Randy turned on the radio. Seventies classics filled the cab and mixed with the occasional sniffle from Clara.

Randy glanced my way. "What are you doing for Easter?"

I hadn't given Easter a thought. My mother used to hide eggs before my father got sick. Then I did it with the little ones—although the joy and excitement had been worked out of me. And then I left. Arthur and I didn't celebrate Easter. Hard to hide eggs in the cab of a truck—and Arthur wasn't the playing type. Let alone the going-to-church type.

"I don't know." I didn't know a lot these days.

"What church does your mama attend? I'm sure they'll have a special service for Easter." Clara latched onto the conversation, her tears having subsided.

"My folks never really attended church. I would go with my grandma, though." I couldn't remember the name of it right then. The church met in an old refurbished school building and shared it with community events.

"Maybe you could go with your grandmother?"

"No. She passed away." I stopped talking as unexpected bitterness pooled in my throat, and I found I couldn't speak anymore. I stared out the window at the blackness, pretending to be distracted and wishing we were there. Clara didn't try to make small talk anymore, and Randy hummed along to "Cool Change" by the Little River Band.

Ten minutes later, we were driving into Elk River. The downtown's buildings were all darkened except for the bar. Two younger guys stood outside, hoodies hiding their features as they approached men entering, probably selling drugs or hoping someone would sneak them a beer. The scene really hadn't changed much from when I was a kid. I never could figure why the police didn't park a man right outside the doors. They'd earn loads in arrest fees.

The early nineteen hundred's architecture of the town mixed with sixties modern concrete offices. The pet store was gone, as was the office supply store. No more arcade—it was a coffee shop. The library still sat on the corner. I'd spent a lot of time there. It was the only place I could go where my mother couldn't nag me and my brother and sisters had to be quiet.

Randy pulled up in front of the gas station. I pointed to a narrow road past the entrance, and he drove up it, past the shop to the house in back. The truck pitched up and down over the ruts on the road. We pulled to a stop in front of the house. The porch light cast a glow on the muddy driveway, sparkling in the puddles. The door opened, and my mother stepped out on the porch.

I climbed from the truck, and we stared at each other. She didn't speak at first, but I thought I caught a look of relief in her eyes. "Macy. Thank heavens." She took a step toward me but stopped.

A tall man with bushy black hair pushed past the squeaky screen door, and stood next to her, hands stuffed into his front pockets. "Hey,

Macy." He nodded to me. I frowned, trying to figure out which shop employee he was.

As I walked closer, I recognized his eyes. He looked like a younger version of my father. "Bobby?"

He cracked a grin. "Hey, big sister." He hopped down the steps and drew me into a comforting hug. "Glad you're home." I started to hug him back, but my mother interrupted.

"It's not nice to keep these good folks waiting. Bobby, get your sister's things." Bobby's arms stiffened, and he pulled away, moving to the truck.

I turned and saw Clara and Randy waiting there in an uncomfortable silence.

"Mrs. Jones, Mr. Jones, this is my mother, Barbara Robinson." I didn't feel right telling her their first names. I had a desire to keep them anonymous and private.

Clara reached out and shook my mother's hand. The forced pleasantry added to the tension building in the air.

"Hey, Mr. Jones. Thanks for giving Macy a ride. How's your truck working?" Bobby put out his hand to Randy and gave it a hearty shake. I could see the approval in Randy's expression.

"Real good, son. Real good." He started handing Bobby my bags, and one by one they were transferred inside the house. I watched each piece, like a chunk of me was being hidden, bit by bit, behind that screen door.

Clara gave my arm a squeeze, breaking me from my morbid thoughts. "You give me a call, now, hear?"

I nodded, feeling closer to her than to the family on the porch behind me.

Bobby reached into his back pocket and pulled out his wallet. He handed Randy a plastic card. "You use it the next time you come by—a free fill."

Randy waved him off. "Now, you don't have to do that, son. It was a pleasure to give your sister a ride, and we had to come this way anyhow."

"I insist." Bobby held out his hand until Randy took the card.

"Thanks. We'd better move on, Mama." He opened the truck door and eased Clara inside. I floated outside myself, watching everything in great detail. Clara gave me an encouraging smile through the window, and then they drove away. A wave of dizziness hit me then, and I realized it'd been much too long since I'd eaten. I steadied myself on the porch railing.

"It's a good thing you got here when you did, that's all I can say." My mother's voice carried an accusation I couldn't quite understand.

Sarcastic remarks formed on my tongue. I needed to eat and go to bed.

"Give her a break, Mom. She just got here." Bobby had never back-talked our mother as far as I could remember. I waited for her to reprimand him, but she didn't.

"None too soon. It's been months since I came to you, Macy." She walked through the front door, and I followed.

Another world of difference met me inside. The front room sported a bright teal wall and ceiling-high entertainment center flanked by bookcases. Across the room sat a couch and two leather recliners. I walked through to the kitchen and sat at the newer maple table, pulling out my lunch sack.

My brother gave me a questioning look, but my mother seemed to take it in stride.

"I need to eat." I took out the remainder of my sandwich and an apple and juice box. As I did, I noticed the kitchen, too, had been repainted and the cabinets refinished. There were new countertops and appliances. A dishwasher? I thought they were hurting for money. "When did you do all this?"

"About a year after you left."

They couldn't get one when I was home—but as soon as their "dishwasher" left home, she bought one.

"Nice." My tone went flat.

"Don't set your mouth, Macy. You remember how rundown everything was. We needed to replace it all. The cabinets were rotting out from under the dishes. We had a horrible leak in the roof that year after your father left us. The stove and the refrigerator went out days apart. The repair man said to get new."

Left us?

"Sorry." I *was* sorry. It wasn't my business what she did to the house. I didn't live there anymore. "I could use some sleep." I got up and waited for her to tell me which room was mine—or if I even had a room.

"There'll be time enough for sleeping after we decide what to do."

"Mom, it's past midnight. It took nine hours to make a seven-hour trip. I really need to rest, okay?" I couldn't believe I was asking permission rather than stating a fact. I'd regressed back to my childhood.

My mother gave me a look I couldn't discern. "You'll need to make some choices in the morning, though, Macy."

I frowned. "I know Arthur still wants me to get rid of the baby, Mom, but I'm not going to do it. He's going to have to listen to reason." There. I'd said it like I meant it.

"I don't know how reasonable he's going to be at this point. He's been waiting for you for three days." My mother put her hands on her hips and gave me a look.

My arms went cold. "He's here?"

I lay in my childhood twin-sized bed, staring at the slight shadows playing over my ceiling. Moonlight suddenly cut through the heavy dark of night. In a couple hours, the sun would rise and fill the familiar space with a gray-pink light. I should sleep, but it wouldn't come. Scenarios of conversations with Arthur filled my mind.

Last night, my mother had expected me to head out to our rig and knock on the door and beg for entry. I corrected those thoughts as fast as I could. The more I stood my ground with her, the more sure I became of my own mind. Until now—now I was alone.

"Lord, are you here with me?" I'd been irregular in my prayers and not even sure he'd been listening these days. The only sounds in my room were my labored breaths as I tried not to cry.

Turning on my side, I stared at the blank wall, trying to remember which posters I had hung there as a girl. There'd been a kitten hanging by its paws on the branch of a tree with the caption HANG IN THERE under it. And I'd had a poster of the latest flavor of cute boy from Tiger Beat magazine. Hadn't I been crazy about Zac Efron?

Funny how when Arthur had proposed, I'd left them all behind as if they'd never mattered. Toby looked a bit like Zac, didn't he? And just about as accessible considering the circumstances.

A sudden tear escaped, and I knew I should get up and face the day. As soon as I sat up, I raced to the bathroom to relieve my bladder. Then I did a quick switch and squatted, waiting for the inevitable. I'd gotten pretty fast at this. I could medal in this event. After throwing up, I showered and dressed. Heading to the kitchen, I found my mother there, already making toast.

She glanced over her shoulder at me and gave me what I interpreted as an empathetic look. "You've got it bad."

"Sorry I woke you." I took a piece of toast from the stack as she poured me a cup of tea.

"I was up already. It's five."

I'd forgotten how my parents would rise before dawn to get the station open in time for commuters. My mother would have coffee and cocoa in large thermos carafes along with several dozen donuts and pastries from the local bakery ready for the first customers of the day. I'd never helped voluntarily.

"Does Ricky still deliver for the bakery?" Ricky had been a good girlfriend of mine before my father got cancer. After that, all my friendships faded away and my focus shifted. Most of my friends had been worried about who liked who, and the styles and music. Raising their siblings and keeping a dilapidated house afloat didn't even show up on their radar.

"She helps bake now, too. Her folks will probably leave her the bakery one day." My mother sounded wistful. Inheritance and investment in the family business was like her moral code.

As I nibbled my toast, I heard the familiar honk from the horn of the bakery delivery van. I peeked out through the kitchen window but couldn't glimpse the van up the drive. Moments later, it drove off.

"Did she leave them outside?"

My mother absently stacked clean dishes from the dishwasher on the counter. "No, your sister is there, getting the coffeepots going."

"Which one?"

"Sarah."

My mother finished cleaning up and left a plate of scrambled eggs and toast on the counter under a lid.

"This is for Brynn when she wakes up." She swiped the crumbs off the counter into the palm of her hand and carried them over the sink. "If you want some of the eggs, go ahead. I don't remember them sitting too well when I was pregnant."

Toby had discovered soft boiled eggs, not runny, suited me fine. But I knew I'd get no such accommodation here. And I couldn't look at a raw egg to save my life. I sipped my tea, saying nothing.

"Arthur should be down soon. If you walk back and meet him halfway, it'd probably go better for you." She gave me a hopeful look. I didn't know what she expected to happen when I spoke to Arthur. I didn't want to start an argument right then, though, so I said nothing. She left the house and headed up toward the store.

After loading my plate and cup into the dishwasher, I stepped out on the front porch, gently closing the squeaky screen door behind me. Part of me wanted to head to the store and see Sarah, since I'd missed seeing her the night before. Or wake Brynn. I didn't know if she'd remember me at this point—so that'd probably be a bad plan.

The crisp spring air cut with pine and cedars filled a homesick part of myself I hadn't known existed. I heard the distant thrum of idling motors and the *ding-ding* of a car driving over the warning line in front of the station. I fought the urge to go ask if they need regular, supreme, or diesel and turned instead toward the back of the property.

In the distance, past a stand of trees, I saw our white rig parked. Just the cab—he didn't have a trailer. He must be headed north to pick up a load. I picked past puddle-filled potholes and slippery grassy mounds. The road seemed to draw out longer before me with every step I took, like a long camera shot in an old movie. A horse out in the neighbor's pasture whinnied, and I jumped. I could hear the buzz of electric fencing humming along both sides of me now.

I stepped wrong and nearly slipped into a mucky hole and caught myself on a wooden fence post, my hand an inch from live line. That'd figure, wouldn't it? Just one slip.

After an eternity of small steps, I stood in front of our rig, shivering in the damp air as cold water seeped into my tennis shoes. I listened for signs of life. My head throbbed so loudly from tension, I couldn't hear much else. So I reached up to knock on the door. Before my knuckles made contact with the cab, the door swung open and Arthur stepped down to face me. His eyes were dark and unreadable. I expected yelling, but he didn't speak. He only stared at my protruding stomach. His eyes reminded me I'd let him down, again.

"I'm here." I couldn't think of anything else to say.

Arthur grunted and moved past me to the wire fence. He leaned on a wooden post and tested it with the toe of his boot before stomping back overgrowth from the field. He'd probably set those posts in the ground with my father. They were loose now, shifting in the wet earth, and would need to be replaced within the year. I watched his back and the tight muscles of his arms. He was still a formidable man—but those arms didn't attract me anymore.

As I stepped away from him, the chopped, yellowed hay stalks from last year's harvest poked through my jeans. I stopped at a farther post, putting us five feet apart, but at that moment it felt like so much more. I leaned against it for support, forgetting the hot lines, and it shifted under my weight. They probably all needed to be replaced.

"You kept the baby." His tone held no emotion, but I could tell by his quiet precision he was angry.

"I told you I would."

Arthur chuckled, but there was no humor in his eyes. "What's happened to you, Macy? You'd never thought of disobeying me before."

"I wanted to be more than someone who obeys you, Arthur. I wanted to be your partner. I wanted to raise our child together." His eyes locked on me, but I didn't look. I kept mine fixed on the horse grazing in the distance, steam rising from its huffing nostrils. It wore training blinders.

"You don't get to choose."

I tried to ignore what he meant. Had I ever been more than his property? I'd thought so at one time. I'd thought so for several years. I was wrong. So wrong.

"I've spoken to Barbara. She's willing to raise the child here with the other kids. I'll send her money every month for expenses." My mother's name sounded so foreign to my ears. My grandmother had called her *honey*, my father *baby*. And she'd only ever been Mom or Mama to me. He said her name with such familiarity, such respect, it unnerved me.

Then panic flashed through me. I knew that tone. The finality of his words hung in the air along with his freezing breath. My fate had been sealed again. Or so he thought.

"No." I said it without hesitation. Some motherly, protective instinct boiled up inside me and tumbled out without my permission. I sounded strong and sure.

Arthur could move fast when he wanted to. Before I knew what was happening, my arms were gripped in his rage-shaking grasp. I lifted my eyes to his in time to see the blaze of anger flash hot. "You'll. Do. As. I. Say." Each word ground out against his teeth.

I became certain, more than ever, I wouldn't. "No." I wrenched away, desperate to protect the life I carried. I tried to run down the muddy, gravel-lined road, but my lumbering form was no match for his speed. I could hear his boots thudding against the wet road, his panting breath, his fingers grasping at my shirt. I wrapped my arms around my lower belly, supporting the baby, not sure I should be jogging, let alone running flat-out at this late stage of pregnancy.

"You stop." He gasped. "Everything's going back to being the way it was." He took a gulping breath. "I need you."

I wanted to scoff, but I didn't think I could manage it. We must have made quite a sight. A middle-aged man frantically chasing after a pregnant woman down a muddied road flanked by horses. A sudden cramp cut under one side of my belly, into my groin, stealing my breath away, intense and relentless, but I didn't stop running.

He was right. He did need me—more than he'd ever like to admit. I completed the picture he had of his life. I read his maps and took care of his laundry and met his physical needs. But it wasn't the way I knew I deserved to be needed. It wasn't mine or my baby's picture. Nothing he could say would make me change my mind. My mother would lose her contracts, the store would close and the shop with it. Maybe she'd lose the house. But I would not go back with Arthur. Not ever again.

I heard a grunt and the grinding sound of boots slipping on wet gravel, then a heavy splat. I turned to look back over my shoulder and saw Arthur laying in the mud, face down. I kept running, knowing he'd be up any minute, screaming and demanding. But as I looked back again, nearly to the house, I saw he hadn't moved. Not a bit.

A battle waged inside me. Most of me wanted to keep going, to run inside the house and bar the door. As I panted and tried to catch my breath, a contraction pulled across my groin. I grimaced and leaned over. The searing pain shot into my hip joint, down my leg, back up and across my lower stomach. It burned to the point I thought I might pass out when it suddenly lessened, and the muscles shuddered with relief. I stood to stretch out my side muscles and the pain threatened again. Down the road, Arthur lay in the mud. My mind rushed with plots and treachery. He could be faking it, waiting for me to return. He'd grab me and force me to agree to his plans. He'd hurt me. He'd hurt Michael.

And even though those thoughts were racing through my head, my legs went grudgingly toward him.

"Arthur?" I called out, but not very loud. In tentative steps, I headed up the road. I heard another voice behind me now.

"Macy? What's happened to Arthur?"

I turned to see a younger girl who must have been Brynn coming toward me. Her eyes were wide in fear.

"He's fallen."

"He tried to hurt you. I saw him." She wrapped her arms across her chest. "He's always been so nice to us. Why would he want to hurt you?"

How could I explain years of abuse to my youngest sister in a matter of seconds? Because now I knew that was all I had left of our relationship. I heard a gurgling sound, and I reached down, pulling Arthur up a bit, but couldn't manage it after my long sprint. He'd been breathing into a puddle, bubbles forming from one side of his mouth, looking every bit like frothy chocolate milk. My muscles shook as I tried to hold him up.

"Help me, Brynn." Together, we took him by the shoulders and turned him on his back. Arthur's eyes were open but glassy. His mouth sagged to the side, and he mumbled at me. The rage in his features had melted into complete fear.

"I'll call 9-1-1." Brynn raced back to the house.

I brushed the mud and debris off Arthur's face with my bare hand. His eyes shifted to mine, but I wasn't sure he saw me. His arms were splayed away from his body, so I drew them closer. I pulled my hoodie off and folded it, putting it under his head. Then I took my sleeve and wiped the dirt from his forehead before pressing it to the gash cut by gravel on the road. Blood and muddy water drizzled down the side of his face and pooled under his neck.

Several minutes passed before I heard a siren in the distance. Arthur mumbled again, and I found myself saying foolish, caring things in response. "It'll be okay, Arthur. Hang on, help is coming. You're going to be okay."

Oh Lord, help.

Thirty-One

Sitting in the waiting room of a hospital had to be one of the worst things in life. I'd been in the very same room when Bobby fell off the back of a big-rig trailer and broke his arm in our garage. My mother was home caring for Daddy, but I'd ridden with Bobby to the ER in one of our worker's cars. I had handed them the note giving permission to treat him. I'd had to call my grandmother to come and give us a ride home hours later when he'd been released. My mother wouldn't leave my father's side—not even for her son's broken arm.

I'd waited there with my mother and brother and sisters when my dad had his last cancer surgery. The time doctors told us he'd never be healed and we were only extending the inevitable by a matter of weeks with chemo.

And here I was again, waiting to find out the fate of my husband. Baby kicked me, and I realized I'd be here again in three more weeks— if not sooner—to give birth. I shifted in my powder-blue chair, and the cushion squeaked beneath me. I'd just read the same line in the magazine in my hand for the tenth time. I gave up and tossed it on the table in front of me.

I stared at a young couple across from me and wondered who they were waiting to see. Maybe a father whose heart had given out. Maybe a child having surgery. Their eyes darted to the door, just as mine did, every time someone walked down the hall.

My mother walked in and handed me a sandwich and a bottle of water. Her eyes accused, even though I was sure Brynn told her what happened. Somehow even this was my fault.

An hour passed, then another. A nurse walked in and whispered to the couple, who gave sighs of relief and followed her away.

Close behind her was the ER admitting doctor. He searched our faces and rested on mine. "Mrs. Stone?"

I nodded and followed him out in the hallway. My mother tried to come, but I gave her a look that stopped her cold. Those baby hormones were really boosting my resolve. They should bottle the stuff.

The doctor pursed his lips as he frowned down at me. I knew what he was thinking. *She's so young. Too young.* At one point in my life, I would have agreed with him. But today I was battle-worn and aged.

"There's no good way to break this news." He glanced down at my protruding stomach and hesitated. "Are you sure you don't want your mom with you?"

Oh, so sure. "No, I'm fine."

"Your husband's had a major stroke. I'm very sorry."

The doctor was already apologizing like it was the sentence being read at a trial, and Arthur had been incarcerated without chance for an appeal.

"Did you give him the stroke medication I've read about?" I had a lot of time on the road to keep up with the latest health magazines.

"I'm afraid those medications work on ischemic strokes, when there's a blockage. Your husband suffered from a severe hemorrhagic stroke. A blood vessel burst causing intracerebral damage. He bled out considerably before we could insert the catheter and clip off the vessel."

My brain had trouble grasping what he was saying. He must have noticed because he followed up with, "We've done all we can."

We've done all we can.

I knew those words well.

Like a magnet, they drew a gasp from my mother, who'd been eavesdropping behind me.

"How long?" It probably sounded heartless to him, but this wasn't a time for sentiment in my mind. I needed to know what to expect.

"It's hard to say. He could live years, still. I'm afraid he's suffered considerable brain damage. He'll never walk again. He'll need to be fed…" The doctor stopped talking. When I looked up to see why, he was moving rapidly toward me at an odd angle, eyes full of concern. The lights dimmed, and my first and last thought had to do with a power outage.

Sometime later, I discovered it was *mine*.

Voices lilted to me through my hazy, blood-sugar-starved brain. I felt a sore spot on my arm and the tickle of an IV line against my skin when I shifted.

"She's always had a weak constitution," my mother said to someone. *I* wasn't the weak one.

"Poor thing. Been through so much." A warm, familiar female voice floated past me. "How long will she be here?"

"Until she's up on her feet again. By tonight, I'd guess." My mother sighed, aggravation and worry dripping from her words. "What we're going to do now is anyone's guess."

Ah. Not worrying about *me*.

I shifted in the bed, making the crinkly plastic liner under my sheet rustle and draw their attention. I opened my eyes to two distinct expressions: worry and blame. Clara held the worried one.

"There she is." She reached out and patted my hand.

"You can't keep forgetting to eat, Macy. It's not good for you or the baby," was my mother's greeting.

"I guess I had other things on my mind, Mother. Like saving the shop, the baby, and my husband."

My mother's eyes shot to the back of Clara's head and then to mine, imploring me to stay quiet.

"What do you mean?" Clara looked back and forth between us.

"I mean Arthur didn't want our baby and has been threating my family for the past several months if I didn't get rid of him."

"Macy, how could you?" My mother put her hand over her eyes as if I'd disrobed in front of the whole town.

"Mother, it's the truth."

"But it sounds so…" She paused, so I finished for her.

"Selfish? Awful? Heartless? Cruel?"

She chewed on the inside of her cheek before answering. "Cold."

"If you want to pretend it's normal for a man to treat his wife and child that way, you go on ahead. I'm done." I shifted in the bed, trying to sit up, but I got caught in a wave of dizziness. Clara helped me lie back against the pillows. My mother grabbed her purse and headed to the door.

"I have to check on the kids."

"Why?"

My question brought her up short, and she paused before continuing out the door. I knew the answer. Even Brynn could heat up a meal in the microwave. She just wanted to leave.

"You need to let go of all those old hurts, honey." Clara clucked her tongue at me. I focused on her for the first time.

"You don't know what you're talking about." The anger in my words and her surprised face shamed me. "I'm sorry."

"Now, now." She brushed her fingers over mine and settled back in her chair. "You've got to think of your baby."

"He's all I'm thinking about anymore."

"And the baby's father."

Anger surged again. I hadn't known how mad I'd become. "Arthur doesn't love my baby. He didn't even want him to live."

I waited for Clara to be shocked, but she just continued to watch me.

I shook my head. "You can't possibly understand."

Her eyes sparkled at my words. "Maybe not, maybe not." Clara glanced at the tray near my bed, and for the first time I noticed a covered plate. She lifted the reddish-mottled plastic lid from the dish, and I spied overcooked mixed veggies and a slab of gray meatloaf. The aroma of canned peas gagged me.

"Well, that's just…" She grimaced. "Awful. Isn't *that* awful? Would you like me to go get you something appetizing?"

The only thing I wanted was Nick's mashed potatoes and gravy. I would have killed for a slab of chicken-fried steak, too, with garlic toast. My stomach growled at my thoughts, and Clara laughed.

"I'll take that as a yes." She picked up her purse. "Now, you sit there and I'll be back with something decent. Pretend to be asleep when the nurses come by." She gave me a wink and left my room. What I really wanted was Toby to show up with something just right. For Toby to show up at all.

I turned my head to the side and caught sight of my drip-dripping IV and counted the droplets of fluid flowing into my arm. Somewhere around one-hundred, I drifted back to sleep.

Thirty-Two

Something wonderful—a meaty, savory, aroma—beckoned me. I cracked my eye open to make sure a nurse hadn't snuck into my room to trick me into eating their washed-out food. Instead of a nurse, I spied Clara dumping the food they gave me into a plastic grocery bag and popping the lids on several glass containers. The tantalizing aroma of stewed beef and carrots shimmied around my nose. I watched as she dumped the stew on a mound of fluffy mashed potatoes, scraping every bit of lumpy gravy from the dish.

"That smells amazing."

Clara didn't turn my way, but I saw a grin crease her aging face. "Good, good." She put the plate before me, and I watched as the buttery potatoes were engulfed by the volcano of veggie and meat goodness swirling and melting the sides of the fluffy mounds. My mouth watered, and I gulped.

She rolled the table around to me, and I pushed the button on the bed to raise it. I lifted the water glass, tinkling with melting ice cubes, and took a large swig before starting on my meal.

"Where," I said in between bites, "did you get this incredible food?"

Clara pulled the chair closer to my bed and lifted her own container to eat.

"You didn't make this, did you? How'd you get home?"

"I called Randy and told him it was an emergency."

"A stew emergency." I laughed.

"A friend's emergency." She leveled her brown eyes on mine, and I remembered the state I'd been in not long ago. Pregnant, faint, husband had a stroke. The facts settled over me, suffocating me. I took a deep breath and tried to chase away the claustrophobia.

"You have a lot to think about, and you can't do it on an empty stomach." Clara stated it in such a matter-of-fact way I drew confidence from her.

"I guess after I eat, I'd better find Arthur and assess the damage."

"I think you'd better pray first."

Pray? "I guess so."

Clara nodded and continued eating. "God's got a plan for you and for me, it's best to ask him to help us work these things out. As much as I'd like to do things under my own steam, I often make hasty choices. That's not his way."

I tried to think of what God's way was for all of this. I came up empty.

"There's things you don't understand." I shook my head, sure I'd never be able to explain the intricacies of my family and the situation with Arthur. Frankly, I didn't have the energy to even try.

She nodded. "Your brother Bobby filled Randy in this afternoon at the station."

My hackles rose. "Bobby's got no right to tell my business to anyone."

Clara put up her wrinkled hands in a subduing manor and shushed me. "He didn't say anything disrespectful. He's worried about you and the family and the business." There was something more, but Clara didn't divulge it. "Randy got so mad at your husband. You know, you're just about the age of my oldest granddaughter. Randy could be your daddy—and he's near Arthur's age."

The wonderful tasting food went stale in my mouth, and I put down my spoon, looking away.

"Sweetie, the reasons don't matter anymore. What you need to do is focus on what you're going to do now."

The reasons didn't matter? All I'd done for the past several months was consider who did what, and who was to blame. My mother, Arthur, even me. If I understood whose fault it was, wouldn't that help me come to terms with it? I looked up, expectantly. I wanted her to tell me what to do. I really did. Being my own woman, making my own choices had grown old. I obviously wasn't any better at it than my mother had been.

Clara just looked back at me. She wasn't going to tell me anything.

I sighed loudly and leaned back against the crunchy, sanitary hospital pillows.

The doctor chose that moment to come in and give me a reprieve. "Something in here smells better than hospital food." He gave Clara a mock reprimanding look, but his eyes crinkled at the corners. Then he turned to me. "Are you up to hearing about your husband, now?"

"Yes." Maybe if I had all the facts, it would help. I sure hoped so.

"He's awake and asking for you. As soon as you can, I'd like to have you wheeled to his room. It's only about four doors down. I can even move you so you're in his room with him, if you'd like."

"No." The word was out before I'd given it any thought at all. I knew I couldn't sleep in the same room with Arthur.

"Okay. If you're able, let's wheel you down there. I know it'd comfort him a great deal to see you."

Doubtful.

Clara stayed quiet but followed us as the doctor pushed my chair through Arthur's doorway and up to his bed. He had a large bandage wrapped around his head and several IV tubes coming off his strapped-down arms.

I gave the doctor a questioning look.

"He's not thinking clearly. We don't want him to rip out his lines."

I nodded, knowing how stubborn Arthur was about, well, everything. If he wanted those lines out, they'd come out, no matter how it hurt.

I rolled closer, and one of Arthur's eyes focused on me. The other lulled to the side.

"He's lost his left side. After rehab and time, he'll likely gain control again of some of his facial muscles. We're not sure of his speech, though."

"You said he was asking for me."

The doctor looked sheepish. "I'm sure he would have if he could. What man wouldn't want to see his wife, especially his pregnant wife?" He gave me a warm smile I didn't return.

Arthur groaned, and I looked straight at him. "This man."

Clara made a disapproving sound.

The doctor shifted his weight from one foot to the other. "I'll leave you alone for now. We'll start occupational therapy in the morning." If ever anyone made a hasty exit, he did.

Clara cleared her throat. "I'm heading home now. Randy's downstairs waiting for me. I'll come back tomorrow. Sounds like you'll spend the night here, after all." She gave my shoulders a squeeze.

I wanted to beg her to stay, but I knew she probably would, and that would have been selfish of me. Clara shut the door behind her and left me with Arthur and his ventilator and his lazy, guilty eye. At least I hoped he felt some guilt. My own seared through me, leaving a dryness in my throat. How had I come to this place?

As I watched him, I subconsciously drew contrasts between Arthur and Toby. I'd lined them up in my mind: Compassionate for Toby, uncompassionate for Arthur. Caring for Toby, uncaring for Arthur. Responsible for Toby, irresponsible for Arthur. Selfless for Toby, selfish for Arthur. I mean, when I thought of it, who else would go to jail to protect their father? A father that had mistreated him and his mom his whole life—who'd gotten a young woman pregnant—and now lay helpless, the victim of a stroke brought on by that selfishness.

At the last thought, my hand flew to mouth and tears welled in my eyes. Toby and I were in the exact same spot with the same kind of person. We'd both made sacrifices we probably shouldn't have to protect people in our lives who hadn't protected us. Who, when it all came down to it, were trying to hurt those they were supposed to protect when they needed it most. Danny and her baby didn't survive.

We would.

Arthur waited. I didn't know where to start, but no matter what, I wasn't going to be a willing martyr anymore. Before I could speak, he mumbled. I leaned closer but couldn't make it out.

"I can't understand you."

Arthur's eye winced, and he groaned. I knew that sound. Anger. I'd had enough of his anger.

"I don't know what they've told you, but you've had a stroke." I laid it out there for him. "It's going to be awhile before you'll speak again." I didn't mention the walking.

His eye drooped toward my stomach and back to me, a question there. It didn't make any sense to me at all. Why would he suddenly care? It couldn't be.

"You still want me to get rid of the baby, even after all this?" Incredulousness welled inside me, but soon dissipated as he shook his head slightly—which ended up looking like a drooping toddler's head falling asleep in their car seat instead of a clear no. I hadn't a clue what he was trying to tell me. I wanted to run, fast and hard back to my room. Safe.

My eyes focused on my wheelchair and the IV hanging on the pole behind me. I wouldn't be running anywhere any time soon. I could roll, though, right out of there. He'd cast me off, I'd do the same. He had good insurance. Let someone else bathe him and nurse him. I'd soon have a baby to care for. I needed to conserve my energy.

The ugliness of my own thoughts startled me. This wasn't who I wanted to be. Could I ever explain to my son how I left his disabled father in a hospital to be cared for by strangers? A wave of dizziness swirled through my brain, and all I wanted to do was ride it out of there. I needed some distance and time to gather my thoughts. I needed to pray, like Clara said.

God seemed an enigma. My grandmother said he loved us all and never left us. Clara obviously knew him well. But all I had was the white-haired father-like figure of my childhood hanging ominously over us all, and my father was dead.

"I need to go rest, Arthur. I'll be back tomorrow." I began to wheel backward away from the bed when Arthur's mumblings grew more pronounced and desperate, but still unclear.

I shook my head. "Maybe tomorrow things will be easier for you."

A tear tickled from his eye, but I couldn't tell if it was emotion or a physical reaction. I reached over and wiped his slack cheek, and he did something that completely surprised me. He leaned into my hand and closed his eye and began to shudder and sob past the breathing tube. He moaned, and something stirred deep in my soul. He mumbled and groaned the same pattern over and over. I held my breath, not believing my ears.

It sounded like, "Sorry."

Thirty-Three

I stared out the window of my mother's store, watching Sarah monitor the pumps. The rain came down around her in sheets, but she didn't seem to notice. She met each customer with a smile. Every now and then one would come inside and grab a cup of coffee or a snack.

I straightened the maps in the rack before moving over to the broiler. I turned it on and started stocking it with hotdogs so they'd be ready for the lunch rush. The odors of thousands of cooked tube steaks whooshed out at me when I opened the door, and my stomach turned. I wiped down the two microwaves and restocked napkins and plasticware.

When I was a kid, I'd watch the hotdogs heat and glisten under the elements. I loved them and burritos and about anything I could cook in the store. It was like the feeling you got when you stayed overnight in a motel with a small kitchenette, or camped in a trailer as a kid. It had been my own little wonderland of independence.

I made my way to the refrigerated section and noticed the cups of precut fruit and side salads covered with cellophane. My mom's idea. They probably sold pretty well to the truckers. It only took a week of constant fast food to make a trucker yearn for fresh. Well, most of them.

Arthur's habit of eating in truck stops and diners was hard to break entirely. In the beginning, it'd been pretty amazing for me to eat out so much—at least for a while. Because of my father's illness, we'd stopped eating out, stopped going places. Stopped living. All the money we had went back into the business or medical bills.

I'd escaped to what I thought of as the rosy days. I felt loved and cherished as Arthur took me to several of his favorite eateries on our way east. About a month in, I realized that was all he would probably ever be taking me to. And somehow I'd put a mystical, romantic spin on it.

I wandered to the other rack of novels nearest the counter to straighten them as Sarah entered with a handful of cash for the register. I watched her from the corner of my eye as I aligned the books and reorganized them. A few had covers hearkening back to the seventies, with daisies and blurred photos of romantic couples on the front. The pages were edged in yellow or red and made crunching sounds as I flipped them. As I was about to comment on the classic collection, I spied something shocking. A pocket Bible. Several, in fact.

"What's this?" I held it up to Sarah and thought I saw a blush on her cheeks.

"I…" She cleared her throat. "I thought that folks might like one for the road."

My face must have shown the amazement I felt. "Mom let you?"

"She only comes in to balance the register at night. Bobby runs the shop, and I run the store." She sounded defensive.

While I wasn't sure where I stood with God—especially with Arthur lying paralyzed in the hospital, and everything in my life up in the air—a growing respect built for this girl who'd become a young woman in my absence.

"Grandma always taught us about Jesus, remember?" Her voice echoed the same awe I carried.

"I remember." This wasn't the first time I'd wished I'd been a better learner. My hands brushed over the Bible as I searched for a price tag. "How much?"

"I give them away." Sarah's quiet answer stilled me.

Before I could comment, the *ding-ding* of another car pulling in for gas drew her attention, and she ducked out of the store to meet the customer.

Free. I could afford that. I tucked it in the back pocket of my jeans and continued to wipe off oily fingerprints from glass and straighten things. The door to the store opened and closed, but I didn't look up because I figured it was Sarah again.

"What are you doing here, child?"

The reaction I had to Clara's voice was just like when I'd played red-light green-light as a kid. I couldn't move for several seconds. Then, as if someone yelled green light, I continued on my path and tossed garbage in the can near the register. "I'm helping out in the store." I cast a sideways glance in her direction.

Her eyes showed surprise. "Why aren't you at the hospital?"

"Why would I be there?" Resentment I'd stuffed down all morning long resurfaced. I tried to clear my throat to hide the bitterness but failed.

"I realize he's not perfect, but…" She stopped when my head snapped up, daring her to finish.

"But what? But he never wanted our baby? But he practically bought me from my mother? But he abandoned me in the middle of nowhere?" The last one I added for drama. I'd have loved to be back in nowhere with Donna and Nick and the known daily expectations of working in the diner. As lonely as I'd been.

Toby's face filled my memory, and I shoved it away.

"Well." She sighed. "Look at me, trying to give you advice." She clucked her tongue and walked over to the coffeepots, pumped a cup full of Columbia blend, and put a dollar on the counter to pay for it. "Glad you're feeling better." She patted my arm as she passed.

Her comforting touch stirred a need inside me as it had on the bus. I wanted my grandma and her wisdom. I wanted someone to tell me what to do, what to think.

"Wait. Please." I walked closer to her. "I'm sorry."

She turned her honey brown eyes to mine. "Oh, dear one, you've been through so much. What do I know, anyway?"

I glanced out the windows, making sure Sarah was tied up helping customers. No one would interrupt us. "Tell me what to do." Desperation slipped a noose around my throat.

"Oh, sweet girl." She wrapped her warm arms around me, and I fell to pieces, sobbing.

I'd cried since Arthur left me. Many times. But this was different. Something broke loose in me, ripped from my clamped-down heart, shook free of the prison I'd built to protect myself. A wail of grief tore from my throat.

Macy

Clara's arms tightened, and she pulled me back through the store, through the storeroom, and outside to the gazebo we kept for families who wanted to picnic under the trees rather than fill their cars with messy travel food.

I sat down next to her on the wooden table. Clara's arm never left my shoulders the whole time. She reached into her sleeve and pulled out a small package of tissues.

"Here now. Blow."

I did. "Tell me what to do." My voice shook as I wiped the tears from my eyes.

"I can't do that."

I knew it. No one knew what I should do. Or if they did, they didn't want to tell me. "I can't see him."

"Okay." She patted my leg.

"You don't get what he's done." A shudder passed through me as I tangled with my emotions. A truck revved its engine, sputtered, and died over in the shop.

"Does it matter?"

What a question. Did it matter what Arthur had done? "Shouldn't it?" I leaned away from her.

"He's the daddy of your son." She shrugged. "He's your husband. You made a commitment to him. A covenant."

"But he didn't hold up his end."

"So you can cancel your side?"

Weren't these all the same reasons I'd given to Toby? Why had my convictions suddenly changed?

Everything springing to my mouth stuck there and died. Suddenly all I could see were Arthur's eyes, full of fear. I wasn't so bitter I couldn't feel sorry for him. Was I?

"You're glad he's being punished."

My head shook no, but inside, wasn't I? I'd felt very justified getting dressed yesterday morning and leaving the hospital without looking back. There wasn't any way he could follow me. When the nurse asked if I'd like to see him, hadn't I said no and meant it? All the way to my bones.

"What if he's not being punished? What if, no matter what kind of man he is, he was going to have a stroke and end up in the hospital?"

Clara nodded her head, as if thinking to herself—or agreeing with someone I couldn't see.

"What do you mean?"

"If he'd been a wonderful man who'd cared for you and cherished you like he promised, and he'd had a stroke, where would you be?" She rubbed her wrinkled hand over my back, like a mother comforting a hurt child.

"That's different. I'd be at the hospital."

Clara nodded. "I've lived a long time and loved a long time. My husband wasn't a perfect man. He did things wrong—so did I. We were both two selfish people in love who had to learn to be selfless." She laughed. "What a long haul that was." Leaning in, she whispered, "I don't regret a minute of it. Do you know why?"

I shook my head. So far the only marriages I'd witnessed were mine and my mother's—not exactly stellar examples.

"It helped me stretch and grow. I learned to be forgiving. I learned to let go of the little things and work on the big ones. I let go of my own expectations and looked to his." She glanced at the boarded ceiling of the gazebo, and I knew she spoke of God. "Marriage helped me learn to be sacrificial."

My spirit balked at the idea. I walked to the other side.

"I'm not learning about anything like that." I crossed my arms and stared out at the evergreens and the glistening grass. "I've given up enough."

Clara chuckled. "What if you were asked to give up everything?"

"God wouldn't want me to." I turned to look at her. "My whole life I've been giving up—my whole life, things have been taken from me. My childhood, my father, my family, my freedom. He wanted to take my child." I took a steadying breath. "I'm done."

A smile of understanding crossed her face. "I hear you, baby." She walked over and hugged me gently. "But what if God's not done?"

Thirty-Four

Arthur had been in the hospital for two days. I hadn't been back. I filled my head with all sorts of reasons, but Clara's words haunted me. What if God wasn't done? Up until now, God had been far away, watching me like my brother used to watch TV. Bobby would take the remote and preprogram two channels so he could flip back and forth. If nothing was on in between commercial breaks, he'd add a third. Flip, flip, trying to keep up, but not really noticing all the details. What if God wanted more from me, and he wasn't just flipping the channels on a supernatural television, going through the motions and keeping an eye on folks here and there? The concept frightened me.

I had never thought of God as accessible. I'd prayed, sure. I wondered what I was supposed to learn from all this—the whole point of life was to learn something, right? Now I was beginning to wonder if that wasn't the whole point at all. Maybe God was more than the ultimate teacher of irony.

I paced around my mother's property, walking past the horses, along the back drive, and ended up staring at our truck. Funny how the thing I'd loathed still felt like home. My gaze focused on the field and the frolicking foals chasing one another as their mother munched grass and acted indifferent.

I opened the cab door and climbed inside before I'd realized what I was doing. I didn't take the driver's seat—that was never my spot. Instead, I settled into my own. The aroma of Brut and Armor All filled my senses. I pushed aside some papers on the dash, kicked off my shoes, and put my feet up, a familiar position for me. Seven long years I'd sat there and been his co-pilot.

Something poked me in the backside, so I reached into my pocket and extracted the small, personal Bible I'd gotten from the store yesterday. I'd read parts here and there last night. Mostly in Matthew. A lot of the stories from Sunday school came flooding back to me. The sower and his seed stuck in my mind the most. I'd pictured Jesus casting seed into the rocks, into the sand, onto the fertile soil. I could see the weeds coming up and choking it off, the wind blowing it away, the few left behind doing their best to take hold and grow.

Maybe some of it had taken hold in my life at one point, but there'd sure been plenty of weeds choking me and winds blowing my feet this way and that. I stared at my feet on the dashboard. They were always running away from wherever I was, as fast as they could.

I'd never taken the time to ask God what he wanted for my life. Not once. I barreled ahead, my focus on escape and independence. A lot of good that did me. Now I couldn't even make up my mind about visiting my ailing husband in the hospital. For the umpteenth time, I wished I'd never tied myself to Arthur.

"I was only sixteen." As soon as I spoke it aloud, I knew I didn't really have an excuse. I'd been watching Sarah in charge of the store, helping customers with gas and purchases. She did it all. When my mother stepped in and tried to give her suggestions, I recognized the look in her eyes. Sarah knew what to do as well as my mother—and maybe she was better at it because she liked doing it. My mother, for all her worries to keep the store and station, really didn't like it there. If I didn't see it as a kid, I sure did now. She resented everything about the shop, about the store. The only thing she really cared about was paying those bills and keeping the family afloat.

Sarah was sixteen. Old enough to know better and do better.

Baby shifted, pushing up under my ribs, and I knew my time of sitting with my feet up high was over. I sat up straighter, patted my stomach, and any self-righteous thoughts I had about my mother fled as I remembered working in the diner and my willingness to do everything I could to keep us safe.

I leaned back against the seat, staring at the knobs and controls on the dash, wondering if I could take over Arthur's routes if I managed to earn my commercial license. At the same time, flitting images of Michael next to me on the long rides from one town to another, screaming at the top of his lungs, went through my mind. There'd be no way I could handle him and a huge, heavily loaded rig through all sorts of weather. I'd have to sell. Barring a miracle, Arthur wouldn't be driving. Anything. Ever.

A book under the console caught my attention. I picked it up and found the lists of Arthur's contacts. I'd never paid much attention to it, but now I flipped through the pages and saw several familiar names—names belonging to customers who'd stopped giving my family their business.

I grabbed Arthur's cell. It still had a battery level, but I hooked up the charger just in case. Flipping it open, I started calling the names of those I knew who'd cut themselves off from my mom. The first was Henry Rollings Trucking.

I scrolled through the saved numbers on Arthur's phone and found it. I held my breath, not knowing if Henry answered his own calls.

"This is Henry." He used his first name. It must have been a personal line.

"Mr. Rollings, this is Macy Stone, Arthur's wife." My tongue suddenly stuck to the roof of my mouth. I'd called without a plan of action. *Lord, please help me.*

"Yes, Macy. How's that old dog doing?" I could almost hear the leer of appreciation in his tone. I wanted to hang up on him, but instead, I forged ahead.

"Not good, I'm afraid. He's had a stroke."

"You don't say? I'm so sorry."

"Thanks. He's in the hospital nearest my family's station."

"That's tough. Arthur being down with everything else happening up there must be difficult."

"Everything else is fine." I wasn't sure what he meant. Had Arthur told him why he'd asked them to quit working with my mom? My face flushed hot with embarrassment and anger.

"Oh good. Everything's well in hand? That's a relief. You know, switching our routes for these past few weeks have actually cost me money. I really need your stop on my route. I'm sure you need us, too. Good to hear."

Something didn't seem right to me. "Well in hand?"

"Of course. You tell Arthur I'll have my trucks heading back up to your family station now that everything's been repaired."

"Repaired?" My head spun as I tried to keep up with the conversation.

"Sure, now the tanks have been replaced. Arthur told me about the underground leaks. I'm sure the EPA was all over your station. They're sticklers, especially now."

The tanks.

I looked down the contacts and saw the letter T listed next to all the canceled contracts.

"Right. Everything's back up and running smooth. It was actually just a misunderstanding. There are no issues with the EPA."

I hung up after a few pleasantries and started calling the others with a different tact altogether. This time, I let them know the tanks were fine after all and they could add our stop back on their routes. I knew perfectly well the tanks were fine, because they'd gotten the EPA approval only a year before I left. They were only about ten years old, so there wasn't a reason in the world they'd need to be replaced.

In an hour's time, I'd gotten back all our old clients—and told them Arthur wouldn't be pulling deliveries any time soon, either. A reluctance to admit aloud that Arthur would never drive again kept me from telling the others about his true condition. As I slipped the contact book back inside the console, my Bible tumbled to the floor and conviction filled me. I looked up at the ceiling.

"Thanks, God." I tucked it back in my pocket, grabbed our expenses ledger, and climbed down out of the cab. The crisp spring air filled my lungs, leaving the sweet tang of pine and cedar in my mouth.

Without Arthur's regular delivery contracts, things were going to get really tight. I was pretty sure my mother couldn't afford to pay me. And I was due any day—no one would hire me at this point. I ran a hand over my extended belly, remembering I was about to be a single parent. Because, either way, it looked like I was on my own.

A visual image of Arthur lying helpless in the hospital formed in my mind. A severe twinge of remorse raced through me. Whatever had come between us, I was still his wife. His threats, though serious sounding, had been little more than a poor attempt at bribery. I'd given up my job, though, to race back and save my family. He'd known I would. He'd also known I wouldn't do it for *him*.

My marriage had come down to manipulation.

I'd read in the papers where people were so bitter at the moment of divorce they no longer mourned what could have been. But I did. I wondered what our life together would have looked like if Arthur had loved me more than himself.

I'd read last night about the Word of God being sown in our lives, but I'd also read about how God hates divorce. I wasn't foolish enough to believe God would want me to stay in a place of danger for me or my baby—but Arthur wasn't in any position to hurt us now.

Did anyone deserve to be deserted and alone like he was?

I trudged back up the muddy road, the ledger under my arm, my hands tucked down deep in my pockets surrounding Baby. The baby's things hadn't come from Donna yet. I'd need to head into town and buy some diapers and supplies.

I went through the backdoor into the house, shutting out the sounds of spring winds and midday traffic. The tick-tock of the grandfather clock met my ears as I pulled out a kitchen chair and opened the ledger.

What I saw shocked the air from my lungs.

Money. Loads of it. Not enough to live on for more than five years—but still, *five* years. And we owned the truck outright. That's right, *we*. He'd put the truck in my name, too. What had Arthur said about saving for retirement? He could have afforded to buy us a little place on the coast. He could have cut out a few longer routes, become a family man, and still retired. The truck was worth thousands by itself.

The front door opened and closed. Bobby walked into the kitchen with my mother following close behind.

"We're not going to be able to pay the gas payment. If things get much worse…" She stopped when she caught sight of me.

I pulled the ledger closer and put my jacket on top of it.

"I don't suppose you've gone to see Arthur yet today?" My mother's voice held more hope than condemnation.

"No."

She sighed. "If he's still not speaking, then there's no hope of him convincing our clients to come back. We're ruined." She sank down into a chair, despondent. Despair came easy to my mother.

"I've already taken care of it."

Both Bobby and my mother's eyes showed surprise.

I shrugged. "I found his client list and read some notations. He told everyone we were getting our tanks replaced. Arthur was bluffing. It wasn't ever a permanent shut out—they would have all come back eventually. Now they'll be back faster."

My mother leapt to her feet and hugged me, laughing in relief. "I knew if you came back, everything would be okay!" I hadn't realized how nice it would be to have my mother's arms locked around me. I leaned into her embrace.

"See, I told you it'd be all right." Bobby tipped his baseball cap at me. "Now Macy can divorce Arthur, keep her baby, and we can get on with life." He sipped his coffee as if he'd said nothing more monumental than it might rain that day. But as soon as he said it, I knew.

I wouldn't leave Arthur.

Thirty-Five

I stood outside Arthur's hospital room, unable to enter, as if an invisible force field held me at bay. My fingers twisted and untwisted my hair so many times I'd gotten it in knots. I reached inside my purse for a brush and straightened it out. I smoothed my dress. I checked the informational pamphlets on a nearby stand. But I didn't go inside.

A nurse excused herself and pushed past me into his room. She pulled the curtain across his bed before I could glimpse his face. Another nurse came in, and they changed his bedding and gave him a bath. Still I stood outside, an observer.

What was I doing here? I didn't owe him anything. My legs itched to turn around and escape.

As soon as the thought passed through my mind, I knew it might not be true. Clara planted the idea of a covenant with me, and I'd looked it up. I didn't like what it said one bit. I'd made a promise to my husband, but I'd also made it to God. And while I wasn't sure yet where that was taking me, I knew I'd better not be burning any bridges quite yet.

The nurses balled up towels and sheets and moved past me when they were done.

"He'll see you now, Mrs. Stone." Somehow they knew it was me. Now Arthur knew, too.

My legs moved like leaden weights as I negotiated the shining linoleum and approached the curtain. As I pulled it back, I saw a man aged. Arthur sat propped up by pillows. He had IV lines hooked to one arm and a blood pressure cuff on the other. The heart monitor beeped. He stared sideways, keeping his eyes on the parking lot and the road beyond, watching the cars and trucks come and go.

"Hi."

Arthur turned his head slightly toward me, bobbing to the side as he did. His left eye and the same side of his mouth sagged and watered. His right eye focused on me. Recognition flashed. He mumbled.

I pulled up a chair and sat next to his bed, staring at his hands, at the floor, at everything but his face. Minutes later, I looked up and saw he still stared at me. I wanted to explain why I hadn't come yesterday. Or the day before. But there seemed little reason to lie so early in our conversation.

"The doctor said you've shown some improvement."

Again, he mumbled. He moved his right arm, reaching out to me, but I shied away. His arm dropped back by his side. He didn't try again. I held his gaze.

"I contacted all the companies you put off of us and told them the tanks were fine. They assured me they'll be back at the beginning of the month." I wanted him to know he held no power over me anymore.

He glanced away from me. A tear slipped from his eye, but I couldn't tell if it was remorse or guilt. Or maybe just moisture. I'd never witnessed a repenting Arthur, so I had no guidelines.

His eye shifted back to mine. He grunted. Maybe that's all I'd ever get from him. The nurse brought in a tray with a cup of thick liquid and a straw as well as a sandwich and juice for me.

"I brought you in some lunch. Don't want you passing out again." She motioned toward the cup. "Would you like to help him eat?"

Handing it to me, she bent the straw and urged me with her eyes. I knew she meant well, but she had no idea how hard it was to be there.

"Thanks, I've got it."

The nurse left us alone and I moved to slip the straw in between his lips. This wasn't something I'd ever expected. I suppose I should have, considering our age differences, but I hadn't. As Arthur's lips grasped the straw, as best he could, I flashed back to my mother feeding my father in much the same way.

By the time he was done sipping, a line of sweat formed on Arthur's forehead, and my hand shook. Dizziness threatened, and I remembered the sandwich and juice. I put down the cup and unwrapped the turkey on wheat. It tasted manufactured, nothing like the sandwiches Nick sent me home with.

I swallowed hard. "I miss my job, the restaurant, my friends." I tried not to think of Toby, but instead lumped him in with Nick and Donna. "Nick sure knew how to cook." I leveled my eyes at him again. "At least you left me in a safe place."

Arthur groaned and glanced away. What could he say? More than that, what did I want him to say?

"I lived over the restaurant. See this dress?" I pulled on my skirt. "It was their daughter, Danny's. She's dead." I wasn't accusing anymore, just sharing. "Sad how she died. She was pregnant, too." I shifted in the chair. My back had begun to ache sitting there for so long, with so much stress.

"Donna liked to push a bit too much, and I didn't care for the mayor, but everyone else was nice and accepting." I stretched and walked to the window, but the discomfort didn't get much better. "I didn't realize how much I'd missed living in one spot." I turned to him. "I know that's not your thing, but when you recover, Arthur, I'm not going back on the road with you permanently. I need a place of my own." I hadn't the heart to tell him he'd never be on the road again, but that wasn't the point of my conversation. I wanted to lay the groundwork for the future. No more pushing me around, no more manipulating me.

Arthur mumbled what sounded like an agreement. I knew it couldn't have been—our whole relationship had been about what he wanted, not what I wanted.

"I had another friend, too. Toby. He really cared about me." I didn't know what possessed me to tell him about Toby right then. "I'd never had a friend like him before." I'd never betrayed Arthur, but I knew, deep down, I could have. I wanted to clear the air of everything. "He took really good care of me." I took a shaky breath. "He loved me."

All the times Toby served me food, took me to the hospital, carried me, and listened to me came rushing back. "Why couldn't you have done that for me, Arthur?" I started to sob. "Why couldn't you have been the man I needed you to be?"

Arthur shook his head a bit, he mumbled, another tear fell, and he reached out to me again with his right hand.

"It didn't have to be this way." I gasped for breath, dizzy with anger and regret. My back ached something awful. I couldn't find a comfortable position. I stood up, hoping to relieve the discomfort. My emotions swirled out of control, and a sharp pain shot through my back and around my groin.

My knees buckled out from under me, and I hit the floor, hard. "Oh!" Liquid poured down my legs and puddled under me. "No, not now. Not now." Panic filled me as I tried to find my focal point and breathe. Arthur mumbled rapidly, his hand searched the bed for a call button. The foot of the bed began to rise. He hit the other button, over and over, and the head of the bed lowered. I thought I heard him cuss.

A nurse came rushing in and scooped me up. Another nurse shuffled me to a wheelchair and rolled me out of Arthur's room. I could hear him mumbling and grunting. If I hadn't known better, I would have thought he was worried.

As the nurse wheeled me into the elevator and up to the birthing wing, I could only think one thing: STOP.

All of this needed to end. I wasn't ready. My husband lay in the hospital, incapacitated. Not to mention I didn't have a thing with me. No diaper bag, no overnight bag, no clothes.

In Bridgeville, I'd had everything I needed. An apartment, a stroller, a car seat—even though I didn't have a car. I had a doctor and supportive friends. I never pictured bringing home Baby to my old bedroom—naked. All the hope I mustered sank within me.

Why did this keep happening? Every time I had things under control, something tore it from my hands. Pain built, ebbed, and hit again. Natural childbirth. *Seriously?* Who thought that up? I couldn't do this.

"Can I help?"

My eyes lost focus, but my ears honed in on Clara's voice. My hand moved with a life of its own, gripping hers, holding fast. I wasn't about to let go.

"There, there, child. All will be well."

"How did you know?" I panted and gritted the words out, one by one.

"I was praying for you this morning. I felt the Lord leading me down here—I thought to check on Arthur—but I can see he had a different purpose now." She patted my arm.

"Mrs. Stone?" The unfamiliar voice cut through my anguish. "Would you like this woman to stay?"

"Yes," I hissed.

Three hours later, I'd transitioned, and Baby had shifted into position.

Clara, still at my side, hummed some sort of hymn—familiar, but I couldn't place it. Another contraction hit, and she gasped and wiggled her fingers.

"Take it easy now, I've got arthritis." She chuckled, but I knew I'd hurt her. She patted my hand. "You listen to me. I've done this three times. The best advice I got was to breathe."

As I did, my death-grip relaxed. As I listened to her hum, my pain decreased enough for me to speak. "Drugs."

"You could, baby, but I'll tell you, they gave me a shot that left me all dizzy and disconnected. I couldn't talk—so they thought I felt better. It hurt just as much after as before."

The idea of being in pain and not being able to talk—I couldn't imagine how much more trapped I'd feel. An image of Arthur, laying alone, head bandaged, unable to move or speak flashed in front of my eyes.

The doctor moved into the edge of my vision, pulling on scrubs. "Too late for that." She motioned for the nurse.

Another contraction hit, then another. The roller coaster cart kept going higher and higher, ratcheting up with no sign of stopping. Where was the respite in between I'd read about? A burning pain tore through me. I felt my knees being moved apart, my hips being moved down farther on the bed.

"Here he comes."

No. Wait. I can't.

Clara's arms surrounded my shoulders and lifted me. The bed hummed to life beneath, meeting my back in support.

"Macy?"

Somehow the doctor's voice, calling me, made its way to my brain. I nodded.

"You need to push now. The next time a contraction hits, you bear down."

As soon as she said it, a contraction like no other struck. I bore down. The relief I needed met me there. I wanted to push again—anything to get rid of the pain.

"Breathe, now, breathe!"

Make up your mind! I couldn't breathe and push at the same time. She was nuts.

The heart rate monitor beeped rapidly. An oxygen mask strap lowered over my head, around my face. The cold hiss of oxygenated air startled me and tickled my nose.

"The baby needs oxygen, and so do you. Breathe deep, now." The nurse sounded like a sergeant major. I obeyed.

"Good."

"Michael?" I'd inwardly called my son by his name, but now the name came out fully formed as fear pushed past the pain.

"Who's Michael? I thought her husband's name was Arthur?"

Clara spoke for me. "She's worried about the baby."

"Macy, you keep breathing deep and pushing hard—Michael's going to be fine." My hope grasped hold of her words, and I prayed she'd be right.

Thirty-Six

I awoke the next morning with Michael swaddled in the bassinet next to me. He slept soundly, making tiny noises of contentment. I waited for the wash of nausea which always accompanied my waking, but there wasn't any. It'd been so long, I fully expected the vomiting to continue. As the nurse came in with a breakfast tray, I joyfully announced, "I didn't throw up this morning!"

She didn't seem as excited as I was. She motioned toward the baby. "You'll need to nurse him again as soon as you can."

I'd read all the literature, but I hesitated. He'd only been asleep for a couple hours. Weren't there wise words about never waking a sleeping baby?

"He needs to move fluids through to clean out his system. And it will help you bond." The nurse handed me Michael, and he shifted against my breast, nature kicking in as he recognized my scent.

I loved him immediately. The minute they laid him on me last night, my world had settled into clarity. I would do anything to protect him, go anywhere to keep him safe, love him forever. I started to nurse him and spoke in soft tones, assuring him of my devotion.

The nurse whispered, "You're a natural. I'll leave you alone. If you need anything, hit the call button."

I kept my eyes on Michel and looked up as she left. What I saw startled me. Packages of diapers and gift bags covered the couch. There were blankets, a large teddy bear, and a stroller, too.

At first I thought my things must have arrived and my mother brought them over—but these were new things, in shiny wrappings and sporting gift cards. Tears of gratefulness streamed down my cheeks as I remembered my last thoughts about bringing Michael home naked. I could offer him nothing, but there was someone else who knew my worries without my speaking them aloud, and he had provided.

On the table nearest me sat a bouquet of flowers. I slid sideways, regretting my movements a bit because I seemed to be sore everywhere. The books didn't tell me giving birth would work every muscle I had to the max. Although if they had described it all in greater detail, no one would ever dare to get pregnant in the first place.

I pulled the card from the vase and read the inscription. "Many blessings on this happy day, Love Donna and Nick."

How'd they know? Did Toby know?

I'd rightly put distance between Toby and me. He had things to work out, and I was married. But it didn't mean I didn't miss him or wish to talk to him. He'd been the best friend I'd ever had. He'd loved me.

A tear slipped down my cheek, then another. I shifted Michael to my other breast and kissed his head in the process. I'd never thought about how being married—or who I was married to—would affect my whole life, or my child's life. What a mess I'd made of things. My conflicted conscience tossed my emotions this way and that. How could I regret marrying Arthur but be grateful for Michael at the same time?

A soft knock sounded on my hospital room door. Clara poked her gray head inside and gave me a big smile. "Didn't wake you or the little one, did I?"

"No, we're awake. It's breakfast time." I tucked the blanket over my shoulder, trying to be discreet but failing miserably. Clara came over and showed me how, speaking softly to me the whole time, erasing any embarrassment I had.

"What a beautiful boy. Strong boy."

I'd never felt cozy or proud when my mother or siblings were admired, but the sense of pride and warmth filling me with her compliments made me sit taller in the bed. A grin broke across my face—as if I'd had anything to do with who he was or how he looked.

"Does Arthur know?"

I sank back down. I'd been subconsciously pretending I was a single mother. Hearing Arthur's name made me feel like someone ripped the bedclothes from me, exposing us. "I'm not sure."

Clara looked up at me, her wise eyes saddened. "I know this isn't easy, but he should see his son."

"The son he wanted to get rid of?"

The animosity that followed my words choked me. I'd promised myself I'd be loving and peace-filled for Michael all the days of his life. I'd already failed, and he hadn't been out in the world for twenty-four hours yet. As if he sensed my tension, he squirmed and let out a small cry. I shifted him and started to swaddle him when I felt the wetness of his diaper beneath my hand.

I tied my nightgown closed, swung my legs over the side of the bed, and put Michael in the bassinet. Heading to the couch, I grabbed a package of newborn diapers and baby wipes.

"Can I help?"

"No. I'm familiar with changing diapers." There. Bitterness again. My shoulders slumped. Hadn't Clara stayed with me through the labor, let me squeeze her hand to dust, and sat with me an hour after he was born? "I'm sorry. Again."

Clara gave me soft smile.

I reached down for the wipes and noticed a new little outfit. "Clara, do you know where this all came from?"

"The women's ministry at my church. I told them there was a new mom going through a hard time."

"Why would they do that? I don't even attend there." They probably wouldn't want me if they knew everything.

"Because you have a need, and they want you to know that God hasn't forgotten you."

I took a shuddering breath and shook my head. God should forget about me.

"What's on your mind, baby?"

"I've made such a mess of my life, Clara. I've prayed God would fix it all. But he doesn't. In fact, it seems to be getting worse." Glancing down at Michael, I regretted those words, too. "Except for Michael, I mean." I changed his diaper, wrapped a clean blanket around him, and lay back against my bed, holding him close.

"God can't erase our mistakes or their consequences—how I wish he would. But he can help you change your heart and make something good out of it." She chuckled. "Although, his making something good can take awhile."

My head hung low. I knew she was right. As much as I wanted a magic-genie-in-a-bottle-god, I would rather have the One True God I'd been reading about in the Bible. The One who wanted to be in a real relationship, not a distant pen pal.

Pushing back my hair, I fingered the oily mess crowning my head and could only imagine the amount of filth crusting over my body.

"Could you watch the baby while I take a shower?" I knew I'd be able to think better once I was clean.

"Sure. Let me get settled on the couch and you hand him down to me."

After handing Michael off, I grabbed a fresh gown and hobbled into the bathroom. In the mirror I spied dark circles, exhaustion, and amazingly spiky hair. The women on TV shows always looked fresh and rested after birth—even on the most dramatic shows. But then, they had professionals to fix their hair and makeup.

I stepped in cautiously, leaning against the shower wall as the water sprayed down, washing away the sweat and blood. Images flashed in my mind of the birth, the fear of losing Michael, the grief of having no husband to share this with.

Arthur. Could I trust him, and would he care?

"God, I'm not strong enough to do this." My spongy tummy, emptied of Michael, increased my sense of loneliness. An idea tickled in my mind, and I knew I didn't have to be. "I've gone my own way for the last time. I'm tired of doing it my way. I can't do it without you. I'm so sorry for all the wrong I've done. Please forgive me. Jesus, will you help me? I'm so alone."

And then, I wasn't. The God of my childhood, the Savior of the world, was there for the asking. Gratefulness filled me. I never had to be alone again.

Salty tears streamed down my cheeks as I soaped my hair, my body, and rinsed it away. Looking down, I watched the blood and suds pool and wind around the drain, until finally the water ran clear and clean.

Stepping from the shower, dizzy and weak, I leaned against the wall, its coolness pressing against my cheek. As I dressed, I caught a glimpse of myself in the mirror again. Dark circles and exhaustion still hovered, but my eyes held a new hope.

Back in the room, Clara waited, humming one of her hymns to Michael, who slept soundly. She glanced up, her eyes widening in concern at my hunched-over state.

"You need to eat something, child. Climb into bed and have your breakfast."

The nurse came in to check on me, taking my vitals and quizzing me on going to the bathroom, my soreness, and checking my bleeding. She pressed against my abdomen—I knew she wanted to help me recover, but it hurt.

"Make sure you finish that food, and then try nursing your son again." She made notes on my chart and gave me a slight smile, parting her mouth as if she wanted to add something else, but didn't.

I asked her instead. "How's my husband today?"

I hadn't called him my husband in a long time. Not like that—like he belonged to me.

"He's doing better. I think he's worried about you."

I wanted to dispel any concerns she had, but Clara interrupted me. "Could you please bring in a wheelchair so Macy can show him the baby?"

Whenever Clara spoke, her tiny frame and tone carried such authority no one questioned her.

"Of course, ma'am." The nurse ducked out for a moment and came back, pushing the chair near the bed. "I'd rest for a bit first. Get your blood sugar up and give your body a bit of time before bringing on any more stress."

I gave her a nod and took bites of cold egg and toast. After the nurse left, Clara shuffled over with Michael.

"Where do they find this stuff?" Her lip curled and covered her nostrils to block out the unsavoriness. "I'll bring you back a nice meaty, iron-rich burger and green salad this afternoon. I know just the place in town to get one. You need to eat more protein." She swayed, humming to Michael.

I continued to eat. "I worked in a diner."

"Did you? Miss their food, do you?"

I grinned. "Yes. Nick made the best chicken-fried steak and mashed potatoes."

"Real ones?"

"Everything was real there." I released a sigh, and my eyes filled with tears. "They cared about us, me and the baby."

Clara murmured sympathetically.

"And there was Toby."

An empathetic smile crossed her face. "Treat you real good, did he?"

It was all I could do to nod. I'd never spoken aloud about Toby and my feelings all this time, except to Arthur. I thought if I kept it to myself, then I wouldn't have to admit how I cared.

"He wanted me to run away with him."

She reached out and took my hand. "I know it's hard to hear, but you did the right thing. Somehow you're going to have to learn to trust the Lord in what's happening here."

Tears spilled down my cheeks unchecked.

"If he hadn't cared..." I stopped. Wishing away my experiences wouldn't do any good. Part of me was glad Toby cared, and the other half resented it because now I knew. I knew what that felt like.

"I know, baby. We can be fooled into thinking life's fine if we don't look past ourselves—but when something comes along to reveal it isn't, it's hard to take." She laid Michael in my arms. His barely-seven-pound form snuggled closer, and he made sweet cooing sounds. She put her hands on my head in a gentle caress and closed her eyes.

"Lord, please take these burdens from Macy, if you will. But if not, help her carry them and give her your peace and strength to carry on. Amen."

No one had ever prayed over me. Humbled and honored, I took her hand. "Thank you."

"I'll be back in a couple hours with your lunch. You feed your boy and get a nice nap. Then we'll go see Arthur."

My head snapped up. "You'll go with me?" Relief washed me from head to foot.

"You're not alone, Macy." Her words carried a double meaning that echoed with me throughout the day.

Thirty-Seven

As Clara rolled my wheelchair down the hall, closer and closer to Arthur's room, I fought the urge to shove my stocking feet against the slippery linoleum and turn us around. It would have made quite a picture, too. The only thing keeping me from trying it was the baby—I didn't want him to think of me as a chicken. Plus, I might drop him in the melee.

We pulled up outside Arthur's room, and I heard mumbling and grunting from inside. The door whipped back, and the attending doctor stopped short of running into us. "Oh good. I'm so glad you're here. We've been trying to keep him calm, but ever since you left last night, he's been very agitated."

A frustrated groan and more mumbling emitted from behind the curtain. Fear fled, and suddenly I needed to see if Arthur was okay. I motioned Clara ahead and we rounded the curtain, pulling up next to the bed. Arthur looked pale and thinner than yesterday. His gaunt face, strained on one side, lax on the other, cradled frenzied eyes. As his gaze locked on me and Michael, his grunts quieted and his form relaxed.

"I'll be back in a bit." Clara patted my shoulder, and I heard the door slide closed behind her.

Arthur's right eye drifted from Michael to me and back to the baby again. Using the bed with one hand, I pulled us closer to him. I reached out and touched his arm. He sighed, relaxed, and closed his eyes, falling into a deep sleep. I climbed from the wheelchair to the recliner near his bed and closed my own eyes.

An hour later, Michael fussed us both awake. The room temperature had dropped, so I pulled the extra blanket from Arthur's closet over us and cuddled down to feed the baby. I tried to hum a tune, but failed miserably. No one wanted to hear me sing—I hadn't a clue why I thought humming would be any better.

Feeling watched, I looked up into Arthur's alert face. I pulled the blanket closer, hiding away my nursing.

"Feeling better?"

Arthur grunted. This would be our relationship from now on. Me peppering him with yes and no questions and him grunting. I closed my eyes against the desperate thoughts racing through my head.

I opened them again, finding him staring at the baby, a curious look on his face.

"Michael. I named him Michael."

"Miiiii," he mumbled. His face grew red, and the vein on the side of his head pulsed.

"It's okay."

He shook his head and grumbled something I couldn't decipher.

Michael finished nursing on one side, so I shifted him to the other. My breast ached, as the books foretold, so I knew my milk was coming in. My mother hadn't been able to nurse—business and unwillingness killed her desire to try—so I wasn't sure if I'd be successful. Seemed as though Michael and I were a perfect fit, though. I pulled the blanket higher, not wanting Arthur to see.

He watched anyway, and then shut his eyes again, seeming to sleep. I had a very clear image of our life together. I'd spend the next three years feeding, changing, and washing Arthur and the baby. Maybe I'd get them on the same schedule?

The phrase "coming full circle" took on a new meaning for me. Sobs shook me to my core, and I pressed my free palm to my mouth to stifle them. How could it be the very thing I ran from was what I'd returned to, but more so, and more awfully?

Once Michael finished, I stood and moved to the window to look out over the parking lot. Groups of people came and went under me with no idea I looked down on them. "Jesus? I don't think I can do this." I held Michael up so his tiny head fit into the crook of my neck and rhythmically patted his back. I continued to cry and pray until the door pushed open. Assuming the nurse had returned, I wiped my tears and turned to face her. Instead, I found my mother there.

"When I didn't find you in your room, I figured you'd be here." Her gaze rested on Arthur for a moment, sadness filling her eyes, and then it left, like drawing a curtain over her emotions. I wondered if she felt about hospitals like I used to.

They were about to become a daily part of my life.

"Your things arrived today, so I unpacked and washed a couple outfits and brought the car seat. But turns out, I didn't need to after all. Where'd you get all those gifts?"

"Clara's church." I moved to the recliner and sank down into it.

"Why'd they do that?" She smiled at the baby and moved closer.

"To be nice." I thought for a moment. "How did Nick and Donna find out about the baby?"

"Donna wanted to be sure you made it home safe and called. I told her you'd had the baby."

My mother's eyes looked hungrily at Michael and I pulled him closer. "It was nice they sent the flowers."

She nodded and pushed her hair back from her face. She wiped her hands on her jeans and held out her arms. "Can I hold him?"

When Clara asked to hold Michael, I didn't think twice about it. When my mother asked, apprehension must have shown on my face, because she paled and then tucked her hands back in her pockets. "Never mind."

I made a lame excuse. "He's just fallen to sleep. Maybe later?"

"Sure." She turned to Arthur. "How's he doing?"

"Not great. He can't speak."

"That'll come in time."

I sighed, wishing my mother didn't toss out false hope like candy at a parade. Every now and then it'd fly true, but most of the time, she missed her mark.

"Well, it could." She sounded exasperated. What was it about mothers and daughters where each one thought they could read the thoughts of the other? Maybe we could. Tension mounted in the room, and I found myself wishing she'd leave. Instead she took a seat. "What are your plans?"

My head shot up. "Plans?"

She cleared her voice. "Yes. Like where you're going to live and how you're going to manage care for Arthur."

Where was I going to live?

"I thought…" I stopped. "I mean, can't I stay until things settle down?"

"For a bit, I guess. But you need to find a place of your own. I can't afford to feed and clothe you, let alone cover his hospital bills." She tipped her head Arthur's way.

I'd forgotten she didn't know I had money. She still thought of me as a child—a child with an invalid husband and newborn baby, but a child nonetheless. I'd been thinking of the emotional support more than the financial. Silly me.

"Don't worry, I'll take care of it." I set my mouth, anger swelling.

"You don't have to get upset, Macy. I only want what's best for everyone. As soon as you've gotten into a routine, you'll see, it'll start to feel normal." She cleared her voice and looked down at the floor.

"Did you tell yourself that when Daddy was dying?"

Her face shocked white, and her mouth trembled in rage. "How dare you?"

How did I? *Easy.* I sat up taller. "If I didn't know better, I'd say you were pleased by the turn of events. What did I ever do to you to make you so spiteful?"

My mother bit her lip, and a single tear pooled and streaked down her cheek before she cuffed it away. "I stayed by his bed, night and day. I fed him, bathed him, changed his diapers, treated his sores. I reeked of urine and sickness for months after he'd died." She wrenched at her hands in her lap as if they were still repulsive to her. "I wouldn't have complained, but he never thanked me. He never appreciated any of it." A sob tore from her throat. "And I could have lived with that, but he'd ask to see you, every day, as if what I did didn't matter."

Blood pounded in my ears and I gasped. He'd wanted to see me? The thing I'd wanted most was to be with the person who loved me the easiest. "Why didn't you let me in?"

"Because he was *my* husband. I gave up everything when I married him. I loved him—but he never appreciated me. He didn't love me."

My head shook in tiny convulsions. "I heard him," I choked. "I heard him tell you."

Macy

"No. No matter what he said, if he did, he wouldn't have left me here in the middle of nothing running a stinky gas station I never wanted. I gave up college, I gave up my dreams. You don't ask someone to do that. You just don't—and then go and die."

I'd suspected there was more to her story than I'd learned. Disappointments, bitterness, anger—but right then, I didn't care. It had been true—she'd really kept me from him. I knew my father loved me and the other kids equally. I could see it in his eyes, in the way he did things with them, the gentle touches and encouraging words whenever they tried new things. But we had a connection, a special understanding. We never spoke of it, but it was there. Maybe it was because I was his firstborn. We loved to fish together off the bridge over the Elk, or take long hikes up into the woods to watch the wildlife. He'd share things about his childhood and tell me stories. Sometimes we would get the giggles for no reason at all. It used to make her angry. I never knew why until now.

She'd been jealous all those years. No wonder when Arthur offered to marry me she'd jumped at the chance. A prickle inside told me it wasn't so easy, but right then I wanted to wallow in my fury. The sun shifted behind the clouds, and the room went darker. I sat shaking with disgust, unable to form a coherent thought.

"Ouuu," Arthur mumbled from the bed. We both jumped, having forgotten we'd had an audience.

He glared at my mother and pointed a hand toward the door. "Ouuuus." He was telling her to leave.

I'd forgotten for a moment my mother had turned Arthur down for my father. It could have as easily been her sitting here in this recliner, preparing to nurse him for the rest of his life, as me. Either way, she would have ended up nursing her husband and been tied down.

"You'd better leave. He shouldn't be upset." Until that moment, I hadn't cared what Arthur wanted, and I didn't much—but if that would get her to leave, all the better.

"Fine. I'll go. Let me know your plans to move out, Macy." She lightened her words as if she hadn't broken my heart and Arthur's in the same moment.

I wiped at the tears on my cheeks and shifted Michael in my arms before turning my attention to Arthur. It'd been the first time I could remember since our engagement that he'd protected me, and he was doing it incapacitated from a hospital bed.

Compassion filled me. Nothing was easy. I looked back on my television-watching days, where everything wrapped up in an hour or less, where happy endings were mandatory, where the plot's twists and turns could be advertised with household cleaners and insurance policies.

There'd been a time in my youth when I would have chased my mother down in the hall and demanded to understand her. But now, I didn't have the energy to care. I made a silent pact with the Lord that I'd never do that to Michael.

I turned my attention to Arthur. "Do you need anything?"

Arthur nodded and waved a shaky hand at the water glass. I moved Michael to the bed, cradled him in between Arthur's legs and reached for the glass to refill it from the pitcher. As I held the cup up and positioned the straw between his lips, he took slobbery sips, losing much of it down his chin. I moved my other hand to close his lips around the straw and he took deeper gulps. Then he nodded and sighed, satisfied.

I put the glass back down and went to move Michael.

"Nohw."

"You want me to leave him?" I didn't expect Arthur to have a change of heart about the baby. But he nodded, and so I sat on the edge of the bed, making sure they were both stable. The sun broke through the clouds, casting a bright streak over the floor, lighting the room to the point I winced at first, but didn't close the curtains.

Arthur hummed a soft tune, rocking slightly, and we sat there together, bathed in sunlight, exhausted from life, hoping tomorrow would be a little better.

Thirty-Eight

"You ready to go, sis?" Bobby had the last of the baby's things under his arms, shifting his gaze out the door. He had better things to do—but I was grateful he came to help.

The nurse came flying in with a wheelchair. "All set then?" I took a seat, holding Michael in my arms, and we trundled down the hall to the elevator and then out to the pull-through in front of the hospital.

After the nurse checked to see if the car seat was installed in Bobby's truck properly, we pulled out of the Sacred Heart lot and headed home. I glanced up at Arthur's hospital room window, seeing the GET WELL balloon swaying over the heat register. Misgiving shivered through me, but I pushed it away. I'd be back soon to check on him. I had to get home—or find us a home.

"Have you heard of any rentals in the area?"

"Huh?" He glanced my way, surprise on his face. "You just got home."

"Mom…" I stopped. Bobby, Sarah, and Brynn had a different relationship with our mother than I did. "Mom thought we should get settled soon and start a regular routine." I remembered the doctor's orders about Arthur needing physical therapy daily once he'd been released. "Also, I need to buy a car." I took a deep breath. "But first, I need to get my license."

"You don't have one?"

I almost laughed. "I never finished my hours of practice before we got married. And once we were married, Arthur drove the rig. I can practice on the property and then take the test."

"He never taught you to drive the truck?"

"No." I didn't mention that Arthur didn't think I was smart enough to do it. *You'd lose your head if it wasn't hooked on.* He didn't trust me to handle the truck.

The words hung in the cab. If Bobby thought anything of it, he didn't let on. For me, though, it helped form another picture of myself. And not a great one. Michael let out a small fuss, and I quickly tucked his bright green infant pacifier in his mouth.

"I'll ask around. You'll need something easy to get Arthur in and out of. And a wheelchair, right?"

A heaviness sank down on me, pressing me into the seat, nearly through the truck floor, to the gravely road below. "Right."

"Probably a minivan. I'll put the word out. You don't want one from out where we are, though. Our road kills vans. The shocks and transmission will already be shot. You'll want to buy one from in town."

"Got it." Bobby knew his stuff. He was very much our father's son. The idea made me smile. "Dad would be really proud of you."

Bobby shot me a white, toothy grin. "You think so?"

"Yeah. I think so." I punched him in the arm.

"I really like running the shop. Going to mechanic school would help me out a lot. But Mom says there's no money. I can't run off, she needs me." He bit his lip.

"Would you like to?" An idea started forming in my mind.

"Sure. And I'd like to take some business classes, too. I could take all the pressure off of Mom if she'd let me. But you remember how she can be."

Did I ever. "Maybe I can talk to her."

We drove past a bank of older houses, and my eyes scanned the streets. As much as I liked the peace and solitude of the country, it wouldn't be realistic for me to live out there so far from medical help.

"Sorry things have worked out this way for you." Bobby's deep voice cut through my plans.

"It's okay."

"It's not." He flashed a look sideways before concentrating on the road again. "When you married Arthur, I was too naive to realize how young you were." He cleared his voice. "I realize now things were rough." He paused. "Why'd you do it, Macy?"

"I really thought it was the best decision at the time. We were in love." Or so I'd thought. "I could blame it on youth, Bobby, but that's a cop out. I wanted to leave home, and Arthur gave me the opportunity." I didn't say I wanted to get away from our mother, or from the responsibilities of raising her children for her, or from the daily boredom of my life, or the aching, gaping hole left when Daddy died. I didn't resent Bobby, Brynn, or Sarah any more than I could resent Michael. It wasn't their fault.

"Do you regret it?"

For some reason, his question made me laugh. "I'm going to say something really stupid and cliché." I reached over and tucked the blankets around Michael. "No. Because I have him."

Bobby drove on, satisfied with my answer, and I closed my eyes. A bump in the road brought me back to the present. We were pulling into the driveway of the house already.

I stretched. "Thanks for the ride."

After Bobby pulled up to the front steps, he put a hand on my arm. "Whatever you need me to do, I'm here for you." The gravity of his words, the piercing look in his eyes, told me he meant it.

"Thanks." I squeezed his hand. "I'm glad I'm not alone."

My mother opened the front screen, but her eyes swam in misgiving. Brynn and Sarah came around from the front of the store carrying balloons, excitement shining on their faces.

"Welcome home!" The girls started to jabber about being aunts and fighting over who got to baby-sit first. My mother unloaded my things and carried them inside the door, setting them by the window. I got the point.

Bobby left for the shop and Brynn for a friend's house. Sarah gave me a hug and went to the store, leaving Mom and me. "I'll contact a realtor after I feed Michael." I moved past her and closed my bedroom door between us. Much to my surprise, a rocker sat in the corner of my room—the rocker my mother must have spent hours in when Bobby and I were babies, and that I spent hours in later rocking Sarah and Brynn.

As I settled in and started to nurse, she knocked on the door.

"It's open." I pushed back and forth, not making eye contact with her.

"I thought you'd like it. You could take it with you."

When I left. I got it.

"I'd like to take my bed, too." I wasn't sure how long Arthur's money would last us, especially with all his medical bills, so I didn't want to replace things I didn't need to. Maybe I could find another furnished place, like I had over the restaurant. An ache resonated in my chest.

"It's all yours. I was thinking of knocking out this wall to expand the living room, or making an office for Bobby."

I glanced up at her, wondering why she waited until I was home to demolish my room. "Speaking of Bobby, I think you should let him go to school."

Mom gave me a *don't start* look, but I continued. "He's going to own this place someday, isn't he? A bit more burden on you now would free you up later and make him more ready to take it on."

"I never wanted this for him." Her voice faltered. "I thought someday we'd sell and retire."

"What's wrong with being a mechanic? He loves it, and he's good at it."

"I wanted more for him."

But not for me? "And Sarah loves working in the store. She's really good with people. I don't know what Brynn's good at yet, because we haven't had time to get reacquainted."

"It's easy for you to say because they're not yours. When Michael grows up, do you want him to work in a garage for the rest of his life?" Resentment rang in my bedroom.

I looked down at Michael, wanting to give a thoughtful answer. I'd been very happy waitressing. It wasn't for everyone. But I'd loved seeing the regulars every day and listening to their conversations. I liked knowing how someone took their eggs, or that their wife couldn't cook like Nick, or how they spent their birthday in the diner because all their family had died, and they didn't want to be alone. I wanted to be part of their Thanksgivings and Christmases. I liked slipping them an extra piece of pie, or giving their shoulder a squeeze because they'd had a cruddy day.

Being part of their makeshift family felt more like home than this did.

I looked deep into her eyes. "No matter what Michael chooses to do, I hope I support him. Because if he loves it, then it's not a waste."

Her mouth hung open as if I'd insulted her. Then she sniffed. "Good luck with that." She turned to leave.

"Let him go to school. I'll pay for it." I hadn't meant to say anything. I'd snuggled with Bobby on cold mornings before the furnace kicked in. For weeks after our dad died, I'd held him late into the night while he. I fed him breakfast and did his laundry and got him off to school for three years. I'd given up my dreams for a fast escape. I didn't want him to lose out on his.

"How?"

"I've got to sell the rig." Everything started to come together.

"You'd do that for Bobby?"

"It's his and your best chance." And maybe Sarah and Brynn's, too.

"What about all Arthur's medical bills?"

I shifted Michael to the bed, propping him between two pillows so he couldn't roll over. "I have some money in savings, and Arthur has insurance from the union. We'll work it out." I yawned.

"If I let him go, he won't come back." Her voice, barely audible, shook. It cost her to admit it. Fear drove my mom. I'd never noticed it before—but it hung around her eyes and mouth, drawing them into tight, untrusting bundles. Maybe that's why she'd been attracted to my father. I couldn't remember him ever saying he was afraid of anything.

"Bobby will come back. He loves this place."

My mother started to leave, and then turned, watching me lay down next to Michael. Her eyes softened. "I'll think about it."

"Good." I curled up, ignoring her. Complete exhaustion stole me away and took me to a dark, quiet place where no one wanted anything from me.

Thirty-Nine

Bobby found me a car by day two. The car had been left at the garage for repairs and then the owner reneged on payment, so Bobby kept it for a loaner. He said I could use it until I found something permanent. It wouldn't hold Arthur with his wheelchair, and all the baby gear, but for now, it would get me back and forth. Everything came back to me—maybe I'd absorbed information just watching Arthur drive all those miles. It only took me couple weeks driving around the property to get the knack again. Good thing it was an automatic.

The glowing red sign over the DMV counter flashed my number and I went up to take the exam. She took my information—which now consisted of a marriage certificate, birth certificate, proof of residence and social security card. I couldn't believe how hard it was to prove who I was. She wrote it all down and pointed me to a kiosk with computers. No more written tests.

I sat down and began. Most of the answers came to me fast. I knew all about the rules of the road. Something good had come from my traveling across the country for all those years. Local laws were a bit more complicated, but I did okay. Missed two. I could live with that.

I went back up to the counter and she gave me a smile.

"Good job. Let's get you signed up for the driving test." She started to move away, but I stopped her.

"I already made the appointment."

She checked the register. "Well, then, you sit on down and I'll tell the instructor you're ready."

A few minutes later, an older man, clipboard in hand, motioned me to follow him out to their test car.

"I'm Josiah Williams. I'll be your examiner today." We climbed into the car and he had me back up, drive around the lot, park and pointed me to the main road.

Every once in a while he'd make a note on the clipboard. As I drove down the road, I felt the need to fill the tense silence with conversation.

"So, how'd you get into this line of work?"

"I used to teach it at the high school, but that about killed me." He made a note. "Now, I just see if you know what you're doing rather than risk my life with those kids. Eyes on the road please." He made another note.

The conversation didn't do much for my tension levels, so I stopped trying. As we pulled back into the lot, he showed me where to park. I turned off the engine and handed him the keys, holding my breath.

He made a couple more notes and then signed the bottom before handing me my copy. "You did quite well, Mrs. Stone. Don't forget to check your mirrors when pulling out, and changing lanes." He put his hand out and shook mine. *I did it?*

"Head on inside and get your photo taken for your temporary license."

"Thanks. So much." I watched him walk back inside the DMV and a sense of pride and accomplishment filled me. I sighed. I'd done it. I'd passed.

Another accomplishment to prove to Arthur I wasn't just capable, but more than able to handle things. He'd abandoned me, but I found a job. I stood up to him about keeping Michael. I took good care of him, too.

And now this. I could drive. "Yes!" I spoke in triumph to the sky, holding up my test to the heavens to show God I'd done it. As I headed inside, a little voice tempted me to pack Michael and our belongings in my loaner car and drive off, not look back. Nothing could stop me now.

The other voice, the one growing stronger every day, told me that it wasn't right. That, even if Arthur didn't deserve it, I should show him love. Because I didn't deserve it, and God loved me.

The next day, as I entered Arthur's room, I realized how normal this routine had become to me. I'd grown numb to the hospital sounds and smells. Arthur gave me the customary grumble. But when I wheeled Michael's stroller into the room, he turned away. I ignored his indifference and situated us by his bed. I sensed his moodiness as easily now as I had before. Although, when we were stuck in the truck together, I felt much more reluctant to talk about it.

"What's wrong?" I moved to his chart and read the notes. The nurse came in and gave me a soft smile. I'd grown used to that, too. Sympathy from most of them, disgust from a couple. Nurses and doctors seemed more willing to look at us as humans in a difficult situation, rather than judgmental like the rest of the world. One or two assumed Arthur was my father, but they only made that mistake once.

At one time, I would have been troubled—but that was before a double-dose of reality. Now I needed people who were on my team, and if they weren't, I had no place for them in my life. I had no trouble standing up for myself. And if they didn't show us respect, I asked for them to be reassigned.

"Looks like he's refusing food." I looked at the nurse. "Can't you just hook another line up, or a feeding tube?" I handed her his chart. Arthur gave a groan of protest, but I ignored him.

"The doctor feels Arthur needs to come to terms with things. We'd rather not force him right now. If he doesn't improve, we'll have to decide on the next steps. For now, he's well hydrated, and his vitals are good." She hung the chart on the end of his bed and checked his lines, blood pressure, and listened to his chest. She gave a frown and listened again. "I hear a couple rattles in there. I'll have the doctor come by and listen."

She peeked in at Michael sleeping soundly in his carrier/stroller. "He's a lovely boy. He looks like you."

I thanked her, and she left.

People said things like that to make you feel prouder. Or because they couldn't think of what else to say. I thought Michael's red hair was beautiful—my mother, on the other hand, said I should ready myself for a stubborn, willful child. The tone in which she said it got my back up. She'd already decided not to like him—at least that's how it appeared to me. She kept warning me about him, as if this helpless three-week-old baby being born would have a negative effect on the whole of my life. I gained more and more insights into her personality, almost daily.

I didn't think she ever wanted to be a parent.

I hadn't either. I'd never imagined myself wanting another baby after raising three of hers for years. But the minute I knew about him, I'd changed. I said a silent prayer that whatever came, I'd never make Michael feel like anything less than a blessing in my life. No matter what.

I moved around to Arthur's other side. His sheets were wrapped around him, and one foot stuck out. I touched it and felt the cold, dryness of his skin. The slight aroma of urine and sour body odor told me he needed to be bathed.

I'd seen the nurses racing here and there, overworked, and knew it'd be hours before they had time to help. I could do this. I grabbed the blue, square hospital pan from the counter at the sink and filled it with warm water. I took two washcloths and pulled out the baby shampoo from the diaper bag under the stroller. It'd been a sample given to us by the hospital, but I hadn't used any yet.

Reaching over, I opened the heat register further, trying to keep him from being chilled. Then I set to uncovering and undressing him. I used the sheet to do one section at a time. As I washed and rinsed each part of him, I flashed back to the first bath I'd given Michael.

Arthur shifted under my hands, and I knew if he could kick me out of the room, he would.

"It's okay. For better or for worse, right?" He didn't relax, and I heard the taint of falseness in my words as they echoed in the room. It hadn't been better when he'd left me at the diner.

I continued to work my way up his body, uncovering and recovering him to keep him warm and lessen his discomfort. Empathy stirred within me as I shifted my gaze from Michael to my husband, seeing him broken in a way I'd never associated with him before. It didn't disturb me as it once would.

I lifted one of his legs, then the other; one arm and then the other. I'd replaced the water in the tub three times before moving on to his head, then dumped it entirely and filled the pitcher. After lowering the bed, I moved his pillows and made sure he could still breathe. Then I took the cover off one and rolled it behind his neck.

"Is this okay?" We made eye contact for the first time, his lazier one locking on mine with the same intensity as his healthy one. They held shame but gratefulness and something else I couldn't pin down. He slurred and nodded, a sound I'd come to understand meant yes.

I pushed the tub under the back of his head and started to shampoo his hair, rubbing the tips of my fingers over his head, sudsing his hair and massaging his head. The very act felt more intimate than we'd ever been, and tears built in my eyes as well as his. I blinked them away and poured warm, clear water from the pitcher down over his hair until it rinsed clean. I towel dried him and took away the wet pillows and towels. Then I sat him up and gave his scruffy face a shave. After we were all done, I hit the call button, and a nurse came in with clean sheets. I took notes as they changed his bed and helped him redress.

I turned away as they dealt with his catheter, and instead took care of Michael. I knew I'd have to learn how to care for him there, too, but I'd done enough for the day.

As they left, one of the nurses smiled. "You're pretty good. You hardly got any water on the sheets. We can always use assistants."

I shook my head and wondered how I'd find time to do such a thing. Worries besieged me as I sat down to feed Michael. I would have to work to pay for the extra care Arthur would need, and then who would stay and take care of Arthur and Michael? Would I even make enough money to pay for their care?

After feeding Michael, I changed him. Arthur's eyes were on me, but I didn't look up. I knew what he was thinking. I felt it too, the shift in our relationship. Braving my fears, I glanced up at a much cleaner and peaceful-looking man. His head had drooped to the left, exhaustion setting in. I put Michael in his carrier and moved to Arthur.

"Are you cold?"

He murmured his yes, and I pulled the blanket up over the sheet, tucked him in, and pushed the button to lower the head of the bed a bit. He sighed and closed his eyes.

"After your nap, you need to eat." Every now and then, I sounded like my mother. I gritted my teeth against the idea. If Arthur heard me, I couldn't tell. He could be pretending to sleep for all I knew. But then the deepening breaths of slumber rose, and I knew he'd rest for several hours.

After being up and down with Michael all night, and bathing Arthur, I needed a nap, too. I turned off the overhead light and pulled the curtains before climbing into the recliner at his bedside. I pulled my jacket up around me and let my mind wander.

Last year at this time we were trucking across the country, making deliveries, sleeping in truck stops and the occasional campground. We'd take long walks together, and he'd tell me things about his childhood—nothing overly personal, just tales and remembrances. He knew everything about mine. We lived separate lives, out in the world among people, but visiting with others was a rare occasion.

Until I'd been at the diner a while, I'd never realized how a solitary life ate at my spirit. I loved being around people, I loved activity—craved it. The biggest fear I'd had wasn't that Arthur would return, but that I'd lose myself to him all over again.

Thoughts of my cute apartment, the soft bed, the dancing lights from the marquee scattering over my ceiling came unbidden, along with tears of grief for what I'd lost. And Toby. Had Toby told his parents he wouldn't lie for them anymore? Had he stood up to the town?

I remembered his beautiful house and the big oak in the back—such talent and promise. The moment where we pretended we didn't owe any obligation to anyone but ourselves—the moment I knew how wrong we were. I missed him so. Glancing at the sleeping Arthur, his once bulky form fading to a thinning, aging man, guilt surfaced, but I shoved it away. Toby had been a friend when no one else would. He'd gone to great lengths to support me, feed me, care for me. It had been the first time anyone had loved me unconditionally since my grandmother—and I'd always be grateful for that. And I'd always regret that I couldn't return his love because I'd given mine away foolishly to another.

Glancing at Michael, I hoped I could impart knowledge and wisdom to him that I'd never gained—well, not until it was too late. I wanted to protect him from the world, to keep out evil, to shut him in a cocoon where all he'd feel was acceptance and love.

As soon as I thought it, I knew I could never do it. Not on my own.

"God?" I glanced up at the ceiling, as if waiting for him to answer. "Please take care of Michael. You've gotten us this far." I tried not to cry. I didn't want Arthur to wake and see me so vulnerable, praying to a God he never believed existed. The sobs came anyway—I blamed the exhaustion, the turmoil, but deep down, I knew I'd tapped a new level of grief. I wanted to tell someone, anyone, about the Father I'd discovered—the one teaching me, holding me, and providing extra strength for me.

Arthur shifted and uncovered his leg. I got up, wiping my eyes on my sleeve, and tucked him in again, tighter, pushing the blanket against the rails of his bed. Earlier, as I uncovered and recovered Arthur, all those parts of myself I'd kept hidden away were being uncovered and recovered, too. And like Arthur, as they were uncovered, God washed them, cared for them, and tucked me in again.

Forty

"I found some listings." My mother tossed the rentals section of the newspaper, covered in red circles, down in front of my cereal bowl.

Brynn and Sarah's eyes widened, and Sarah sighed before cleaning up her breakfast dishes. "Why does she need to leave, anyway? She just got home." She rinsed her plate and loaded it in the dishwasher.

"Yeah." Brynn came around behind me and settled her chin on my head. "I love being an aunt. I don't want Macy or Michael to leave."

My mother cleared her voice. "Listen, Macy needs to find someplace where she can live closer to town. It's eating up her gas to go back and forth every day like this. And she needs to plan for when Arthur can leave the hospital."

"They can move in here." Brynn smiled at her own brilliance, but it faded fast.

"No." Both my mother and I spoke at the same time, loudly.

I picked up the paper. "Thanks, Mom. You're right. It's time. But, I don't need your help. I've already found a place." I hadn't really, but I'd seen one on my drive to the hospital the past week. I'd been putting off making the call. Today, I'd stop and check it out.

When I was younger, I thought once I'd had a husband (and now a child), I'd quit getting my back up with my mom. But I didn't think it'd ever go away. I knew for certain, because even if she'd found the best place in the world in that paper, I wouldn't go look at it.

So much for growing up.

I gathered my things and Michael and headed out the door. As I loaded us into the little car, I saw Bobby leave the shop and realized there was something else I needed to do. As he walked, he popped the top of a soda before sitting down at one of the tables. I drove the little car over to him, rather than remove Michael from his carrier again.

Rolling down the window, I gave him my best smile. "Hey, so any word on a van?"

Bobby bit the inside of his cheek. "No. You know you can keep this thing for as long as you want." He gave the tire a nudge with his steel-toed boot.

"I need a van."

"For Arthur?" Bobby let his skepticism show.

"Yes, for Arthur. Why?"

He stood, tucking his hands into his pockets. "Listen, I saw him yesterday. I don't think…" He sighed to a halt. "Never mind. I'll keep looking." Bobby turned away to head back inside.

I reached through the window and grabbed his arm. "What?"

Bobby's eyes filled with sorrow. "I don't think he's leaving that place, sis. Or if he does, it'll be to a care home." He put a big hand on my shoulder. The smell of gasoline lit my senses, and I flashed back to my father, his kind dark eyes, his mellow ways. "You've got to face facts."

"I can't. I don't know what else to do." My voice trembled.

"I get it." He rubbed my back. "You've got to keep doing what you're doing. I just don't want to see you get hurt."

I didn't have the heart to tell him it was way too late to worry about it now. He kept looking down at me, wisdom and warmth in his eyes. Somewhere along the way, someone stole my eighteen-year-old brother and replaced him with a man.

"Thanks."

Bobby nodded at me and headed toward the shop. I shifted the car and pulled out, more resolved than ever to find a place to live and move before any more changes happened in my life.

We drove into town, and I turned down a side street I'd taken by mistake the week before. My mind had been wandering, and I'd turned on the wrong block and ended up driving by a cute little gray house. I found it again and pulled up in front. I unbuckled Michael and climbed the steps, looking around. The FOR RENT sign listed the address next door.

I peered into the warbled antique glass windows of the front room, spying some built-in cabinets, a dining table, and a tiny kitchen beyond. The carpet was low pile—perfect for a wheelchair. Although Bobby's words were still tumbling in the back of my mind, I subdued them and wandered to the renter's house and knocked on the door.

A tiny older woman answered the door. She had near purple hair, soft and wispy, pulled back into a loose bun. She gave me a curious glance but then settled all her attention on Michael. "What a lovely baby. So precious. What's his name?"

"This is Michael."

"Oh, sweet baby. Sweet baby." She seemed to forget I was there, then looked up rather startled to see me. "What can I do for you?"

"I'd like to see your rental."

"Are you married?" Her eyes scrutinized me.

"Yes, ma'am."

"I'd bet he'd like to see it, too." Her voice lilted up at the end.

"I'm sure he would, but he's in the hospital right now."

"Oh, dear." I'd never heard anyone *tut-tut*, but I'm pretty sure that's the noise she added at the end.

"In fact, when I do bring him home, I'll need to put in a ramp for a wheelchair. My brother can do the work, and I'd pay for it all."

"Oh, dear, what a hard road you'll be riding." She patted her lips with her well-manicured fingers until her eyes lit. "Actually, there's a ramp up to the backdoor. My last tenant used a walker. I never went that way, myself. But I'm almost positive it would be wide enough." She pulled a ring of keys from a hook on her wall near the door. "Let's go take a look together." She motioned for me to follow her. "I'm Mrs. Rigsby." She held out her hand to me.

"Macy Stone."

"Lovely name—Stone. Settled. Strong. Foundational." She murmured the last two as if making a mental note. I didn't correct her misconception. My kind of stone sank, tumbled, hung heavy around necks and weighed me down. I cast off my thoughts and concentrated on Mrs. Rigsby—who looked every bit like a much older June Cleaver. My little hopeful heart beat a bit faster.

We wandered through the grass of her yard, to a chain-link fence and gate between the properties. She swung up the screeching latch, and we entered through, up a paver-lined walk to the back porch of the rental.

"Are you from around these parts?" She walked up the ramp to the backdoor and pushed the key into the deadbolt.

"My mother, Barbara Robinson, owns a gas station and convenience store out in Elk River."

"I never go out that direction."

So much for my connections to the community.

"Although, some folks from my church live out that direction." She gave me another look before entering the house.

I followed her inside the mud room, and we closed the door behind us. The house smelled of age and Carpet Fresh, but not moldy or musty. We walked past the L-shaped kitchen on the right, lined with carved, white painted cabinets. The window over the sink faced the side fence and Mrs. Rigsby's yard. I didn't see any way to roll a wheelchair through the narrow kitchen, but I didn't give up hope. I passed by the first bedroom on the left, then the second. They looked very roomy. The living room and dining room were combined, but I didn't mind. It'd make it easier to move Arthur around.

"What about the bathroom?"

"It's back by the mud room."

I turned around and headed back the way we came in. I opened the door and held my breath in excitement.

"As you can see, my last tenant and I remodeled his bathroom to accommodate his walker."

Indeed. The shower was a roll in and had a folding seat and sprayer nozzle. Perfect.

"I think this will be just right. I'll take it." We'd figure out the kitchen. Bathing Arthur in that room would be a breeze.

Her eyes widened. "But I haven't even told you how much it is, or any of my other conditions. I don't rent to just anyone."

Michael took that opportunity to fuss. "Hang on, sweetie." I shifted him in my arms. He'd want to eat soon.

"What a cute little man." Mrs. Rigsby brushed Michael's knuckles with her fingers. I usually felt protective when strangers tried to touch him—and they had—but not with Mrs. Rigsby.

"Do you have children?"

Mrs. Rigsby's eyes watered. "I did. He passed away when he was eight. A sweet little brown-haired boy." She pulled a tissue from her sleeve and dabbed at her nose and eyes. "He'd bring me violets from our garden every day."

"I'm so sorry." I touched her polyester-clad arm, feeling the fake silky sleeve rake against her bone-thin arms underneath.

"We never had another child. We wanted to, but it never happened." She sniffled. "I'm sorry." She shook her head. "It's been fifty years. You'd think I'd be used it by now."

"I don't imagine you ever really get over the loss of a child." I knew I couldn't. If I thought I loved Michael before his birth, it was nothing compared to the protective feelings I got now at the thought of losing him, or having him taken from me.

She motioned me to follow her into the back bedroom and moved the sheer curtains aside.

"You can see there's a nice long drive to the carport and a paved sidewalk to the backdoor. You shouldn't have any trouble wheeling him inside." She dropped the curtains back in place.

"It's perfect. Like I said, I'll take it."

"I'll need you to fill out the application—I've got to do a background check. It's only a precaution."

I nodded and followed her back out and to her house. She put a pitcher of iced tea on the table and poured me a glass as I filled out the form.

"I'll need first and last month's rent, and a cleaning deposit. The carpets are newer, and I'll pay to have them cleaned once a year. If they are soiled more often, I'll expect you to pay for them to come every six months." Mrs. Rigsby looked over my application.

"That sounds fair." Six months. A year. I couldn't fathom living there for that long, taking care of Arthur. A shudder built inside me, but I fought against it. Tears threatened, but I blinked them away. If Mrs. Rigsby noticed, she didn't say. Michael began to fuss in earnest, and I knew he was done being patient.

"I'll call today or tomorrow if you're a good candidate." Her eyes locked on Michael's whimpering face. "Sweet boy." She cleared the glasses away and walked me to the door. "Thanks for your interest."

I nodded and headed back to the car, settling in to feed Michael before heading to the hospital. The warmth in the car seeped into me, calming my nerves. A voice in my head reminded this wasn't how life was supposed to be and my eyes filled with tears once again—this time I let them fall.

I glanced at the window of Mrs. Rigsby's house and knew that wasn't the life she had planned. Her son's life wasn't supposed to end so early, but it had. I needed to let go of what I thought life was supposed to be, and concentrate on what life was.

I prayed God would give me the strength to do that. Fast.

Forty-One

I heard Arthur's mumblings and groaning down the hall long before I reached his room. As I rolled Michael's stroller in, two nurses were leaving.

"I'm so glad you're here, Macy. He's refusing to eat again and won't let the occupational therapist do her job." Shelia, his day nurse, looked as relieved as she sounded. The other nurse gave a grimace and shot a grumpy look at Arthur before leaving.

"Sorry." I pushed the stroller over by Arthur's bed and saw his eyes lock on the baby.

Sheila gave me an encouraging smile. "Don't mind her. She's a filler today, and Arthur spilled his food all down his front and the floor with his jerking around."

I regretted being so late.

"Is this how he always is when I'm not here?"

"Yes. You have a calming effect on him." Shelia said it like she assumed I'd feel a sense of pride and peace in how my husband relied on me. Instead, it made me tired. I shook it off and adjusted my attitude.

She left the room, and everything went still except for the restless shuffling of Arthur's fingers on the sheet. I pulled up my chair and checked Michael. Sound asleep. My gaze returned to Arthur. "Why are you giving everyone such a hard time?"

Arthur didn't look at me. I might have imagined a shrug. It was hard to tell.

"If you're going to get better, you're going to have to eat." I held out the cup of thickened liquid, straw pointed at him, but his head lulled away. I put it back on his tray and sighed. "I found a house for us today." I hadn't meant to mention it to him—not until it was for sure—but here I was, spilling my guts.

The comment obviously surprised him. His head shifted and his gaze rested on me, questioningly.

"You can't stay here forever. We've got the future to think about."

His eyebrows furrowed, and then tears started streaming down his cheeks.

"What is it?"

He mumbled over and over again, but I couldn't make it out.

"Slower. I can't understand."

"Not…deserve…no." His sobs came more rapidly as the words mushed out.

Arthur had never been the type to discuss feelings or share his thoughts with me. Ours had been a relationship of hierarchy. He was in charge, and I was the one taking orders. The romantic love I'd believed we shared had dissolved. Seeing him broken and desperate wrenched something free in me, but I resisted.

"We're married. That's what a wife does." I didn't want him to think there was anything more behind my caring for him than there was. But even as I spoke the words, I knew they weren't entirely true.

I'd read about Jesus the night before and how he loved me unconditionally. And that's what I was supposed to do for Arthur. I whispered a silent prayer for peace. I hoped one day I could look at him as my *husband*, not the manipulator he'd been. But I knew right then there were no guarantees. There were only the promises made, the covenant entered, and even if he never loved me the way I longed for, the way I should be, I'd still take care of him. And maybe one day learn to love him again.

A renewed strength filled me, and I reached into the bottom of the stroller and pulled out my Bible. As I flipped open to where I'd stopped reading the night before, I took a cleansing breath. If God could reach me and make my feet stop running, maybe he could reach Arthur, too, and make him the man he should have been.

Arthur listened intently as I read for a couple hours, and then he fell asleep. Once again I found myself curled up in the recliner, watching the two men in my life nap. Not for the first time did I find the situation ironic.

I'd always imagined an independent life—one I could direct to take me to where I'd wanted to go. But now I no longer knew where that was, or how to manage getting there. That fantasy of the open road, my husband and I casting our cares off and focusing on each other—it'd never happened. And now I wondered how selfish those plans had been in the first place. I closed my eyes, trying to shut down my brain and save those worries for another day.

After our nap which somehow left me more tired than rested, I headed home.

I didn't go right in, though. Instead, I microwaved a burrito in the store and moved us to the picnic table area.

Brynn came out of the store, grinning, waving a slip of paper. "A lady called and said you got the house." She handed me the note, and I gave her a hug. Her smile faded. "I wish you didn't have to leave." She gathered Michael up out of his carrier and held him close, snuffling the top of his head. "He smells so good."

"Now he does." I smirked.

"You know what I mean." She gave him kisses under his chin and Michael gave her a lopsided smile. As a cool breeze whipped up, she pulled the blanket around him tighter. "Can I take him inside and cuddle him?"

"I'm sure he'd like that."

Brynn loaded Michael into his carrier and headed into the house, leaving me behind in the unusual quiet. No trucks revved in front of the station, no automotive sounds came from the shop. I heard a hawk call, drawing my attention to a path through the trees I'd forgotten about. I climbed down from the picnic table and followed it, pushing through the bushes and overgrowth, my feet quiet on the pine needles. The sweet cutting smell of budding spring leaves and the sun-warmed earth filled my senses.

As the path opened up to a run-off pond, memories flooded back of my last time here. It'd been on my wedding day. I'd come down to tell my father good-bye—not him, but the memory of him. It had been *our* place. Besides the hiking and fishing trips, we'd come here and sit on the downed logs and toss rocks out into the water. I'd share about school and friends and what I wanted to be when I grew up. He'd been such a good listener. We'd search for the best skipping stones— smooth, thin, no rough edges. Then we'd share a thought and skip a stone—each taking turns counting off the hits, each trying to outdo the other as our stones reached farther and farther across the pond.

Without noticing I'd been doing it, my eyes searched until I found three or four that might do. I squatted down to inspect them, caressing each one, checking for imperfections, feeling the weight of them in my hand. When I found one that fit perfectly between my fingers, that settled comfortably in my palm, I cocked my arm back and snapped my wrist, setting it free. It skimmed over the glassy pool, bouncing. I counted them off aloud, as if he were standing there with me.

"...ten, eleven, twelve." The bounces came so rapidly I lost count, then it bit into the water, sinking from sight, joining the hundreds of companions who'd gone before it. I wiped at my eyes and looked for another offering.

My father once told me it took hundreds of years for the water and sand to erode a rock to skipping perfection. At first it would be hard and unwieldy, like any old rock—but when conditions were right, the hard edges would be worn smooth and perfected. Like me.

As the idea shot through my mind, I sank hard to the log behind me. I rubbed the next rock with my fingers, feeling its smoothness, brushing the excess grit from its sides. Leaning over, I rinsed it at the pond edge. The mud drifted away, revealing a sparkling mica-covered stone. Holding it up to the sun, I watched as the light reflected off the flecks. Instead of skipping this one, I dried it on my pants. The brightness and color faded dull—but I could still see the potential beauty. This one I tucked into my pants pocket to save.

One day I would give it to Michael.

I knew my father wasn't there, but I told him what had been happening. Somewhere along the line, I quit talking to him and switched to my heavenly Father—now I knew he heard me. I made firm plans, decisions about what would happen next. But this time, I prayed about it first.

I'd stay married to Arthur. We'd live in the little house—maybe I'd even offer to buy it from Mrs. Rigsby one day. And over time, I'd figure out what to do for a living. I didn't have to know everything right away. All I needed to do was trust God would work it all out as long as I kept my eyes on him and not on me.

The suffocating feeling I kept having whenever I thought of losing myself by caring for someone disintegrated. I knew it might come back, but I was determined not to let it rule me anymore.

After tossing one more rock, I headed back to the house and went inside. The baby was crying, so I entered my bedroom and found Brynn trying to calm him in the rocking chair. As she rocked, she spoke sweet words, but I could see the panic around her eyes. Nothing lit up the nervous system like a crying baby. I put my hand on her shoulder.

"Everything's okay. He's hungry."

Brynn gratefully handed him back to me. "I changed him, rocked him, burped him, nothing helped."

I gave Brynn a sideways hug. "You did great. After I move, you can come and baby-sit for me, okay?"

Brynn's eyes lit up.

"I need to feed him and call Mrs. Rigsby. Then I'm going to have to track down some furniture for my new place. You can help with that, too, can't you?"

"Sure." She grinned. "We can start packing tonight."

As Brynn moved around my room, collecting things on the bed, my mother walked in, a strained look on her face. Had she been unable to make the bills after all? But as the grave look in her eyes deepened, I knew it must be something much worse.

"Is Bobby okay?" I remembered the uncharacteristically quiet garage. I should have gone to check on him. I laid Michael down in his carrier.

"Bobby's fine." She swallowed. "It's Arthur."

Forty-Two

Nothing seemed real. The world shifted, and here I was at my husband's bedside again. The ventilator filled and compressed, the soft whooshing sound mixed with the beep and hum of other machinery all working to keep him alive. Hadn't I been there a few hours before, reading to him?

My mother came in and handed me a cup of coffee. She sat down on the couch next to me, and we continued our vigil. The stroke this time was massive. There was little hope, and yet I did. I took my mother's hand in mine.

"Would you pray with me?"

She stiffened.

"You don't have to say anything."

"Sure," she relented, holding my hand and closing her eyes.

"God..." I didn't know what to say. I'd never prayed with anyone before except Clara, and she took the lead. "Arthur's in bad shape. Would you heal him? But most of all, please love him and help him know he's not alone. Amen."

When I opened my eyes, I saw tears in my mother's. "I never wanted this for you." She pulled her sleeve of her sweatshirt down and wiped at her eyes.

I handed her the tissue box. "It's okay."

"No. I convinced myself it was the right thing to do, letting you marry him. But as soon as you drove away, I knew I'd been wrong." Her shoulders shook with emotion. "I'd been so caught up in my own grief for so long, Macy."

I took her hand and squeezed it.

"I didn't know how we'd take care of the bills or the kids and it seemed like the perfect solution. I'm so sorry." She blew her nose. "What I did would have broken your father's heart. Your grandmother certainly never forgave me."

I needed to take the pressure off, I needed to tell her the truth— something I'd only come to understand days before. "Mom, even if you hadn't said yes, I would have run off with Arthur. I wanted so badly to get away. As much as I could sit here and blame you—as much as I *have* blamed you—I made that choice."

Her eyes cleared, and she focused on me. "Really?"

"While Daddy was dying…" I choked. "I felt like everything came down on me."

"I'm sorry."

I put my hand on her arm. "I forgive you." And I did.

"I shouldn't have shut you out. Your father was everything to me." As she said it, a new horror dawned over her face. "I should have loved you kids better."

"We all do what we can." I meant it. I'd realized something else, too—that my mother had gotten caught up in her own plans, just like I did. And they'd gone south, just like mine had. "I was looking for any avenue of escape—when Arthur proposed, I convinced myself that was the right one, and took it."

She pulled my hand closer, under her arm.

"When I fell in love with your father, nothing else seemed to matter. I told myself he'd give up working on cars and go into business. We'd move to Seattle and buy a grand home. I'd go to art school." Taking a tissue, she blew her nose. "Then we'd have a child or two, and I'd paint in my studio and sell my works in the local galleries." Her voice grew wistful. I'd never known my mother wanted to be an artist.

"But he wanted to be a mechanic."

She nodded. "He loved working on cars. Loved it. He'd lose himself in it. And then I got pregnant with you." She shrugged. The rest was history.

"It's not too late." My mother was only in her fifties—young enough to start over, to start again.

"Maybe."

"The kids will be grown. Bobby's already there."

My mother sat up, her back straightened with conviction. "I'm going to send Bobby to school. And Sarah and Brynn, too. Whatever they want, I'll support them."

I smiled. "They'll be very relieved and happy to hear it. Make sure you send them where they feel led to go, not where you think they should go."

She laughed, but there was a bitterness lingering. "I have a feeling they'll all want to live on that property forever. They'll marry and bring their spouses home."

"And you'll be a grandmother and get to watch grandbabies grow."

Her eyes sparkled with unshed tears. "I'm already a grandmother." She looked over at the sweet sleeping baby in the carrier at my feet. "He's a lovely boy, Macy." Regret laced her words. "I'm sorry about that, too."

"I didn't give him up. I couldn't." I tucked the blanket around him tighter.

"If you had, it would have been my fault."

My forehead furrowed. "But I didn't listen to you or to Arthur." I glanced over at my husband. "And if I had, it would have been my fault, not yours." I'd learned no one could make me do anything I didn't want to do. I could use them as scapegoats for the rest of my life—but really, the only one to blame for where my life had ended up was me.

"Still." My mother took my hand in hers. "Whatever you need, Macy, I'm here for you. If you want to stay at the house, we'll work it out."

"I've got a house lined up. It's perfect for us—even has a roll-in shower." My voice trailed off as I wondered if Arthur would ever use it. My mother pulled me toward her and shifted me into her embrace. My face cuddled into her neck, and the familiar whiff of her perfume, her warmth, her love cascaded over me. Her hand petted the back of my head, drawing me closer, and I drew my knees up over hers as she rocked and cradled me on the couch. Tears streamed as I sobbed, and the sounds of her comforting words and motherly shushes lulled me to sleep.

I dreamed about Arthur. We were driving up a long pine-tree-lined highway listening to the radio chatter in the background. His strong hands gripped the wheel, and he hummed a tune. The ashen, sunken complexion was gone, and his eyes sparkled at me in a way they hadn't done for years. I heard Michael make a cooing sound and realized he was in between us, strapped in his seat, replacing the center console. Arthur laughed—so freely, so unlike the man I'd hardened my heart against.

"I love our boy." He reached over to chuck Michael gently under the chin, and then to me, caressing my cheek. "I love you, too, Macy. Always have." His eyes saddened. "I should have waited until you were older. We should have talked more. I should have trusted you. I was afraid of change, afraid of what it would all mean to us."

We were so at ease. I let the feelings I'd squashed down for so long bubble to the surface. "I love you too, Arthur."

"Perfect love drives away fear." His voice grew grave, even as his eyes filled with unshed tears.

"I read that to you last night."

He nodded and looked at the baby. "Make sure he knows." He reached down and caressed Michael's head. Then he gave me a grin before gripping the steering wheel and hitting the gas pedal. Our rig barreled down the road, faster and faster, all the world around us becoming a blur of green and brown, but I wasn't afraid. I was laughing.

I awoke to a haze of beeping machinery, panicked voices, and blurred vision. I couldn't shake off my dream. A team worked over Arthur's bed, shouting out orders, pulling up machinery, tossing back blankets. My mother gripped my hand in hers. Everything slowed down. Nurses ripped open packs of IV needles, a doctor shouted for an injection. I held my breath, wondering which was real and which was dream. Was I awake at all?

Michael began to cry, and my mother changed his diaper and outfit then handed him to me with a blanket. I fed him as the team moved with more caution, moved slower. And then Arthur's nurse, Shelia, gave me a long look, sadness creasing her face.

On medical television shows, the doctors would pull the loved one aside and put a strong hand on their shoulder and break the news. The lead would take the information stoically and then slow tears would trail down their faces.

That didn't happen.

"No!" I choked on my scream, and my mother held me back to keep me out from under foot while they turned off one machine after another, removing the needles and lines from his body, covering him up, making him appear comfortable once again. As I relented, she took Michael from me and left the room, her face buried in his blanket, her own muffled sobs echoing down the hall.

Shelia came over, grief in her eyes. "I'm so sorry, Macy. We tried, but there was too much damage this time." She hugged me, but I didn't feel it. Then she left me alone.

After all the activity, the silence hung in the room like one of their heavy heated blankets—comforting, but paralyzing. It reminded me of the time we were caught in a tornado on one of our runs. We ran on foot, along with the rest of the drivers, from the road to the underpass. The sound was like a locomotive engine bearing down on us, thundering and grinding and then, as it passed over us, deafening silence. We could only hear the sound of our own breathing and the whimpering of children as they buried their faces in their parents' chests. And then the roar was gone, leaving the calling card of devastation in its wake.

I stepped now through the strewn wrappers and wires, the medical waste and blood spots and urine that would be mopped away after they took Arthur to the morgue. Already his body was shutting down, becoming an empty shell of who he'd been.

I picked up his already-cooling hand and held it in mine.

"We started off wrong, Arthur, but we ended it right. I'll miss you. I'll tell Michael about you—that you were hard working, that you were dedicated. That you loved him." I put his hand back down, smoothing out his fingers, memorizing their shape. I remembered their power as they'd first held mine and then as they'd gripped the steering wheel. All the struggle of the last few months was gone. His face was full of peace. I'd never seen that look before. No agony, no grimace, no anger. Just peace. There was only one thing left to do. I hadn't voluntarily kissed him for over a year. I did then.

Hospital staff came in with papers to sign and directives to agree with. I was given a packet of information and a large plastic bag with all of Arthur's personal items in it. His old gold watch, his bent wedding band, the red plaid shirt and Wrangler jeans were tossed inside. His hand-carved leather belt with a gaudy trucking buckle jangled as I opened the sack and breathed in the scent of his cologne. It was a great improvement over the smell of antiseptic and sickness.

I moved away from Arthur, from the bed, from the recliner I'd spent so many hours in. I passed the curtain, pulling it closed.

My mother met me in the hall, her hand outstretched. "Let's go home."

Forty-Three

The sun warmed the back of my neck as I dug in our garden plot. It wasn't as big as the one I grew up with, but it'd be enough to supply Michael and me with some fresh vegetables, and most importantly, tomatoes. I loved the feel of the dirt, its cool gritty dampness clinging to my warm hands, the earthy, peaty smell.

Michael made a cooing sound, and I looked up to see his smiling face as he jerked his small rattle back and forth, every now and then shoving it toward his face where he'd mouth it. He giggled at me.

"Just wait, one of these days you'll be here, helping me weed."

He laughed again as if he didn't believe me.

"Well, my son, let's plant some peas and beans and carrots here, and"—I craned my back, looking at the side of the house—"we'll put the tomatoes over there."

Michael must have thought my plans were sound, because he went back to chewing on his toy and making small, contented noises.

After finding all the rocks I could, tossing them in a pile for later use, I rolled the gas tiller I'd borrowed from my mother over to the plot and turned the soil. The rich blackness filled me with hope. Some clay, but overall not bad. My little yard would soon boast a nice, full garden—one I hoped to share with Mrs. Rigsby. She'd been such a dear in the past three months, arranging meals for us from the ladies at her church. Of course, Clara helped. Funny they'd known each other all those years ago, and had become fast friends once again. I'd only ever had one grandmother in my childhood, but now as an adult, I had two. And they doted on Michael.

I hadn't started attending church with them yet, but I would one of these days. Mrs. Rigsby would come over and I'd surprise her with a yes when she least expected it. I hoped Michael would grow up with God rather than having to be chased down by him.

The tiller ground the dirt and chucked up clods, making an awful racket. I glanced at Michael and laughed at his mesmerized expression. He loved all things noisy and mechanical. Maybe he'd follow in Bobby's footsteps? There'd be worse things than him working with his uncle in the family business.

As I turned off the machine and leaned it against the maple, I heard footfalls on the cement path behind me. I thought one of the kids must be visiting. Kids—I had to stop thinking of my sisters like that. They were more grown-up now than I'd been at their age.

"You've got a nice place here."

My hopeful heart kicked to life at the sound of his warm voice, even as the rest of me froze to the spot. I'd never expected to see him again. Ever. I turned to face him, holding my breath, afraid he wouldn't really be there after all. He stood there, blond hair ruffled over his forehead, eyes full of hope, edgy hands tucking in and out of his pockets.

I did my best to look calm and unsurprised, but I'm sure I failed. My fingers found the ends of my hair and started to twist madly. *Breathe, just breathe.* Toby walked up the rounding path toward me and stopped when he heard Michael babble. His eyes filled with awe and wonder.

My own filled with tears, because that was the look I knew he'd have if he ever saw us again.

"Wow." Toby squatted down in front of the carrier. "Hey little man." He reached out and reverently brushed his fingers along Michael's cheek. "He's gorgeous. He's got your hair and your eyes." His voice said *I told you so.*

"And Arthur's hands." They were, too. Huge for an infant, fingers bent in the same manor. I prayed they'd do good work and bring blessings to his family one day.

"Nothing wrong with hardworking hands." Toby chuckled and came over to me. He stood a couple feet away, but something in the air, some kind of gravitational energy, tried to pull us closer.

"How did you find us?"

His hand reached out to mine but pulled back. It'd been months, so much had happened, it was wrong of me to expect us to pick up where we'd left off. At the same time, his hesitancy hurt. Would I ever be rid of my double-mindedness? To ward off my feelings, I tucked one hand in my pocket, but the other betrayed me and kept twisting my hair.

"I saw the obituary."

"How?" Had he been watching the local paper? "Did Donna tell you where I'd gone?"

"No." He sighed. "I left town not long after you did. No one would hire me, even after the truth came out. So I applied for jobs at a couple Spokane and Seattle architectural firms and got one. I've been here ever since."

I couldn't believe it, and yet, having him here, standing in our little yard, felt like the most natural thing in the world. Then again, something didn't make sense. "Wait, what truth?"

He glanced around and saw the bench under the tree near Michael. "Let's sit down, okay?" As he took my hand and led me over, Toby gave me a sidelong smile.

"What?"

His eyes twinkled. "You were glowing and beautiful pregnant. I didn't think it was possible you could get any prettier."

I could feel the blush rushing to my cheeks. In the past, his compliments would have pleased me but left a trail of guilt behind—because of Arthur. Now, they left a warm path to my heart. But I didn't dare let him know.

"What truth?"

His eyes grew serious. "I thought long and hard after you left. I almost came to the bus station to stop you from leaving." He shook his head. "I knew deep down expecting you to run away with me was wrong. I'd been wrong to lie for my parents, and I had no business drawing you into it. I guess I thought if you went along, it'd make what I was doing seem right."

He stopped, thoughtful. I waited for him to gather his words.

"I got so lonely." His voice cracked, and he looked away, focusing on Michael. "I don't want this to sound hokey, but I started to pray. I'd never given God a thought all those years. We went to church, but it was just a routine with my parents." He looked away, staring off into the distance. "It was just another way for my folks to keep up appearances. My dad would go to church and act like the best guy in the world. But at home, all he did was drink, shove my mom around and blame me for things."

"I'm sorry it was so hard for you." I offered Toby my hand, and he took it like a lifeline, holding fast.

"Even though the things the church taught made sense, I didn't listen. Instead, I covered for my dad, trying to make up for the drinking, and what he did to the family. For what he did to Danny. I tried to fix him, I tried to fix his mistakes and take his blame—but it wasn't my job."

Michael dropped his rattle—a new game between us. I was about to pick it up, but Toby beat me to it. Their eyes met and locked, and Michael took the rattle and gave Toby a huge toothless smile before shoving it back in his mouth again—proud he'd converted yet another player. Toby chuckled softly and turned back to me.

"I knew I'd been in the wrong to cover up the accident, but I didn't know what to do. As stupid as it sounds, I kept hoping someone else would come forward with the truth. In all that time, no one ever did. Not long after you left, I went back to church and talked to my pastor, told him everything, and he prayed with me. After a couple weeks, I worked up the courage to do what I needed to do. I went to my mom and told her I was going to the police station to confess."

I held my breath, hoping his mother had done right by him.

As a tear slipped down his cheek, I knew she hadn't.

"She got really angry. She told me I was ruining everything." He took a shuddering breath. "But I did it anyway."

"What did the police say?"

"That I'd obstructed justice. They tossed me in a cell for a couple days and brought me before the judge. He sentenced me and released me with time served. I got off easy."

Easy wasn't the word I had in mind. He'd gone to jail twice, lived with the condemnation of the town and his family, and he'd survived.

"Then what?" My pride in him grew with every word.

"I told my mom I was done. I put my house up for sale and started looking for work. When word got out around town, some folks supported me, some didn't. But I was able to get a handful of local builders to write recommendations for me, and that, with the truth about my convictions, was how I landed my job in Spokane."

No more hiding. No more pretending. "I'm so glad for you, Toby."

The breeze whispered through the maples and fir trees, carrying a sweetness that only early summer could bring.

"When I saw the obit, I could hardly believe my eyes. It took me a couple weeks to get my nerve up to contact you. When I went by the gas station, I gave your mom a story about us being old friends." He squeezed my hand. "So she gave me your address."

I frowned at him. "When was that?" The orange pickup truck, driving off as I'd pulled in to the station one day had looked so familiar, but I'd talked myself out of it. That had been weeks ago.

"It took me a while to gather my nerve to come." He looked down at his feet. "And I knew I needed to pray about it. I'm done doing things headlong."

"Me too." I bumped my shoulder into his. It was good to know we were on the same page with our faith.

We sat there on the bench, surveying my hard work, listening to Michael shake his rattle and the traffic and someone's stereo in the distance. I was about to lean against him when Toby jerked in his seat, startling both me and the baby.

"I almost forgot. Hang on." He jumped up and jogged back up the side path. A minute later, he'd returned, carrying a small fir tree in a ceramic pot.

"You left this behind." He held it out toward me.

I shook my head, not sure what he meant, and then I saw it. Under one of the branches hung a small Christmas ornament, the white stripes now gray, and parts of the red reflective paint scratched off. It couldn't be. I'd left our first Christmas tree behind in my sooty, damaged apartment, water logged and dying.

"Is that the same one?"

"Sure is. I didn't know if we'd ever cross paths again, but if we did, I wanted to be sure to give it back to you." He put the pot down next to Michael.

"I don't know what to say. I never expected to see that again." I couldn't believe he'd gone back to that mess, past those angry people, faced their scrutiny and blame just to rescue my little tree. "Thank you, Toby." My thanks sounded empty and meaningless in light of what he'd done. In light of *all* he'd done.

Toby shrugged and smiled. Then he stepped closer and tipped my chin up to look at him.

"I don't have the right to ask. I know I've made a mess of things in the past and my track record leaves a lot to be desired."

I gave him my most encouraging smile. "You're not alone."

"We can't start off where we left things, Macy. But I'd sure like to begin again."

My soul sung at his words even as my head searched for a movie, a television show that might sum up our story until now—but there wasn't one. This was our own path, one that would be guided by God, not by selfishness or impatience, one with a purpose and meaning that only he could map for us.

I looked deep into Toby's eyes, and every sound filtered away, every misgiving and mistake disappeared, until all that was left were the four of us—Toby, me, Michael, and Jesus. I leaned forward, and he closed the gap, pressing his lips against my forehead, sighing, as I nodded in agreement.

My life didn't need to wrap up like a movie to have a happy ending. It didn't need to blaze down the highway, escaping in hopes of a better one around the bend. It just needed to stay focused on what the Lord might have for me. And that was enough.

Acknowledgments

First and foremost I want to thank my Lord and Savior, Jesus of Nazareth, without whom I would not be here. He encourages me to get out of bed each day and helps me put one foot in front of the other. He lifts my spirits and loves my soul—I am completely unworthy and eternally grateful. Everything I accomplish is directly related to the power and ability He blesses me with.

To my love, Ken, and little loves, Madeline and Seth, you give me focus and reason to rise every day. I love that you love quoting lines of movies and TV shows along with me and that we all stay up way too late laughing ourselves silly. For all the trials we face, we know we've got the Lord and we've got each other—and that makes hard days easier, and joyful days that much brighter.

To my editor, Roseanna White, thanks for encouraging me to go deeper with my characters and story—but always helping me to keep my voice and intention. I'm so grateful you found Macy and her story worth publishing—and for taking a chance on me again! Thanks, too, to editor Wendy Chorot and her keen eyes and intellect. With an awesome team like you two, no writer could go wrong.

To Melody Roberts, my critique-partner-in-crime: we made it through another one together! And to the rest of my Encourager's Writing Group: Danika Cooley, Louise Dunlap, April Lesher, Kim Kress, Jac Nelson, and Kendy Pearson—thanks for being the best crit group ever.

To my sweet friends who keep me in prayer on a daily basis: Anne Beals, Valerie Becker, Debbie Carpenter, Billie Jo Robbins and Melody

Roberts, thanks so much for holding me up in prayer when I can't even think straight enough to know what to ask for!

To the women who have shared their abuse stories with me through this novel and through *Jasmine*, thanks for being so transparent and honest in your pain and triumphs. No one should have to survive what you have endured. Your continuing to reach out to others who are hurting, being the hands and feet of Christ, loving them and listening to them on their healing journey is inspiring to me.

And to my readers—thanks for reading, for encouraging e-mails and notes, for amazing reviews and all the support. I appreciate you more than you could ever know!

Are you stuck in an abusive relationship—either emotionally, verbally or physically? There are people who want to help. A great place to start is the National Coalition against Domestic Violence http://www.ncadv.org/ Please reach out to trusted people in your community—never stay in a place where you or your children might come to harm.

Discussion Questions

1. Macy had a lot of pressure put on her by her family. Have you ever lived in a situation where others were expecting more out of you than you could give? What did you do about it?

2. Macy married young. Do you think younger people know what they are getting into when they get married? Do you think age has anything to do with that, or do you think emotional maturity plays a bigger part?

3. Have you ever dated (or been married to) a person that mistreated you? What did you do about the situation to change it?

4. Have you ever lost a parent to illness or accident? How did you cope with that?

5. If you're married, what qualities did you look for in your mate? Did you ever look at someone you were dating and realize they'd be an awful parent? Do you think that if people pictured their boyfriend/girlfriend as a parent to THEIR child, they might choose better? Why would that make a difference?

6. When Toby enters Macy's life, she's tempted to have an affair with him based on her mistreatment by Arthur—and the true friendship and comfort Toby offers her. Do you think she handled the situation correctly? What might you have done differently?

7. Macy's mom lived with a lot of disappointment in her life, much of which she chose willingly. Have you ever found yourself in a situation of your own making that was hurtful or harmful? What did you do to fix it? Looking back, would you have made different choices?

8. Do you think Arthur loved Macy, or was he in love with the idea of Macy? Why do you think that?

9. At the end of the story, Arthur comes around and realizes he was in the wrong. Macy got closure in her relationship, but not all abusive relationships get closure. Some just end badly. Have you ever helped anyone through a difficult situation like that? Did they get closure? If they didn't, how did they deal with it?

10. What do you think will happen between Toby and Macy now? What do you hope happens?

CPSIA information can be obtained at www.ICGtesting.com
Printed in the USA
BVOW05s1150250714

360433BV00001B/17/P